Play
Dead

Play Dead

A CRIME NOVEL

PETER DICKINSON

OPEN ROAD
INTEGRATED MEDIA
NEW YORK

Cover design by Mimi Bark

978-1-4976-8446-1

This edition published in 2015 by Open Road Integrated Media, Inc.
345 Hudson Street
New York, NY 10014
www.openroadmedia.com

GEOGRAPHICAL NOTE

The London Borough of Ethelden and Ormiston lies east of that of Hammersmith and Fulham, and west of that of Kensington and Chelsea, and combines many of the characteristics of those two. It does not, however, contain any character who in any way resembles a resident or politician living or active in either of its neighbours.

Play
Dead

AUGUST 1989

1

The new child seized the tricycle and screamed. Denny looked at her in astonishment for a couple of seconds, then his lower lip projected, quivering, and he launched into a bawl of outrage. His face contorted and went scarlet and his body became rigid, except for the arm which pushed flailingly at the aggressor, who clung on, still screaming.

Poppy Tasker watched the encounter with mild interest. It was the sort of thing that happened every few minutes in the play-group, especially when a child turned up who hadn't yet learnt the rules—rules unwritten, of course, and largely unspoken because most of the children's vocabularies were still limited to 'Mine!' and 'No!'. Adult rules did exist, but were different, less subtle than those the children had evolved among themselves to govern such confrontations, the gestures and stances by which one would attempt to take over a toy or piece of apparatus and the other assert primacy of possession. It was these conventions of the instinctive democracy of childhood that the newcomer had ignored.

She had started her scream while still a good yard from the tri-cycle, before Denny had even noticed her approach and refused to yield, but it wasn't that that had aroused Poppy's interest. It was the way she screamed, on a very pure and piercing note, like a magnified electronic timer. When she ran out of breath she stopped, drew a fresh lungful and immediately, without having to work up to it, struck the same note, full volume, spot on. Her face meanwhile remained calmly concentrated on the central act of screaming. She might have been an operatic soprano doing her exercises—Brünnhilde, perhaps, honing up the voice before a sequence of *hoya-hoyas* but not yet working on the character, the bouncing, virginal harvester of dead heroes.

The encounter was broken up by Big Sue, Denny's nanny, and George, the chief play-leader. A strange girl, presumably the screamer's nanny, hovered uselessly by. Poppy couldn't hear what was said because it was almost the only wet day of that fabulous summer and the roof of the hut, a handsome, pavilion-like, circular structure, tended to resonate to the rain, and the children at the Lego table were smashing up the structure they'd been making, banging and scattering the pieces as they did so. Anyway, some sort of draw was agreed, another tricycle was produced and Denny moved slowly off, propelling himself along with his toes on the ground. The screamer climbed on to her tricycle but made no effort to move it, sitting erect and triumphant as if posing for a war memorial.

Brünnhilde, thought Poppy. Wish I felt like going to the opera again. How long? A good four years, not counting that experimental once with dear old Aunt Liz, all pleasure made savourless by having seen Derek and Veronica settle into their seats at the other end of the row in front. She'd known it would happen. He never missed a production of Tosca, but that was what Liz had insisted on seeing, and since she was paying for the seats . . . Did he still go to the Escargot afterwards? Probably. Then home, and bed. Had Veronica yet worked out what female singers did for him, that while they were making love he in his imagination was slowly disrobing that night's diva in the luxury of her hotel room, she still throbbing out arias for him as he did so? It had made his love-making livelier than on non-opera nights, so Poppy had never minded, but now she hoped Veronica knew, and did.

Deliberately she decided to run a fantasy of her own, a new one. Start with the opera—*Figaro*, because he'd never tried opera before and she wanted it easy for him. After the interval they hold hands, his thumb exploring her palm. Not a restaurant. Taxi home through rain-glistening streets. Supper ready, taramasalata, duck salad, bottle of burgundy—they don't drink it all—share one scrumptious pear, calvados, and now they're in the living-room undressing each other and laughing and caressing and sipping from the same glass and spilling dribbles of calvados on to each other's flesh and licking it off. Just the firelight . . .

Hastily Poppy reran a section of fantasy and arranged to have sold the bracket clock after all so that she had afforded to install a proper open fire.

. . . firelight from dry logs, faint wood-smoke. He . . .

He was still too vague (what he looked like, what he did for a job, how she'd met him) for the fantasy to take proper hold. What about a big, craggy man with a very hairy chest? (Derek was smooth as a Canova and Alex merely downy.)

. . . so a softly furry strong obliterating weight on her . . .

'All right if I sit here?'

The voice was nervy, northern. Poppy abandoned the log fire with more regret than she felt for the furry lover, but both had been an effort to keep going. The girl was the screamer's nanny, a thin-faced, small-eyed girl, skinny apart from a disproportionate bust under her yellow T-shirt. A plea to save the whales was printed across these undulations. She wore jeans with the regulation tear on one kneecap, and sneakers.

'Of course,' said Poppy. She could see half a dozen places where the girl could have settled among people her own age. 'You're new, aren't you? I'll introduce you to the others in a minute. My name's Poppy.'

'Never! Oh, sorry, I didn't mean . . .'

'I'm used to it now, but I know it's a shock for strangers, like having different-coloured eyes or something.'

'Oh, I didn't mean . . . only my name's Peony, see?'

Poppy crowed with laughter. She saw several of the girls look across the room and smile. They'd often said they liked to hear her laugh like that, though to her it was an odd, unbidden eruption, not really expressive of the doubts and subtleties of her inner self, a bit like a harmless sort of poltergeist to which a family has become inured but which still manifests itself to surprise strangers.

'All we need now is a Pansy,' she said. 'Come and meet the Nafia.'

'Uh?'

'The regulars. Somebody must have called them that years ago. They'd have been a different lot then, but the name's just gone on. They call themselves that without thinking about it. Who's here? You've met Big Sue—she looks after Denny, the boy who had the tricycle. That's Nell, at the paint-table, with the long hair, all in black. And that's her son with her, Nelson. By the way, don't ask if that's a joke—she called him that for political reasons and didn't realise till after . . .'

'I've got a cousin lives in Mandela Road. You know, Runcorn.'

Poppy nodded, though she knew nothing of Runcorn. Peony wasn't as dumb as she looked, then. None of them were. They might have extraordinary patches of ignorance, but then so, in their eyes, did she.

'Who else?' said Poppy. 'That's Fran in the red track suit. She brings her son, Jason, and a neighbour's little girl, only she hasn't got her today. And that's Laura, the older one, next to her, and now that's Little Sue going across to talk to them—she looks after Peter, there, hitting that ball with the paintbrush . . . Heavens! What on earth can Sue have said?'

The exclamation was involuntary. From across the room Little Sue seemed to have spoken briefly, to Fran rather than Laura, but Laura's head had jerked back and her hand had flown to her mouth. Sue turned away, concealing her, and looked round the room, and by the time she moved Laura was looking down at her knitting, her face invisible.

'Sorry,' said Poppy. 'Where was I? Oh yes, Laura—she's a real nanny—sorry, I didn't mean that, but most of the girls do it as a sort of between job, until they start families of their own. Laura's never done anything else. At the moment she's looking after . . .'

'You're not one yourself then, Poppy?'

'A nanny, you mean? No, I'm a gran. That's mine.'

She pointed at Toby, sitting on the floor a few feet away, enclosed in his own absorption which was like a force-field round him shutting out the wails and shouts and scurryings as he repetitively threaded a length of red ribbon he had found into the funnel of his plastic steam-engine and out through the fire-box. The engine had its own plastic driver and fireman for putting down the funnel, but as usual Toby was more interested in other possibilities.

Poppy looked at him with slightly uneasy pleasure. The pleasure was rational—he was a lovely baby, by any standards. The unease was stupid superstition, but there. He was too good to be true, slept all night, teethed without whingeing, cried for acceptable reasons, finished his plate, shook off colds and other bugs in a couple of days, played with you if you felt like it and by himself if you didn't, and above all put out his arms with a smile of delight to greet you as you came through the door and stumped across to be picked up and hugged. However much reason might tell you to enjoy your luck, unreason squatted always in the dark beneath the stairs mumbling not-quite-audible fragments of doom. When people praised Toby to his face Poppy had a strong wish to shut them up, just as if she'd been a peasant in some mountain hamlet where the evil eye was still a living dread.

'Look at those curls!' said Peony. 'Is it a boy or a girl?'

'Toby, and very male. A right little chauvinist, in fact.'

'You ought to meet my brothers,' said Peony. 'Three of them, I've got, and each worse than the last, and Dad he's worse than the lot.'

She shrugged, smiled and looked away, trying to avoid any attempt on Poppy's part to take her off and introduce her to her own age group. This had happened before, with other newcomers, until they lost their shyness, in fact Poppy tended to be treated by many of the younger nannies and mums as a sort of substitute elder relative, a combination of lonely hearts column, Citizens' Advice Bureau and non-marriage counsellor. She had mixed feelings about this. The acceptance and trust were welcome, and so was the company, though the chat was narrow in its interests. Occasionally there were nuggets of gossip, about their own lives or the doings of their employers, which gave her titillating insights into alien modes of living. The couple of times when she felt she had actually helped with a problem had been rewarding. On the other hand the vague but real assumption on their part that she was different, old, any part of her life that could be called interesting now over, was irritating and depressing.

She campaigned unobtrusively to narrow the perception gap, avoided grannyish clothes, varied her make-up enough to make them comment and suggest, eavesdropped on their talk so as to be able at least to pretend that she'd watched *Neighbours*, learnt to tell Madonna from Michael Jackson from Kylie Minogue, and when it was her turn to provide a joint lunch for some of them and their charges produced frozen peas, chips and baked beans and microwaved fish fingers.

'Oh, oh,' said Peony on a note of warning.

Her own charge, the screamer, had returned, having left the tricycle and then gone wandering round the room in a dreamy way, as though her burst of screaming had for the moment satisfied her lust for domination. Most children coming into the confusion of the play centre tended to cling to their minders, often for several days, before gaining confidence to face their peers. This girl was different in that way, too. Now she stopped at the edge of Toby's force-field and studied his game with the ribbon and the engine. She concentrated. Poppy could sense her energies focusing for another outburst, but did nothing to intervene. Reason told her Toby had to learn that life wasn't all admiration and cuddles, and unreason added that it needed a daily sacrifice of delight to appease the mumbler under the stairs.

Peony did nothing either—too cowed, probably. But at the moment of crisis Tony decided that he had mastered the ribbon-down-funnel phenomenon and that he now needed an audience to whom to demonstrate his triumph. He looked up for Poppy, not having realised that in the process of discovery he had moved a half-circle round the engine and was facing away from her. He was confronted instead by the screamer, at the point of onrush. She would do. (Anybody would in fact do. At Poppy's flat he would reveal his intellectual breakthroughs to her cat, Elias.) He held up the ribbon in front of the screamer's face like a busker about to startle passers-by with a conjuring trick.

The scream stuck. Toby bent to the engine to begin his demonstration, but dissatisfied with the level of her attention turned back and took the girl by the wrist, pulling her down. Docilely she knelt and watched while he slid the ribbon through the engine three or four times, then, as he was reaching in to withdraw it from the fire-box, plunged her hand down the funnel to snatch it back. Their fingers met. They realised what had happened, looked at each other and laughed. It was one of those instants of communicated joy with which small children are programmed to reward their adults, lollipops to make the slavery of child-care worth enduring.

'Jesus!' said Peony. 'I reckoned we were in for a bust-up. Some days she sort of blows up every ten minutes like one of them, you know in that park place, America, was it?'

'Geyser? Yellowstone? Old Faithful, or something.'

''Sright.'

'My father-in-law was a bit like that. You'd be having a perfectly sensible conversation with him and then you'd ask for the salt and he'd blast your head off for ruining perfectly good food. It didn't mean anything. If you'd mentioned the Common Market at that moment he'd have blasted you about that. What's her name?'

'Deborah. Not Debbie. Mrs Capstone wants her called Deborah.'

'I'll try and remember,' said Poppy.

'You don't look old enough for a gran.'

'Thank you very much. Actually I've got three, but the other two are in New Zealand. Not that you've got to be that old to have grandchildren—there must be some grannies under thirty. It's probably in the *Guinness Book of Records*.'

'Dead thick, they must of been. I'm not starting till I'm twenty-eight, and I'll have a girl and a boy, and that's it.'

Poppy smiled—she had no wish to add family planning to her other unofficial duties. Capstone, she thought. The name rang a bell.

Deborah Capstone—you'd have the makings of a formidable woman with a name like that. Deborahs ate Poppies for breakfast . . .

Deborah lacked the scientific bent. Toby would have spent a good ten minutes verifying the hands-down-funnel-and-up-firebox effect, but before she'd finished laughing she was on her feet and looking for other objects to insert. She scurried round snatching up toys regardless of size and shape and whether another child happened to be playing with them. Toby was looking with disbelief at Nelson's yellow polka-dot cuddle tortoise when Nell brought Nelson over to retrieve it.

The tortoise had come from Harrods, the gift of a great-aunt. Nell had removed the label, but even without that the toy was still curiously expressive of values antipathetic to her, lazy, complacent, bourgeois, frivolous. Maybe that was why Nelson had chosen it to be his sacred object—almost from the cradle children seem to be preparing the ground for later revenges. Deborah saw their approach and knew what it meant. The delayed scream erupted.

She stood stock still, firmly in the centre of the imaginary limelight, clinging to the tortoise like a soprano to her lover who has been called to distant wars, letting the sound come. Nell and Nelson halted, but Toby rose and gazed at her in wonder. Slowly he lifted his hand, extended his forefinger and inserted it into Deborah's mouth. The note modulated from C to D flat, then returned to C as he withdrew his finger. His movements were characteristically decisive but gentle and Deborah, rapt in the ecstasy of her scream, appeared not to notice. He repeated the experiment, this time as she drew breath. She found his finger in her mouth and pushed it away.

'More,' he said.

Her mouth was still open but no sound came. She actually seemed unsure of herself. Perhaps it was beyond her experience that anyone should ask her to scream.

'More,' he said again, but she seemed to have forgotten the cause of her outrage. To show her what he wanted he let out a hoot and varied it by putting his open palm over his mouth and moving it away, a trick Hugo had taught him some months ago. She copied him, no longer screaming, nor hooting like him, but singing a definite note, something Poppy hadn't heard other children at that age do. Nell took the chance to ease the tortoise from her grasp. Poppy made the introductions.

Poppy both admired and liked Nell. She admired her for the way she faced the world, her courage in her principles, her sureness of purpose. She lived in a squat. Greenham had been a second home to her. At some point she'd spent a month in Holloway following a destructive break-in at another American base. She joined protests, stood on picket lines, and so on. From chat among the other girls Poppy had gathered that Nell had deliberately decided she needed a child to fulfil her femininity, and had equally deliberately chosen a black friend to be the father. Nothing else was known about him. He clearly didn't live with her and she never mentioned him, or referred to Nelson even having a father. It all sounded egocentric, cold-blooded, almost ruthless, but despite those adverse aspects of the modern zodiac, the act of childbirth had triggered the primeval necessary responses. When she was with Nelson every line of her body expressed her love, her intelligent, aware absorption in her son and his needs and nature. That was why Poppy liked her.

Nelson crooned to the tortoise. The three adults watched Deborah and Toby's game.

'Ah, isn't that lovely?' said Peony. 'She doesn't get on with other children the way she should, always. Mrs Capstone said try here, 'stead of Holland Park where we used to go.'

'Mrs Capstone?' said Nell, sharply.

''Sright,' said Peony, inexplicably defensive.

The social temperature had plummeted. This was clearly not the time to ask either of them about Deborah's mother. In a moment Nell would take Nelson back to the other side of the room, and Poppy couldn't decently abandon Peony and go with her.

'How's things at the commune?' she said, trying to prolong the contact.

'They're going to close it down.'

'Who are?'

'The Council, looks like. You'll read about it in the papers when it happens.'

'What'll you do? Have you got anywhere else to live?'

'I'll find something. It's different from before I had Nelson. I lived under plastic bags sometimes then. Hi, Sue.'

'About dinner tomorrow,' said Little Sue, who had appeared beside Poppy's shoulder. 'I've got Mrs Ogham-Ferrars staying—she's Pete's gran—and she's having some friends in, so you best not come through the house. I'll see the door's open into the park.'

'No problem,' said Nell, beginning to turn away.

'Hang on,' said Poppy. 'I'd have a bed for you for a few days, if you need it. There's only me and my cat.'

'You mean that?'

Poppy didn't hesitate. In a sense she had made the offer only as a way of prolonging the contact, building an extra strand into the tenuous relation between them. Challenged, she found she had told the truth.

'Yes, of course. Gladly.'

'Thanks.'

A squabble had broken out by the paint-table, involving Sue's charge, Peter, so she darted away to help peace-make before Poppy could introduce her to Peony. Nell picked Nelson up and carried him back to where she'd been sitting before. Deborah and Toby were still rapt in their game—a duet now, and sometimes they were stopping each other's mouth to vary the notes, which were further modulated by their giggles. Poppy heard Peony sigh with simple pleasure as she watched them and realised that she had done the same. It was a parody picture of young love, of the exploration of delights and possibilities available to two human bodies. When you sigh like that, she thought, you sigh for yourself as well.

2

'. . . I spy Mother Hubbard,' read Poppy. 'Can you see her, darling? Where is she? Yes, *there* she is!'

She let Toby turn the page.

'Mother Hubbard in the . . .'

'Mummy,' he said and wriggled from her lap. She put the book down and thought, Perhaps I *am* getting a bit deaf. Please not. Don't let anyone say it runs in the family or it's only to be expected at my age.

Toby was already through the door. Now Poppy could hear the noises of Janet bringing her cycle into the hall and stripping off her oilskins, mixed with Toby's cries of welcome. She crossed the kitchen and switched on the kettle. Janet came in with Toby bouncing on her arm. Her face glowed with the lash of rain and her red-blonde hair exploded round it, with odd lank locks that had escaped her crash-hat straggling down. Exhilarated health streamed from her.

Poppy's main feeling for her daughter-in-law, apart from a mild unfocused resentment, was awe, awe for her beauty, intelligence, dynamism mental and physical—she stood six feet and at the cottage would split logs with a seven-pound axe. How Hugo could have dared involve himself with such a Valkyrie, how Janet could have been drawn to vague, cold Hugo, were mysteries—as all marriages are, in the end.

'You must have had a wild ride, darling.'

'One of those days when the wind is against you in all directions.'

'I don't know how you dare.'

'It's fun. Like white-water canoeing. The traffic's the current you learn to ride.'

'But Hyde Park Corner, for instance.'

'Just a big eddy. How's he been?'

'An angel, as always. It's all in his book. He's fallen in love.'

'Again? Who with?'

'A terrifying little hussy with a scream like a steam-siren, called Deborah. Pushing two-and-a-half, I should think.'

'The older woman.'

'It's coming down. Sukie was four. And at least Deborah was just as smitten with him, so he's had a lovely time.'

'They'll have forgotten about it by tomorrow.'

'You can't tell with Toby, can you, darling?'

He had been nestling into Janet's shoulder, relaxing his body into the luxury of mother love, but looked up at the sound of his name.

'Who did you meet today, darling?' said Poppy. 'Deborah?'

'Debba,' he said, putting his hand in front of his mouth for a snatch of the yodelling effect.

'Where's Debba, then?' said Janet.

'Watch it,' said Poppy. 'We've got to call her by her full name. Mrs Capstone's orders.'

Janet was at the working surface making her tea with her free hand. The movement stopped with the kettle poised.

'Capstone?' she said.

'Why does everyone get the horrors when her name's mentioned? Ought I to know? It rings a bell, but there aren't any Capstones in the telephone book. I checked.'

'She'll be ex-directory—she's that sort. Don't you read the papers, Poppy? Don't you watch the telly?'

'Of course I know her name—it's just slipped. You aren't being fair. I listen to the radio all day long.'

Janet laughed. It was well known that Poppy listened to the radio all day long—Radio 3, switching off mentally for the news bulletins and on again when the music started. She watched the arts programmes and wildlife and travel on TV and read the review pages of the Guardian.

'Mrs Capstone proposes to become our second woman Prime Minister. At the moment her Thatchering is confined to Ethelden.'

'Oh, yes, of course! But she isn't really a Maggie clone, is she? There can't be two of them. And she'll have to win this constituency first, won't she? D'you think she can?'

'It's up to you.'

'Me?'

'Did you remember to renew your Labour Party membership?'

'Of course I did, darling. Well, the moment you told me.'

Poppy didn't feel she'd got the sturdy indignation right. It was often like that, talking to Janet, as if the conversation were being conducted on a slightly ill-tuned radio, the words clear enough, but the tones unreliable. All her life Poppy had voted Liberal but about fifteen months ago she'd happened to say she was thinking of going Labour because of the intransigent, self-savaging stupidities of the centre parties, and next morning Janet had pushed the membership form in front of her nose and demanded a cheque. Now Janet looked at her over the rim of her mug, her eyes mocking.

'There's every chance I and Mrs Capstone will be standing against each other at the next election.'

'Oh. I mean Oh?'

Janet ignored the note of doubt. She lowered Toby to the floor and gave him the egg-whisk and a bowl of water.

'At least you've heard that Tom Charleswick has decided not to stand next time.'

'Something to do with loans?'

'Officially it's health. In fact he used his contacts in Town Hall to get them to use a company which pays his brother a retainer to do some so-called creative accounting for them, which turned out not to be legal. The brother's an alcoholic wreck. Anyway, the Tories are going to make hay with it, and that gives Capstone a chance, and that gives me more than a chance. They haven't announced the short list yet, but I've been told. It's me and Bob Stavoli and Trevor Evans. Bob's a good bloke, but a useless speaker as well as being gay—you can imagine what Capstone could make of that. Trevor's not a bad speaker in a ranting kind of way, but he's such a shit, he's let so many people down over the years, and I bet he's got just as many skeletons in his cupboard as Tom Charleswick—anyway, Trish Edwards who's running my campaign says that Walworth Road want me.'

'Walworth Road?'

'Oh, Poppy! Labour Party HQ. In a few weeks' time there'll be a meeting of our constituency General Management Committee to select a candidate from the short list, so you've got to come along and vote for me.'

'I'm not even on . . .'

'Anyone who's been a paid-up member of the party for a full twelve months is entitled to vote. That's why I wanted to be sure you'd renewed your subscription.'

'I see. Well, that's very exciting, darling. What does Hugo . . .'

'Hugo knew what I wanted when he married me.'

'Yes, of course,' said Poppy, hearing beneath the words the tone she had known so well a few years back, like the creak of ice-floes in the spring, the quiet groan of a relationship beginning to tear itself apart. She looked at Toby, happily whisking sprays of water over his green dungarees and the blue lino. Hugo had been an easy baby to love, too, not as bright, but just as cuddly and forthcoming. The change had begun . . . when? He'd been nine when she'd first really noticed. You can never tell what they'll become.

'It affects you in another way too,' said Janet. 'Only if you want it to, of course. If I actually get in I shall give up NACRO, but till then I'm going to have to get my constituency work done in the evenings and weekends.'

'I see.'

'I'm not asking for your bridge nights, of course.'

'When's the election?'

'Depends when Thatcher can dig herself out of the mess she's in. It's got to be by the summer of 1992, so it'll be spring that year, most likely. Possibly the autumn before. You don't sound too keen. I don't want to ask Hugo.'

'No.'

Poppy knew the feeling well. So it had got that far, when even the most reasonable request becomes something you are going to be made beholden for, things you'd have taken for granted a few weeks back.

'And I'll have to find somebody for Saturdays—Hugo will want to go down to the cottage, of course.'

'Why Saturdays?'

'Because there are people around you can't catch other times. It wouldn't be every Saturday, Poppy.'

'No, I definitely don't want to commit weekends, I'm afraid.'

Poppy felt quite firm about this, though it was months since she'd had much by way of weekends away, apart from visits to the cottage. But to close the possibility off would be another bar in the cell window.

'I'll think about evenings,' she said. 'Of course I could do it, but you see . . . well, I love looking after Toby, and it came at the right time for me, but now I'm not sure it's been really good for me. It's sort of narrowing. And ageing. I like the nannies and young mums, and they've been very nice to me, but they have such limited ideas—I know that sounds snobbish, and there's all sorts of things they know and I don't, but . . . and they don't mean to, but they treat me sometimes as if I was a hundred and twenty. I'm going to be fifty in a couple of weeks. If I'd got a proper job it would be at least ten years till I retired. I refuse to let myself become just a granny, and nothing else any more. I need more in my life than baby-minding and bridge evenings and Radio 3. For a start I'm going to get myself a real job, and some new friends.'

'You've stopped seeing Alex?'

'Some time ago. You might as well know, I suppose. I gave him the push. I realised I was never more than a bit on the side for him. He kept telling me his marriage was dead, but really he wanted it still. It wasn't just that he hadn't got the guts to leave his wife—he was comfortable with her, used to her. At first he used to pretend, quite pleasantly, but then he stopped bothering. I wasn't having that.'

'Poor Poppy.'

'Toby got me on the rebound, you might say. But now . . .'

'What sort of a job, though?'

'I'm not unemployable, whatever you may think. First I'm going to go to evening classes and get my German back—I used to be pretty good—and I'll think about learning a third language . . .'

'Much better learn how to use a word processor.'

'Oh, well . . . But just with good German I ought to be able to find something. If I start getting myself together when the courses start—just a few weeks now—I should be able to aim for a real job about this time next year. But I'm going to need regular evenings, you see . . . It's none of my business, darling, but when I took Toby on you were talking about starting another baby around now.'

Janet laughed and stretched and shook her wild hair.

'Can't you see me on the hustings?' she said. 'Size of a double-decker bus. Remember what I was like with Toby? Vote earth mother for a better Britain!'

'I wonder how Mrs Capstone would counter that. I suppose there's lots of different kinds of earth mother. Some of them are pretty sinister.'

'Cruella de Ethelden. She's a Pro-lifer. She'd manage to imply that by rushing round canvassing I was trying to induce an abortion. How long has her kid been coming to the play centre?'

'This was the first time. The nanny said Deborah hadn't been getting on with the children at Holland Park, so she told her to try ours.'

'Fat chance. She doesn't want people saying she sends her kid out of the constituency to play with a nobbier lot.'

'Do you really think so? If Deborah had been happy there?'

'That sort of woman does absolutely nothing that isn't governed by how it can be presented in a press release.'

'Aren't all politicians like that? I don't mean you, darling.'

'I'll rely on you to tell me.'

'I wouldn't dare.'

'But you'd tell me all the same. You can't help letting people know what you think, even if you don't mean to. I know you don't want me to stand for Parliament, but I'm afraid I'm going to, all the same.'

'Yes, of course . . . What will Mrs Capstone do? About Toby and Deborah, I mean? When she finds out?'

'Get a picture into the papers with Toby in a tantrum and Deborah all smiles. Don't worry. The love affair will have blown over before she finds out, I shouldn't wonder. I'm standing as Janet Jones, of course, and Hugo's keeping right out of it, and you and Toby are both Taskers, so she may never . . . What is it, darling?'

The last four words were addressed to Toby, who had whisked all the water out of the bowl, and then spread it around the lino with a J-cloth by way of mopping up. Now, soaked and earnest, he was standing by Janet's leg and beating his closed fist against her kneecap, like a gnome in a picture book rapping on an oak trunk for the resident gnome to let him in. As soon as he'd got her attention he headed for the door. They heard him rattling the gate at the foot of the stairs.

'Bath-time, evidently,' said Janet. 'How I look forward to the day when I can send him off to have his own bath.'

'Oh, you're wrong! You'll find you long for the fun of bathing him.'

'Not me, Poppy. I'm not really an earth mother inside.'

'I must go, or Elias will be ripping the sofa to bits. Shall I ask around at the play centre and see if any of the girls would like to take on extra evenings? That would have the advantage that Toby would be used to them already.'

'If you're sure you don't want to do it yourself. There's no great hurry—the adoption meeting's not till November—but I'd like to get it fixed. Coming, darling! Coming!'

'Saturdays are going to be difficult.'

But Janet was already out of the door.

SEPTEMBER 1989

1

'Scuse me asking, Mrs Tasker, but Sue says you're looking for some-one to babysit Toby. Is that right?'

Laura was sitting on the bench just inside the playground gate. For once she wasn't knitting, and the way she rose the moment Poppy reached the gate made it clear she had been waiting for her to come.

'Do you know someone?' said Poppy. 'No, darling, you go and check the climbing frame by yourself. I want to talk to Laura. I'll be with you in a minute. Sorry, Laura. The thing is I was hoping to find one of the girls from here, because he's used to them, but of course none of them want to do Saturdays. So if you know someone reliable . . .'

'I get Saturdays off.'

'Oh. You mean you'd like to do it yourself?'

'I wouldn't mind.'

'But that would give you no free time at all. I mean . . .'

'It's all right,' said Laura. 'Their age, Saturday's bound to be dif-ficult, what with them all having their young fellows to think of.'

'What do you mean, their age?' said Poppy.

Laura stared at her, and she blushed. It's always a mistake to make jokes to deeply serious people like Laura, but Poppy realised the misunderstanding was her own fault for another reason. She had got the tone wrong, meaning it. She had been whiling away the twenty-minute ritual between park gate and the playground—duck feeding, peep-bo round the rhododendrons, twig along railings, gravel scratching and so on—with a rather successful variant on her furry-lover fantasy, in a cave on some western shore with the sun going down and reflected wave-ripple patterning the rock above. Laura's stare was not of simply surprise. It was as though she had come stumping into the cavern in full nanny uniform and found them at it. 'Miss Poppy! How dare you! No supper for *you*!'

Did Laura herself never enjoy any version of such imaginings? Perhaps that's what being a devoted nanny did to you, funnelling your emotional drives into surrogate motherhood and suppressing what didn't fit. Laura had never done anything else, starting when she was sixteen. She was now in her early forties, at a guess, and would go on looking after other people's babies till she retired. Her current employers preferred her not to wear uniform, but she dressed as close to it as she could. It was typical that she should call Poppy Mrs Tasker, though Poppy had no idea what Laura's own surname was. The two children she looked after, Sophie and Nick, were clean, obedient and beautifully dressed. Sophie, aged almost five, could be bossy towards other children, but Nick, a pretty two-year-old with curly, near-white hair, was vulnerably clinging.

One day, perhaps, one of her appointments would stick. She might be taken on to nanny the youngest of a family with a wide age range—more likely now than it would have been a generation ago, with almost Victorian spreads being achieved through divorces and remarriages and second and third families—so that by the time that child went to prep school older siblings might well have started a new generation for Laura to take over. Then she would simply stay, the family nanny, till her retirement, and that would have been her life, and ranks of sturdy young stockbrokers would attend her funeral. Apart from the children she looked after she seemed to have no existence at all.

Laura's look, compounded by the absurdity of finding herself blushing before it, made Poppy babble.

'It's got to be Saturdays,' she said, 'because that's when you can find people at home. Canvassing, you know, and meeting the party workers. I'll have to talk to my daughter-in-law about it, but I'm sure . . . if you are, I mean. Anyway there's a bit of time still. It's not going to start till next month some time.'

'Oh.'

Poppy heard the disappointment in Laura's voice and realised she genuinely wanted the job, needed it. It was hard to imagine why. She must be drawing a reasonable salary—her agency would have seen to that. And living in with the family she'd have almost no expenses. Perhaps there was an old mother she was helping to keep in a home somewhere. Something like that.

'Going to help Mrs Capstone, is she?' said Laura.

'Actually, no. Please don't pass this on. I haven't told any of the girls because I didn't want Peony telling Mrs Capstone. Toby and Deborah are such friends, you see. It might be awkward. But there's every chance my daughter-in-law will be the Labour candidate at the next election.'

The *Miss Poppy!* look was back.

'Oh, it's all right,' said Poppy. 'We're terribly respectable, I promise you. I've even joined the party, though I've voted Liberal all my life. As a matter of fact my daughter-in-law did it all for me first time, but we aren't all mad Militants, I promise you.'

'There's some of them will rob you blind,' said Laura, one of those mysterious, dark, nursery warnings to which old-fashioned nannies give utterance, carrying all the force of generations of wrong knowledge. Poppy was beginning to wonder whether the convenience of having Laura to look after Toby on Saturdays would be outweighed by the resulting culture confusion inside that small skull when Nick, who had been quietly toeing one of the play-centre trikes up and down the path in front of the bench, left it with his usual and rather frequent whining whimper and ran to Laura. Poppy looked and saw Deborah coming down the path.

Poppy had been half-watching Deborah's activities while she was talking to Laura. A few yards further along the path there was a structure known as the Wendy House, cuckoo-clock-shaped, with big eaves, painted blue and yellow. It stood near the bottom of a slope in the path, down which toddlers more adventurous than Nick used to free-wheel on the trikes. Deborah had commandeered the hut, and just as each child came to a halt she was darting out like a trap-door spider, seizing the trike and stuffing it through the door.

According to Janet, Mr Capstone was some kind of mysterious middle-European entrepreneur, so perhaps this was hereditary behaviour, an attempt to corner the trike market. Peony was nowhere in sight, though it was accepted that all minders had a duty to control the anti-social drives of their charges. Deborah had successfully bullied two tots off their machines with no more than the threat of a scream, and now, with a lull in the use of the slope, was ranging further afield for prey. Poppy rose from the bench and intercepted her.

'Hello, Deborah,' she said. 'Have you seen Toby? Where's Toby? I've lost Toby? Where can he be?'

Deborah didn't answer her smile. Her calm blue eyes stared back in disdain at the obviousness of the subterfuge, then glanced beyond Poppy to where, by the sound of it, Laura was reassuring Nick of his rights to the tricycle. She hesitated. They'd had a really successful game of hide-and-seek round the climbing frame and in and out of the open-ended barrels only yesterday afternoon. Happy and involved, Deborah could be a perfectly reasonable, likeable child.

'Oh, look,' said Poppy. 'There he is!'

Deborah gave in and followed her pointing arm. Toby had finished with the climbing frame and was rolling one of the barrels along the grass. He'd put a beach-ball into the barrel, and was trying to study its movement at the same time as trundling the barrel forward, but his co-ordination wasn't up to the complexities of the posture and as Poppy watched he fell flat on his face. Deborah forgot about the tricycle and scampered across to help.

The empathy between them was extraordinary. Though both, for different reasons, had previously tended to behave as natural solitaries, there was a bond between them whose nature Poppy didn't fully understand. Perhaps Deborah recognised that Toby was somehow not in competition with her, that his interests were such as she could not dominate, nor would he want to dominate her, while she for him had the fascination of glamour and strangeness. It wasn't a unique relationship, of course—a kindergarten version of Arthur Miller and Marilyn Monroe—and Deborah was a very pretty little girl. It was just surprising in babies.

At any rate it took no more than a demonstration trundle or two for Deborah to grasp what Toby wanted and start pushing the barrel while he crabbed along beside it studying the rotation of the ball. They ended with a bump against the larger slide. Toby prepared to shove the barrel back along its course, to give Deborah a chance to study the phenomenon, but she had spotted an unattended tricycle. She rushed off, commandeered it and brought it back. There was a slight Chinese-puzzle element in getting it past the rim of the barrel, and though Poppy could see how it would have to go she decided to let them work it out for themselves. They were still at it when Peony appeared.

'Hello,' said Poppy. 'You don't look that good.' 'Jesus, have I puked!' said Peony.

Everyone had a tan that summer, but her skin was drab grey-brown and her eyes bloodshot.

'Have you eaten something, do you think?' said Poppy. 'Hangover, mostly. My own fault. Shouldn't of let him talk me into trying that brandy. Lethal, that was.'

The name of Peony's Liverpool boyfriend slid conveniently into Poppy's mind.

'You had Randy down?' she said.

'Wasn't him. Imagine Randy eating squid? He'd die! Jesus!'

Poppy could hear the note of smugness under the groans. At least Peony had enjoyed herself the evening before, whatever she was suffering now.

'You'd better take it easy,' she said. 'I'll keep an eye on Deborah. She's no trouble while she's got Toby to play with.'

'Thanks a lot, Poppy. Listen, Mrs C. says I'm to take you back to tea one of these days. Some time she's there. OK?'

'So she can check if we're suitable playmates for Deborah?'

There was something about the idea of Mrs Capstone which made it difficult to keep the mockery out of one's voice, but Peony was in no state to notice. The children were happy for the moment with their barrel, so Poppy got out her copy of *Floodlight* and started to leaf through for language and word-processor courses, distracted by other possibilities. What openings were there, for instance, for a middle-aged, German-speaking, computer-literate dry-stone-waller in Central London? Peony dozed. The children rolled the tricycle in the barrel, and then each other, and then got in it together and wobbled it to and fro. Then they tried a variant of their yodelling game, using the barrel as a sound-box. Poppy began to listen with interest, and when Peony stirred she said, 'Listen. Can you hear? I think Deborah's taught Toby to sing.'

'Uh?'

'He's not just yelling into the barrel. That's a note. Of a sort. Are the Capstones musical?'

'Her Dad is, though it's not my idea. Stuff he'll listen to—like cats being fried alive!'

'Don't! How are you feeling?'

'Not so bad. What's the time? Think I'll take her home in a minute. You won't say anything to Mrs C about me having a sore head, will you? Only she might ask, see. She's like that. I don't want you to get the wrong idea—she's been ever so kind to me. She's not like they say, Poppy—really not, not at home, anyway. Mind you, he gives me the creeps.'

'I'll give you my number, and then perhaps you or Mrs Capstone can ring me and arrange a day.'

When Peony moved to break up the game and take Deborah home. Deborah loosed a bout of screaming, the first of the afternoon, but not as piercing or prolonged as usual, and in the end she settled into her push-chair with a good grace. Toby pecked her goodbye and then meandered about for a while, eventually settling into the sandpit, where he became fascinated by the way that, as he dug, the soft sift from the edges of the hole slithered inexorably back down its sloping sides. Several of the Nafia were on the benches beside the pit, including Laura, who having through most of the summer rather pointedly set herself apart from the girls—the trained and disciplined career nanny as distinct from these unreliable fly-by-nights—had in the last couple of weeks completely changed her stance and seemed to be making a determined effort to belong. The girls, being tolerant, accepted her, as no doubt at home they were used to accepting older and slightly odd relations into their extended families. As Poppy approached she rose and came over.

'You mustn't mind me, Mrs Tasker,' she said. 'There's a lot of very decent people of your way of thinking. I know that.'

'Oh, good heavens, I'm not worried if you aren't, and I'm sure Janet won't be either. I'll have a word with her tonight and we'll talk about it again tomorrow, if you're still interested.'

'Shan't be here tomorrow, Mrs Tasker. Got to take Sophie to the dentist.'

'Oh, Lord, is she starting already? Why must they grow up so fast?'

Laura looked at her, then at Toby sturdy and golden in the pit, then at Nick, bleach-haired, patting sand into a bucket.

'That's the pity of it, Mrs Tasker,' she said. 'That's just the pity of it.'

2

Next day was a return to the full blaze of summer, glare and inertia, bare brown torsos littering the grass, diversions from the usual route to the play centre in search of shade, a sense of tranquillity and well-being and thanks for such a season before winter. Almost all the children were out in the open, moving in random patterns in their bright Mothercare clothes. Poppy helped Toby inspect the climbing frame, then settled on a bench to try and work more seriously on *Floodlight*. She had only three more days to make up her mind about first choices and alternatives before the scrum and frustrations of booking in. She was distracted by Big Sue, Little Sue and Fran on the next bench. Fran was bringing the others up to date on the saga of her neighbour's domestic affairs. Fran brought her own son, Jason, to the play centre, and usually the neighbour's little girl, Winnie, as well, receiving an erratic token payment when the neighbour was in funds. The neighbour had a new man living with her, and a few weeks back her previous man—not Winnie's father—had come back and broken up her flat and given her a thrashing, the police had been called and the man arrested. Yesterday he'd appeared in court.

This was one of the bonuses of bringing Toby to the play centre. Occasionally, amid the repetitions and banalities of the conversation Poppy would be given glimpses of other lives, or scraps of gossip and other social titillations. They weren't often actually startling, though last year, before she'd begun coming, a girl called Jane had been working for one of the protagonists in a thoroughly English headline-making scandal involving sex, insider dealing, a viscount and a feud in a cricket club. Jane had left now, but Big Sue had told Poppy things about the case which hadn't appeared in the newspapers. And more recently she'd heard Big Sue herself telling her friends about her previous employer, some kind of BBC executive, who'd been in the habit of coming home while his son was having his pre-lunch rest and trying to get Big Sue into bed with him. Big Sue was diabetic and earned her adjective but was still attractive in a creamy, cushiony way, so the episode was easy to imagine. Poppy was interested too in the conventions of these exchanges—suppose the man had been her present employer, would Big Sue have been so forthcoming? Probably not. She would have told Little Sue, and perhaps Fran, in confidence, Poppy thought, and that would have been it.

By now Toby and Deborah had joined forces. Deborah had commandeered the Wendy House again, and together they'd rolled a barrel over to it and jammed it endwise into the entrance, like the tunnel into an igloo, so that Toby could carry out a variant on yesterday's acoustic experiments. Further up the slope Nell was helping Nelson use the slide, encouraging him to abandon himself to the pull of the earth and waiting to catch him at the bottom. Her love, his trust, were manifest in stance and gesture. Together they composed an idyll, sufficient to each other, Eden-innocent in the perfect afternoon.

The thought itself must have been the serpent. Poppy sensed a change in the mood on the bench next door. Fran had stopped her recital. The girls had been muttering, notes of doubt and warning, and now their poses stiffened. They were all three gazing steadily towards the clump of trees outside the fence, between the play centre and the pond. She switched specs to see what was bothering them, saw, and joined her stare to theirs. This was how you dealt with this problem.

Rapt in his own interest the man didn't for the moment notice he was being watched. He was a silhouette, black as the tree-trunks against the grass glare and pond glitter beyond the patch of shade. He was slight, and was wearing a short, Burberry-style coat. He had a beard, but his other features were invisible in the shadow. He didn't move. His stance, as he dragged on his cigarette and dropped the butt on to the ground, declared that this was not a casual passer-by, stopping for a moment to enjoy the pretty antics of the children as he might have enjoyed the bright-feathered ducks on the pond, but a watcher, serious, intent, motivated. He seemed to Poppy to be looking at Toby.

Deborah was inside the Wendy House, singing through the barrel. The round bulge of Toby's nappy-padded overalls, where he knelt to call back into the apparatus, was all there was for the man to study. There were no other children near. Poppy concentrated her stare. Any moment now he would realise, turn and go. It always worked. They couldn't stand the focused gaze of twenty women. This sort of thing had happened a couple of times since she'd been coming to the play centre, and then, though disgusted at the necessity, she had found the power of this communal weapon actually exhilarating. Now, with the man seeming to be particularly intent on Toby, she felt only hatred, fright and shock.

In less than a minute most of the enclosure, including some of the children, had joined the gaze. Without looking, Poppy was aware of the accumulation of energies. In her peripheral vision she saw someone wheel a push-chair through the gate, stop just inside and turn to stare too. Now the man's concentration broke. He looked round, mimed a moment of bravado by tapping at his pocket as if for another cigarette and realising that he needed to buy a fresh packet, turned and walked away.

Poppy's heart was hammering. She watched him dwindling into the sunlight along the path by the pond, his pale coat flapping at his hams. The coat looked newish. His walk wasn't a derelict's shamble. She tried to summon up the proper thoughts into her mind—just one of those things, poor sod, something must have gone badly wrong in his life, way, way back . . . (They should be painlessly done away with and buried six feet deep in lime!)

She shivered. The sun, so honest and strong ten minutes ago, had no warmth in it. She was aware of the girls beginning to talk again, a group of them now, five or six.

'I'd like to see them all hanged, that sort.'

'Hanging's too good.'

'If I got my hands on him.'

'Probation's all he'd get, till he actually went and did something.'

'Cut their cocks off, first offence, that's what I say.'

'Got his eye on Toby, hadn't he? You OK, Poppy?'

She looked up.

'It's all right,' she said. 'It's just one of those things.'

'Don't be so bloody soft,' said Big Sue. 'Sorry, Poppy, but it makes me sick, that line. Pussyfooting around with psychiatrists. Not their fault. Jesus! I'd teach him a thing or too if I could get hold of him!'

She meant it, too, for the moment at least. Her big face was a mask of primal anger, the muscles bunched, the dark and usually rather dreamy eyes now hard and glittering.

'Easy, Sue, easy,' said Fran.

'I'd cut their cocks off, then I might feel easy.'

There were mutters of agreement. Poppy said nothing and felt ashamed, partly at the feebleness of her liberal conscience in not attempting to reason with them, but more because in her heart she knew she didn't believe that conscience either. She welcomed the distraction of Nell coming down the path, shoving the push-chair with one hand and with Nelson looking bewildered on the other arm. Nell's face was set.

'It's all right,' said Poppy, 'he's gone. He won't come back. It's just one of those things.'

'See you tomorrow,' said Nell and strode past.

Slowly the mood of outrage subsided. Those children who had noticed anything strange quickly forgot, and scampered and triked and dug and explored as usual. The girls split into smaller groups. Poppy forced herself back into *Floodlight*, marked possible courses and made decisions. Later on a policewoman turned up, summoned by the play-leader, George, on the hut telephone, and took statements. Poppy excused herself on the grounds of her poor distance vision and left early.

The man was waiting for her by the entrance to the park.

She was almost sure it was the same man. He sat on a bench in the rose garden just inside the gate. His head was bowed aside as he lit a fresh cigarette from the butt of an old one. He had a beard and wore jeans and a dark green, thin sweater. A pale coat, folded to show its tartan lining, lay on the bench beside him. Solitary people often used those benches, and Poppy was already past him before she realised that it might have been him.

Waiting at the crossing it was natural that she should turn to watch for the stream of cars to stop. Seeing the push-chair they did so almost at once, but not before the man had emerged from the gate and stood on the kerb, his head turned away as he too watched the traffic. She was aware of him threading between the halted cars to her right as she crossed. She felt angry and frightened, but reasonably in control.

The first thing was to verify that he was in fact following her. Then she must shake him off, or find a policeman, or confront him. Above all she mustn't lead him back to Janet's house in Abdale Grove. She walked up the wrong side of Belling Road to the chemist's, where she bought an unneeded spare toothbrush. Waiting for change she could study the road outside. He'd gone. No, that was him in Frith's opposite. She walked back down Belling Road, past her usual turn, and swung the push-chair round to back in through the door of Jinja's Megastore, a perfectly natural manoeuvre apart from the suddenness of the move. The man wasn't ready. He was still on the opposite pavement and she'd caught him sufficiently by surprise to make him turn his head away and thus collide with an elderly man in a turban who was trudging in the opposite direction bowed down by two carrier bags full of vegetables. Toby was restless by now—shopping didn't amuse him if he couldn't do it himself—so she bought him an illicit packet of crisps.

'There's a man following us,' she told Mrs Jinja at the till. 'That chap with the coat over his arm. Will you take a good look at him, just in case? I'm trying to think how to get rid of him—I don't want him to know where Toby lives.'

Mrs Jinja swung her bulk round to look through the window. The man was in profile now, studying the window of the Halal butcher's on the corner as if choosing a meal. The face was pale above the beard, with a curving nose repeating the curve of the high forehead. Nothing special.

'You must go down to the school crossing and speak to Jim,' said Mrs Jinja in her gentle, toneless voice. 'He is good. There were boys making racial remarks to Farah and her friends when they left school. Jim dealt with them.'

'That's an idea. Thanks.'

She went back to the main road, turned right and right again into Starveling Lane. Jim was at the crossing waiting for school to end. She had never spoken to him but knew him by sight, a stolid-moving, pink-faced middle-sized man. She knew his name because according to Darlene at the play centre he'd saved some child's life on the crossing last term, something to do with a skidding motor-bike. He was standing by the beacon with his lollipop, but seeing her turn the push-chair for the crossing he came into the road, though there wasn't a moving car in sight, and signalled her to cross, accompanying her back to the far pavement. She slowed her pace to prolong the time for talk.

'Thanks,' she said. 'Mrs Jinja told me to come to you. There's a man been following us—Toby he's after. Jeans, green jersey, coat over his arm.'

He didn't hesitate in his stride, look back or question her.

'Spotted him,' he said. 'Straight into the school, through the swing doors. Right, and all the way along the passage. Takes you out past the school office at the senior entrance. Have a good look round soon as you're out. If he's there, back into the office and tell Trixie as I sent you. She'll call the police.'

They had reached the far pavement and stood facing each other. His pale greyish eyes gazed confidently at her.

'That's marvellous,' she said. 'Thank you so much.'

'Don't you worry, love. I'll sort him out.'

He upped his lollipop and turned to recross the road. She pushed into the school, opened only two years back after the fire, now bright-coloured and angular, like a bit of play apparatus for a brood of giants, but already pocked and scarred with the abrading tide of children that sluiced in and out each day. As she turned at the top of a ramp to buttock her way through the swing doors she could see Jim on the far pavement, facing her follower, the embodiment of sturdy civic decency.

Toby had finished the crisps and fallen asleep. The main corridor was almost empty. The feel of a new academic year just started hung in the air. A few older children scurried past with loose-leaf folders. No one questioned her. From the classrooms came the stir and scuffle of books being stuffed into desks, equipment being cleared, chairs reordered. A boy held the far door for her. Out in the street the follower was nowhere to be seen.

She pushed home through side-streets. Since Jim had confronted and presumably accused the man she felt there was no harm in turning suddenly at random to look behind her, until it struck her that to passers-by she might look like a batty old woman running off with someone else's child. There was no way of not crossing Belling Road. If he'd gone back to wait for her there he'd be difficult to spot amid the shoppers. She crossed it and took a roundabout way back to Abdale Grove, pausing on corners to check behind her.

3

Too tired to cook but pleasantly on the edge of wooziness after the second gin, Poppy opened a can of mackerel fillets, cut up the last of the Chinese leaves, spooned on oil and vinegar and told herself it was a healthy meal. What had she done? Walked a mile or so further than usual. Why should fright and anger make her feel as though she'd crossed half a county, physically fought a troop of men, to bring Toby safe home? Radio 3 was Delius, moody-ethereal, so she'd put on a tape of Aida to buck herself up.

A third gin? Wicked, and if she had a third there'd be only a couple more tots in the bottle and she'd be bound to have them too, even if she'd tried locking the bottle in the filing-box . . . Elias rubbed against her calves, purring like an outboard motor. She'd given him the can to lick with a few scraps in it, but the smell of mackerel on her plate roused him from his normal lethargic calm to gluttonous ecstasy.

The doorbell rang. It would be those young men from that scheme, selling dusters and oven-gloves. Poppy balanced her plate on the lampshade, out of Elias's reach, and went to the door trying to think of excuses. There's a limit to the number of ironing-board covers a single woman in a basement flat can wear out in a year.

It was Jim.

'Just thought I'd look round, see you're all right,' he said. 'Mrs Tasker, isn't it?'

'Oh, do come in. I'm so glad to see you. I was going to come and thank you tomorrow. You were marvellous. And I want to know what happened.'

He didn't hesitate but followed her into the living-room. Elias's purr as he rubbed himself against the lamp-standard competed with Caballé. Poppy snatched the teetering plate and turned the volume down.

'That's a cat and a half,' said Jim. 'Shown him, ever?'

'He hasn't got a pedigree. He just turned up at a friend's house three years ago, half starved, and they didn't want to keep him. We thought he was full-grown then, but he wasn't, nothing like. I'm afraid that if I showed him someone might say he was theirs.'

'Not a spot on him anywhere.'

'Actually he's got an invisible black collar under the white. You can only see it when he's moulting. He's behaving like this because of the mackerel.'

'I'm stopping you eating your tea.'

'Don't worry—it's cold. Won't you have something? I've got some gin. Or I could make some coffee.'

'I wouldn't say no to a spot of gin and water.'

'Just water? Not tonic?'

'Water—about half and half.'

'Ice?'

'Bruises the gin, my dad used to say.'

Now that she had the excuse Poppy gave herself a smaller tot than she might have if she'd been swigging defiantly alone.

'Ta,' said Jim.

'How did you know my name? Where I lived?'

'Asked Mrs Jinja. How're you feeling, then? Nasty that was for you. But you told the kiddie's mum about it, acourse?'

'Yes—she's my daughter-in-law. I played it down a bit. I didn't want to frighten her. But you're right, Jim . . . I don't know your other name . . .'

'Jim Bowles. Jim'll do fine. Nobody calls me anything else these days.'

'I'm Poppy. It's silly, but it can't be helped. What was I saying?'

'Me being right about something.'

'Oh yes—it *was* nasty. Afterwards I felt as if I'd, well, had a rape attempt on me, myself.'

'Don't blame you.'

'What did he say?'

'Effed and blinded a bit, and then he tried to make out as he was from the papers, following up a story. Hadn't got a press pass, natch.'

'I keep asking myself what I'm going to do if he shows up again.'

'Came to see you about that. Now, first off . . . Hold it . . .'

He was listening to the music, head cocked on one side and lips moving. Poppy rose and turned the volume up. It was the famous march, of course, but when he started to hum along he wasn't following the main theme.

'Is that the woodwind?' said Polly. 'Bassoon?'

'Trombone,' he said and returned to the music, absorbed as a child. Poppy joined in with the trumpets, far less expertly. Encouraged, he let himself go, bomping and baahing full throat. They were driving into the final *tutti* when Poppy noticed Elias staring up at her with that look of affront and disbelief which cats keep for outrages on their ideas of dignity. She collapsed into laughter. Jim closed with an unperturbed flourish and turned the volume down. Poppy could sense an inner lip-smack of self-satisfaction.

'If I had a fiver for every time I've played that,' he said.

'Was Verdi using trombones as early as *Aida*?'

'Brass band I'm talking about. West London Police Band. I still turn out for them if they're short.'

'What else have I got . . .'

'First things first, Poppy. About if that fellow comes hanging around at the play centre. I'll drop down to the station tomorrow, have a word with Terry Hicks. He'll send someone along to talk to you, Ozzie Osborne, most like. Telephone at the play centre?'

'Yes. George has probably reported it already.'

'Right. Ozzie will know, then. She'll give you a number and who to ask for. And most like she'll drop by off and on for a couple of weeks, walk you home.'

'Oh, Jim, that's marvellous! It's such a load off my mind! I can't thank you enough.'

'Listen to a bit more music, shall we? Not this caterwauling, mind.'

'It isn't caterwauling!'

'And those fellows bawling away like they're showing their tongues to the doctor.'

'1 don't think I've got any proper brass band music.'

'Bet you have, too. Bet you've got old Vivaldi.'

'Yes, of course, but . . .'

'Let's have *Spring*, then, for starters. Some bloody good tunes in there. Anything left in that gin bottle?'

• • •

Buying her *Guardian* next morning Poppy thanked Mrs Jinja for her advice.

'He was wonderful,' she said. 'He didn't just rescue us; he came round in the evening to tell me what to do if the man turned up again. Oh, you know that, of course—you gave him my address.'

'I hope you did not mind.'

'Of course not. Why?'

Mrs Jinja's mouth closed to a purple blob, like a shrinking anemone, in the large fawn face.

'Jim has a certain reputation, you understand me?' she said. 'I was careful to ask Mr Jinja's permission before I consulted him about Farah's difficulty.'

'I think I can look after myself.'

'He has his pension from the police. He does not need the money for being a crossing warden.'

'He says he likes being useful.'

'He also likes to inspect the young mothers who come to collect their children, and to make friends while they are waiting by the gate, and to be asked for advice, and to call round perhaps while the husband is working, and then . . . who knows, Mrs Tasker, who knows?'

Poppy laughed.

'I promise you we spent the whole evening listening to music.'

'You do not object to my telling you this?'

'Of course not. I'm flattered.'

OCTOBER 1989

1

A vast Mercedes was waiting by the far entrance to the park. The chauffeur, blue-chinned, Greek-looking, simply stood and watched while Peony and Poppy collapsed their pushchairs and stowed them in the boot. There was a baby-seat fixed for Deborah in the back, but Poppy had to sit beside her with Toby on her lap, trying to control his impulse to explore every knob and handle. Peony sat in the front with the chauffeur, separated from the rear by a glass partition, and Poppy had the amusement of being able to watch their body language. When people know you can't hear them they tend to forget how much their subsidiary modes of communication express their meanings and emotions. Even the back of the man's head and the way his hands rested on the wheel expressed a ruthless assumption of dominance, while Peony's shrugs and turnings away, hoity-toity but come-hither, were just as speaking. Poppy had little doubt by the time the short trip was over that the chauffeur had been the squid-guzzling brandy-plier responsible for Peony's sorry state a few days ago.

The house was nothing like as imposing as Poppy had expected, nor as large, until she realised that the establishment included the house next door. The two stood in a twisting, cobbled side-street, one of those sudden oddnesses you find in London's inner suburbs, where the rush of patterned development over what until a hundred years ago had been fields and gardens was intruded on by an older shape, some track or lane which had been there for centuries as a thorough-fare when Acton and Kensington were still villages and Kensal still was green. Poppy, in lonely evening walks after her separation from Derek, had passed through it several times and had told herself that she must try and look up old maps and see what its purpose had been but had never got round to doing so.

Deborah had what was effectively her own suite, with day nurs-ery and kitchen on the ground floor and bedrooms for herself and Peony on the floor above. Mrs Capstone had her office on the top floor, Peony said, but she and Mr Capstone lived and entertained next door. There was a little garden behind, paved, with a few shrubs, and beyond that the back of a mews, where the cars were kept, with a flat for the chauffeur above. Deborah instantly assumed the role of chatelaine and insisted on showing Toby her realm, so Poppy kept an eye on them while Peony got tea ready. Interestingly, though the place reeked of wealth, it did so as much by restraint as by ostenta-tion. Even Deborah's bedroom, for instance, didn't have the hoard of toys Toby owned, and there were only a couple of soft animals in the cot, and no dolls.

The bathroom contained a bidet. Toby was entranced. Real taps at his level, with real water gushing out, and a fancy waste-plug oper-ated by a lever. The situation remained under control for about thirty seconds, with Poppy closing the taps and opening the plug as fast as he opened and closed them. Deborah at first hung back. It had apparently never crossed her mind to treat the bidet as a plaything, people rather than objects being her sphere, but as soon as she joined in Poppy had four hands against her two, one for each tap, one to keep the plug closed and the fourth to flail at the rapidly rising water, drenching all three of them and a fair-sized area round the bidet.

'No!' cried Poppy. 'Stop it, Toby! Stop it, Deborah! No!'

But their joint excitement had reached critical mass, feeding each other's, whipping them towards hysteria, a two-tot rioting mob, out of control of the state apparatus. Poppy seized both taps, forced them shut and held them All four fists welted the water. The splash shot into her face. Her spectacles fell. She was soaked, blind. The children whooped with the joy of freedom.

'And what is going on here?' said a woman's voice at the door.

'Help!' said Poppy.

Deborah was snatched away and immediately started to scream. Poppy groped, grabbed Toby and held him to her while she tried to rub the water from her eyes with the back of her wrist and then peered for her spectacles. Their tortoiseshell frames made them invisible on the brown carpet. She patted desperately around. Toby wriggled like a trapped animal.

'More,' he shouted. 'More baa!'

('Baa' was a new word, corrupted from the adult 'bath' and describing all things wet, other than drinks.)

'Not now, darling. Please, where are my specs—I'm blind without them.'

'By your left knee,' said the voice, both brisk and patient.

Poppy shoved them on and rose. The lenses were wet, so all was still blur. Toby threshed in her grasp.

'I'm terribly sorry,' she began, but the rest was drowned by Toby's yell. Why, after days of angelhood, must he choose this moment for a tantrum?

'If you go on like that, Deborah, you will be shut in your room,' said the woman, dim-seen through wet lenses but obviously Mrs

Capstone, though somehow not what Poppy had expected from the public image. Of course the scene in the bathroom was different from the average photo opportunity. Mrs Capstone seemed not to need to raise her voice to penetrate the yells but Poppy had to mouth her answers.

'Toby will stop in a minute or two,' she said. 'I'm terribly sorry. I'm afraid they're drenched.'

'I'll find him something. This way. Close the bathroom door, please.'

They carried the yelling infants into Deborah's bedroom. Mrs Capstone put Deborah down, opened a cupboard and began to pick out clothes. Deborah stood where she'd been placed, concentrating on her note.

'More baa! More baa!' bellowed Toby.

Poppy had never seen him so outraged. Perhaps he had sensed her own discomfort at the visit to this formidable woman's home having begun with such a display of ill-discipline, mess and temper. (Mrs Capstone's latest campaign was for stiffer penalties for football hooligans.) He was making more noise than Deborah, so much so that she must have noticed that she was being upstaged. Her scream continued but the look in her eyes changed. She took a couple of paces forward. Her hand rose to her mouth and moved to and fro, making the note waver.

Poppy knelt and twisted her threshing burden round till he faced Deborah.

'Look, darling. Look what Deborah's doing.'

He took no notice, still wrestling, still trying to make for the door. Deborah came up and put her face only inches from his, yodelling away, and all at once he gave in. Poppy could sense a sort of inner male, 'Oh, well. Women!' He gave one more sulky look towards the door before he set up an alto hoot, stopping and unstopping his mouth with his hand. At last Poppy was able to let go and wipe her specs dry.

The children kept the game up, with variants, while they were laid side by side on the bed, stripped and changed into dry clothes. The noise was possible to talk through.

'I haven't heard her do that before,' said Mrs Capstone.

'It's something they invented. Deborah's taught him to sing, too, after a fashion. She's very musical, isn't she?'

'I wouldn't know. If she is it comes from her father. You're Mrs Tasker, aren't you—his grandmother?'

'Poppy Tasker.'

'I'm Clara Capstone.'

'I'm terribly sorry about the mess in the bathroom. He's never seen a bidet before. He simply has to find out how things work and what you can do with them, but then Deborah joined in and it got out of control.'

'Would he be allowed to play with a bidet at home, supposing there were one?'

'He's pretty good, really. He knows where he's allowed to make messes, and my daughter-in-law organises it for that.'

'I discourage messes of any kind.'

Time, Poppy decided, to rise above the level of acquiescent contrite worm, though it had in fact taken her time to get used to what Janet regarded as acceptable levels of chaos—painting sessions, for instance, in which floor and walls, clothes and flesh, moved towards a sort of visual entropy of puddled blue and yellow smears.

'I brought my own children up like that,' she said. 'Now I'm not sure I was right. Of course it's so much easier with the kind of paints you can buy, and everything washable.'

Mrs Capstone rose without replying.

'There,' she said. 'That's better. You're dry now, Deborah, so you can stop making that racket and we'll go and have some tea. I'll tell Peony to put Toby's clothes in the tumbler and they'll be dry by the time you go home. What about you, Mrs Tasker?'

Poppy fastened the Velcro shoulder-strap on the loaned overalls and took off her specs for a final wipe.

'I'll be all right,' she said. 'It mostly went over my face. I'll steam off during tea. I was going to wash my hair this evening anyway.'

She settled her specs on and saw that Mrs Capstone was gazing at her, openly weighing her up, as if considering whether to hire her as an employee. She did this in a perfectly straightforward way, so that it didn't seem an intrusion on inner privacies. It was the sort of look the young give you sometimes on meeting, those adventurers for whom the decades seem to spread away before them like rich provinces waiting to be sacked. Mrs Capstone still had that look of youth, though she was thirty-nine according to Janet, a child of the squirearchy, reared and educated to marry her kind and breed more of the same. She must have decided that the power which was her birthright had left the ancestral acres, and she must seek it elsewhere for herself, but she still had that look about her, the forthright gaze, the slightly plump assurance, the blonde and tended hair, the good bones.

'More baa?' said Toby hopefully, now that he had a whole set of dry clothes to soak again.

'Tea now,' said Poppy.

It went well enough. Baked beans and ice cream for the children, tea and digestives for the adults. Toby was too interested in his surroundings to feed himself with proper attention, so spread his meal lavishly in the general area of his mouth. Deborah concentrated on eating with the same attention as that with which she could concentrate on her scream. At home she seemed a half-different child, a handful still, but neat and self-possessed.

Poppy, meanwhile, coped with Mrs Capstone's inquisition. Mrs Capstone had that kind of quick, superficial intelligence which needs to be fed a mass of fact which it will then store with great efficiency, so that if they were to meet in a year's time she would immediately know Poppy's name and ask whether there were any more grandchildren in New Zealand and what her doctor son-in-law thought of the health system there. The process wasn't mechanical. She was genuinely interested, within the limits of a not very subtle imagination. Long ago Poppy, faced with the occasional need to account for her separation from Derek and knowing the impossibility of explaining (even to herself) the involved, self-generating network of motives and actions, of understandings and misunderstandings, which had led to the event, had decided it was simplest to say flatly 'He left me for a younger woman.' This was at least true, though really a crude and, in a way, unimportant part of the truth.

Mrs Capstone sighed, shook the blonde waves and said just as flatly 'They will do it.'

There it was. Life. Airlines overbooked flights. Maintenance engineers failed to keep appointments after you'd waited in for them all day. Boys hit tennis bails through neighbours' conservatories. Men left wives for younger women. Not impersonal facts, but all worth a perfectly genuine brisk sigh. It was easy to see why Peony had found her kind.

'But your son is still in England?'

The awkward moment was coming. Not that Poppy intended to lie, or even to conceal the truth if the conversation came anywhere near it. Mrs Capstone was perfectly capable of handling the trivial contretemps with complete aplomb, but the danger was that she might be able to make something of it later, to Janet's disadvantage.

'Hugo, yes. He's in charge of the legal list at an academic publisher's. I can't say . . .'

'Deborah, no!'

Poppy turned her head and saw that while Deborah had finished her ice-cream Toby, having smeared large dollops round his cheeks, was now engaged in seeing whether by piling what was left in his bowl up into a mound he could convert it from its semi-liquid state back into its original solid. Ice-cream wasn't regular fare at Abdale Grove; so this wasn't an experiment he'd been able to try recently. Absorbed, he seemed not to notice as Deborah leaned across and scraped a blob of ice-cream off his face. The spoon paused in mid-air at her mother's command. Then, with a look of defiant smugness, she popped her booty into the neat round of her mouth. Poppy laughed. Encouraged Deborah reached out for more.

'You can put her down now, Peony,' said Mrs Capstone. 'I think Toby's really finished too,' said Poppy. 'Shall I clean you up, darling?'

'Num gone?'

'Yes. It melts if you don't eat it up. That's why you have to keep it in the fridge.'

He nodded and let her remove the bowl and wipe his face with kitchen paper.

'He can't really understand that,' said Mrs Capstone.

'No, of course not, but he likes to have things explained. He knows there've got to be explanations. It's no use just saying "Don't touch. Hot." You have to tell him about electrons jiggling around to make it hot or something like that.'

'You're lucky to have the time. You were telling me about your son—Hugo, you said—law publishing. I imagine that's been . . .'

Rescue again, and what for an instant Poppy thought was a theatrical mask being poked round the door.

'Daddydaddydaddydaddydaddy,' squealed Deborah and rushed across the room. The man picked her up as he came in and held her bouncing on his arm and yelling his name. The mask effect had been only an accident of light, enhanced by the angle at which he had held his head. His features were acceptably human, though emphatically modelled on the large head, with strong black eyebrows slashed across prominent brows, a bony nose and a wide, hard mouth. He was of medium height but very broad-shouldered, the sort of build no tailoring seems to fit. His pale grey suit looked expensive but was still under strain.

'We're having a tea-party, darling,' said Mrs Capstone. 'Do you want Peony to warm you some milk?'

'No, thank you. I came to say I have to go to Trieste. I shall be back on Thursday.'

The voice was harsh and flat, reviving the mask effect—hidden actor inside the tank-like body, behind the modelled visor, using a mechanical vocaliser. Nobody knew much about him, Janet had said. No wonder.

'What time do you land?' said Mrs Capstone.

'Eighteen-fifty, supposedly.'

'That'll do, provided you're not more than forty minutes late. I'll have your dinner-jacket in the car. If you're later than that Constantin will meet you in the Mercedes and I'll go direct to the Coombeses in your car.'

Deftly he tilted Deborah back, caught her by the ankles and swung her to and fro pendulumwise in front of him with her dark hair streaming down. As her laughter verged towards hysteria he flipped her over, crouched and set her on her feet. Clearly she sensed he was about to go, but instead of screaming tried to prolong his interest by showing off her new trick, singing on a pure high note and using her hand to make a flutter effect. Toby at once joined in. The result was discord, but Deborah altered her pitch to make it tolerable.

'Did you hear that?' said Poppy. 'That's what I mean about her being musical.'

'Mrs Tasker says Deborah is musical, darling,' said Mrs Capstone.

'Even when she screams she's really singing,' said Poppy. 'Like a prima donna.'

'When prima donnas scream, they scream,' said Mr Capstone, evidently speaking from experience. 'I'm afraid I have to take Constantin with me.'

He tousled Deborah's hair as he rose.

'No, that won't work, darling,' said Mrs Capstone. 'We need him to . . .'

'Can't be helped. You'll have to make some other arrangement.'

'But really . . . !'

'I haven't time to talk about it now.'

Mrs Capstone kept her voice and face under perfect control. Poppy merely sensed the surge of anger.

'Well, if you've got to have him . . . In that case . . . I'll get my diary and we'll sort things out in the car. At least then I can drive it home.'

'If you're free . . .'

His glance at Poppy registered that she was of no interest or importance.

'I'll need to go in ten minutes,' he said, and left. Deborah made no attempt to delay him by clinging, though she looked for a moment as if she was thinking of trying the effect of a scream. Mrs Capstone rose.

'I hope you don't mind,' she said. 'My husband's a busy man, and I don't see as much of him as I'd like.'

The charm seemed unforced, though no doubt a lifetime in politics would coarsen the act.

'I quite understand,' said Poppy. 'Toby will have a lovely time investigating Deborah's toys.'

'She doesn't have as many as some children. I don't believe in that, but . . . oh well, why not, once in a way? Put plenty of towels down in the bathroom, Peony, and they can play with the bidet again.'

2

When she got home Poppy found Nell sitting on the steps down to her basement flat, reading a cloth book to Nelson.

'Hello,' she said. 'What's the matter? Have you been waiting long?'

'Council are closing the commune. Tonight it's going to be. They wanted to take us by surprise but we got told.'

Poppy saw a crammed old rucksack in the corner under the arch made by the steps up to the house above.

'I'm so glad you took me at my word,' she said. 'I was afraid you mightn't. Come in and we'll make a pot of tea.'

'Tea would be great. Thanks a lot, Poppy. It'll be just two or three days till we can sort something out.'

'That's fine.'

Elias tolerated Toby, but viewed other children with deep distrust. As Poppy opened the kitchen door he rose royally from his cushion on the dresser, purring with the prospect of food, but seeing Nelson he assumed a look of affront and stalked out through the cat-flap. Nelson, a gentle and sweet-natured boy, gave a coo of delight and ran to the glass door into Poppy's little back garden, pressing his nose close against the pane so that he could watch Elias taking out his resentment on what had once been a lilac but had degenerated into a scratch-pole with occasional sad leaves. Poppy made tea, found biscuits, showed Nell how the cooker worked so that she could warm milk for Nelson, put out half a can of Whiskas for Elias and led the way back to the living-room.

'I'll sleep in here,' she said. 'I've done it before. There's room for both of you in my bed, and we'll get more privacy that way.'

'Oh, no, that isn't right.'

They argued about it, but Poppy was firm. Nelson was a quite different character from Toby, who by now would have discovered the gas-tap and the telephone and the TV controls and Poppy's sewing-machine, which she'd had out three weeks now, meaning to finish shortening the yellow skirt she'd bought for the holiday with Alex that hadn't happened. Instead Nelson, clutching his tortoise with one arm and sucking from his mug in his other hand, made cautious forays round the sofa, looked under cushions more as if he was checking for booby-traps than hoping to find buried treasure, and at last, deciding that this was a safe, or at least neutral, environment, began a quiet game of peep-bo over the arm of the sofa. Despite his caution he didn't seem to Poppy a boring child. His face was humorous and intelligent. When he was still you could almost sense his thought processes, much more abstract and flexible than Toby's. His puzzlements and wonders were whys, not hows. When Elias at last padded into the room, sulky and suspicious, Nelson gave his crow of delight and his dark face shone with interest, but he allowed Nell to hold him still and simply watched Elias

climb on to Poppy's lap and settle there, glowering. While Poppy
stroked Elias reassuringly Nell led Nelson over. Slowly he put his
nose close up against the cat's, squinting into the green, resentful
eyes, touched the white paw with a gentle hand and allowed himself
to be distracted back to the sofa.

'There,' said Poppy. 'That wasn't too bad, was it, Elias? They aren't
all little Genghis Khans.'

'What's the time?' said Nell. 'Hell! Can we have the telly on? Bet
we've missed it.'

'Yes, of course. What?'

'News South-east. Soon as we heard the Council were coming we
rang round the media. Look! Must have missed some of it.'

A street scene, policemen, officials, two large semidetached houses
with ornate but damaged stucco, boarded lower windows, a barricade
of iron bedsteads across the front door, faces at the upper windows,
beards, T-shirts, a banner across the frontage 'E & O COUNCIL—
THATCHER'S THUGS'.

'. . . had hoped to take the squatters by surprise,' the voice-over
was saying, 'but evidently the news had been leaked and the Council
officials, who refused to be interviewed, have decided against a violent confrontation. Negotiations are now taking place. Meanwhile
the squatters have allowed a BBC camera crew into the so-called
commune.'

Cut to interior scenes, a tidy bedroom with three mattresses on
the floor, a kitchen with women preparing a meal in large pots, a
communal sitting-room with a group sitting cross-legged on the floor
folk-singing, a notice-board. Zoom in to a blown-up news photograph with speech balloons drawn onto it *Private Eye* fashion. Mrs
Capstone getting into the big Mercedes, the chauffeur holding the
door, Mr Capstone in profile on the other side of the car. Poppy's TV

wasn't good enough for her to be able to read the caption in the balloon, but she laughed all the same.

'What does it say?' she said.

'Can't remember. People kept changing it. Wasn't that good.'

'I've just been having tea with her, you know. I was pretty scared, but I liked her much more than I expected.'

Nell said nothing, but stared at the TV, though the item about the squatters was signing off.

'That's one of the difficult things,' said Poppy. 'I mean, it seems to work out that often you like people you don't agree with and you don't much care for people who've got what you think are the right ideas. I like you. I like you a lot, as a matter of fact. I love to see you with Nelson, but I expect I'd be very uncomfortable with a lot of your ideas.'

'Liking doesn't matter.'

'Oh, I don't agree. I think all those things matter more than anything, love, friendship, liking, affection. You don't mean to tell me that when Nelson grows up and starts thinking for himself, you're going to stop loving him if he thinks differently from you.'

'Please, Poppy. I don't want to talk about it. The answer is yes. If that happens. But till then. That's why it's so important, having him now. I don't want to talk about it. Please.'

There was distress in her voice. Poppy longed to reach out, to hug her to her, the daughter in need she hadn't got, not masterful Janet, not Anna, deliberately self-distanced on the far side of the world.

'OK, but just remember if ever you want help,' she said. 'Now I'll change the subject. He's pretty extraordinary to look at, don't you think?'

'Who?'

'Mr Capstone. He was standing on the other side of the car. I believe nobody knows much about him, though Mrs Capstone's opponents must be digging away like mad. He doesn't look English, does he?'

Poppy could sense an inner sigh as Nell decided to come out of her carapace and play a guest's part in keeping the conversation going.

'He's a Romanian, or maybe Bulgarian—something like that. What you've got, you see, is a corrupt capitalist system over here and a corrupt so-called socialist system over there. They make out they're enemies, but really they need each other, so as to keep things the way they are, and that means they've got to do deals with each other. The systems don't mesh, of course, so you've got to have people in the middle to sort things out. That's what Capstone does, taking his pickings along the way, and that's just about as much as anyone knows.'

Poppy was impressed. Janet hadn't known that much.

'Do you know how they met?' she asked. 'It seems an unlikely kind of marriage.'

'He's got money. She's posh, got a lot of the right friends.'

'I suppose you do need someone to fund a career like hers, but I'd have thought it still wasn't worth the risk, taking someone like him on. He looks such a pirate.'

'She's one, too. They're the same kind, under the accents.'

'I wonder. Of course she may be, and him not. I saw him for about three minutes. For all I know he's got the soul of a book-keeper inside. He may be a mystery man, but perhaps he's just mysteriously ordinary, and behaves like that to stop people realising. I think that's the only picture I've seen of him, the one they showed.'

'Expect he didn't notice the camera was there. Tired, love?'

Nelson was now lolling against Nell's knee with his thumb in his mouth, gazing at Elias with heavy-lidded eyes. 'Would he like a bath?' said Poppy.

'Oh, you'd love that, wouldn't you, poppet? Baths are a problem in the commune. Have you got an egg for his supper?'

'I stocked up yesterday, luckily. What about you? I expect you're a vegan or something. I'm afraid . . .'

'Stereotyping, that is, Poppy. If you want to know, I'd eat steak every day, good and rare, supposing I could afford it.'

'Best I can do is canned stew. Now let's go and sort you out for the night, and I'll clear a drawer and get a few of my clothes in here. And if you want to telephone your friends and find out what's happening at the commune . . . I suppose they haven't got a telephone . . . don't laugh at me . . .'

'You're doing fine. And thanks, Poppy. But as a matter of fact, even if this hadn't come up I'd have been leaving the commune.'

'Oh. I thought you were a sort of founder member.'

'Things change. I don't want to explain. It'll only be a couple of days till I get something else lined up. Is that OK?

'Yes, of course.'

'Thanks a lot, Poppy.'

OCTOBER 1989

1

The chairs were hard, the hall stuffy, the audience sparse. It was not Poppy's kind of music, but a woman on her Polish course had been handing out free tickets and she'd felt it would have been feeble not to give it a try. Now she closed her eyes, trying to concentrate all her inner energies into the single sense of hearing. The first piece was an extended fanfare, an enjoyable mess of loud noise going nowhere in particular. It might have sounded more shaped and purposeful, she thought, in a different acoustic, with long echoes. The second piece was called Famine, and was described in the programme note as a political suite. Each short section started with a member of the ensemble reading some item to do with Ethiopia—a government statement, a UN report, an eyewitness account, a medical text about malnutrition—and then beginning a solo with the other members joining in one by one. The programme note explained that how they did this and what they played was partly dictated by the composer and partly chosen by themselves according to formulae she'd laid down. The music was clearly very demanding on the performers, with ceaseless shifts of tempo and volume. Poppy could discern no key, but she worked at listening almost as conscientiously as the performers worked at playing. When the piece ended she decided it hadn't been worth her time, or theirs.

In the interval she rose to rest her back and stood against the wall. The audience—youngish, casually earnest—mostly seemed to know each other, but the woman who'd given her the ticket didn't seem to be there. She felt let down by this.

Her lack of empathy with the music seemed to emphasise her solitariness.

She was trying to eavesdrop on a group who were discussing some kind of confrontation with what sounded like a religious leader, a guru with inadequate charisma, perhaps, when a man's voice, flat and gravelly, said 'You weren't, I take it, actually asleep? I wouldn't blame you.'

Poppy had been so wrapped in her isolation that it took her a moment to realise he had spoken to her. She turned and saw it was Mr Capstone. Though inconceivably out of context there was no mistaking his totem-emphatic features.

'I was doing my best to listen,' she said.

'To what result?'

'A bit disappointing, I thought. There were bits I quite liked— that funny little five-note twiddle that kept popping up in unlikely places, like the rabbits on the Peter Pan statue, I decided.'

She hummed the phrase. The predatory mouth turned out to be capable of a smile.

'A good image,' he said. 'Sentimental kitsch.'

'But it didn't belong. I think that was the trouble. I don't think she really minded or understood about the famine. That's probably uncharitable—I'm sure she minded but she didn't understand.'

'You may exercise your charitable bent if you wish. I think she neither minded nor understood. I would guess she has a politically activist partner or patron whom she's trying to conform to. We've met before, haven't we?'

'I brought my grandson to play with Deborah. I'm Poppy Tasker.'

'That's it.'

He made no excuse for not having recognised her, though it wasn't surprising. Her presence at a function like this must seem quite as unlikely to him as his did to her.

'Do you think it's worth staying for the second half?' he said.

'I've got to give it a try, or I'd think less of myself. It's not really my kind of music—I stop just before Tippett, I'm afraid, but I feel there must be something there if I listen the right way.'

'Why did you come?'

Poppy explained, and finished with a shrug and a laugh at having to present so inadequate a reason to a serious concert-goer. A solitary girl smoking in a doorway turned her head at the sound. Mr Capstone nodded and looked at her in silence, consideringly, for several seconds.

'If I were to stick it out I could give you a lift home,' he said. 'You presumably live in our area.'

'The other side of the park. But I'll be quite all right on the Tube.'

'I was in two minds in any case.'

The piece that comprised the second half was by another composer, also a woman. To Poppy's joy it began with the hornpipe from *Pineapple Poll*, played with great sparkle and gusto until things began to go astray, a couple of wrong notes, then braying trombone slides, then the tempi falling apart until what had been recognisable music degenerated into what to Poppy sounded like mere mess, though the players were still reading from their scores and playing with what seemed to be full concentration, indeed effort, until the semblance of a key and beat emerged, and there was *Begin the Beguine* with the full yearning schmaltz. Then that too was allowed to fall apart, collapse and become chaos. Poppy concentrated with all her intellect on trying to follow some kind of thread through the tangle. The Beguine was still in there somewhere. Was the hornpipe? The Fauré *Credo* emerged, then something Poppy didn't know but which sounded like one of the other Bachs, then *Blues in the Night* with a saxophone taking the Bessie Smith part, and so on. The last clear passage was of course *God Save the Queen*, but that too degenerated into a chordless bray which then deliquesced with instrument after instrument dropping out until all that was left was a penny whistle piping right at the top of its register. Then silence.

At least it was something to talk about in the car, a low, softly upholstered, glossy, powerful object, an Audi or something.

'I'd have to hear it several times before I could decide if it was anything more than a joke,' said Poppy.

'It would be worth the effort?'

'I've probably got more spare time than you. Yes, I think so. It's too much fun first time through, spotting what's coming next, like one of those Christmas quizzes in the *Observer*, but I think I might get to like the original bits for their own sake. I thought I was just beginning to hear shapes and patterns. It's a new language. I've just started Polish, and at first there didn't even seem to be syllables. It's like that.'

'You play an instrument?'

'No—in fact I don't know much about music—the sort of thing musicians are taught, I mean. I had totally unmusical parents and I didn't go to the sort of school which does much about it without being prodded. But when I married and my husband started taking me to the opera . . .'

'Not here tonight?'

'We've split up, but anyway he'd have hated it. He likes a stage to look at, and things happening, and singers. He used to get miffed when he saw me sitting there with my eyes shut—you know what tickets cost—so I started getting the records out of the library and listening to them before we went, over and over, teaching myself . . .'

'Have you eaten?'

'I'll scramble an egg when I get home.'

'Enough for two?'

'Oh . . . if you like. It's not at all . . .'

'Scrambled eggs will do. Heard any Stockhausen?'

'Only on radio, and even then . . . Isn't there something called *Hymnen*? It goes on for ever, voices chanting, with tiny variations . . .'

'You have to be there. Radio's no use, or records. They are just pushing sounds out to anyone who happens to be listening, so the experience is dissipated. Go, and the sounds are moving inward to each listener, focused, concentrated. It is the reverse experience.'

'I see what you mean, but I don't know if I think like that. I agree that actually going to a concert forces me to concentrate, but I don't . . .'

'Not what I meant. The thing, the performance, of course exists as much as a book or a painting exists, for as long as the performance lasts. But none of them—performance, book, painting—is complete, is fully existent, until I experience it . . .'

It was difficult for Poppy to pay attention and at the same time run through the steps needed to scratch together a supper she wouldn't be ashamed of There were five eggs, a few rashers of bacon, the carrots should still be presentable, that pot of pesto—was there still a tin of peaches? He expected her to do her share of the talking, keeping her up to the mark with his abrupt, almost ferocious questions and comments.

'What have you got against Tippett?'

'I didn't mean that. I expect I'm not quite ready. Teaching myself, you see, starting with the easy people like, you know, Mozart . . .'

'Mozart is easy?'

'No, of course not. He just seems easy when you're starting. He gives you enough to keep you happy, straight off, even if you know nothing about it. It's like the sort of wine you like when you're eighteen . . . If you want wine with your eggs we'll have to stop and buy some.'

'Milk for me.'

'Oh, I'm almost out. Mr Jinja will be open. On the corner after the next lights.'

'So you're not ready for Tippett . . .'

The flat, normally so cloistral in its half-basement at the end of the cul-de-sac, seemed to vibrate with the energies of his presence. Poppy showed him into the living-room and lit the gas.

'My kitchen's too small for two,' she said. 'If you don't mind waiting. I'll be about ten minutes. The loo's opposite. Tell me if you don't like cats and I'll shut Elias in the kitchen.'

'I like cats. May I have my milk at blood temperature, please?'

Poppy heard him use the loo while she cooked. The sound reminded her of nights when Alex had come. No, this wasn't going to be like that. He wanted to talk about music—it was clear Mrs Capstone was unable to satisfy *that* need, at least. Poppy liked to think of herself as an efficient user of her kitchen, and now made a point of putting the simple meal together with a speed that would impress him, the eggs on wholemeal toast, the bacon grilled crisp, the carrots sliced lengthwise to dip in the pesto. When she carried the tray through she found him sitting in her armchair with Elias purring on

his lap. It is ridiculous the things about which one can feel a twitch of
jealousy, but for size alone they made a fitting pair.

'You're honoured,' she said. 'He doesn't do that for everyone.'

He allowed her to wait on him, then ate in silence. As with music,
he seemed to concentrate all his attention on the matter in hand, so
Poppy stayed silent too. He finished by drinking his milk.

'Thank you,' he said, as he put his mug down. 'Exactly right.'

'Coffee?'

'Not for me. What do you make of my daughter?'

'Oh, well . . .'

'The truth, please.'

'You've got to remember how much they can change. She's obviously a difficult child now, but she may simply be getting through
that phase of her life. I have a friend whose daughter lived a really
vivid, weird, private imaginative life until she was about seven, and
seems never to have had even a moment of mild fancy since. She's
thirty now. I'm biased about Deborah because she gets on so well
with Toby. It's as though there are two people in there, one being
extremely self-willed and capricious, and the other standing back and
rather coolly watching the effect she is having.'

'Her psychiatrist says she is fighting to make a space for herself.
My wife and I are considered to have strong personalities.'

'I expect there's something in that. I don't know. I don't get the
impression she's an unhappy child. Anyway I wouldn't have thought
there was a lot you or your wife or anyone else could do about it.
Deborah will be what she chooses to be. I do think you can mess
children around by having theories about them. My husband was
brought up rigidly on the Truby King system, and it made . . . oh,
you don't want to know that. I think you should do whatever really
feels right at the time, and in particular show that you love them.

I thought you were doing fine when I saw you with her the other day.'

'That's very helpful. You'll come to another concert with me?'

'Oh, I'd love to, but . . .'

'I would appreciate a companion who is prepared to think about music. Not necessarily talk, but think, recognising it as a cerebral activity. I can't always be sure of my free time, so it would mean asking you at short notice.'

'I do evening classes on Mondays and Wednesdays.'

'Polish, you said?'

'I'm only just starting. That's Mondays. I do German on Wednesdays.'

'Why Polish?'

'Because the course fitted in. My German's fairly good, but I wanted a third language, partly to see if I could and partly to help me get a job. Polish worked out best, and besides, I thought, with such a lot happening there—it's terribly exciting, isn't it, even for a political innocent like me.'

'It is the major event of our lifetimes.'

'Do you know Poland?'

'I am Polish by origin. My original name is unpronounceable in English so I chose a new one.'

'It's still a very unusual one. There aren't any in the phone book.'

'I didn't wish to share my name. But you will be able to practise your Polish in the intervals of the concerts.'

'I've only just started. I certainly won't be up to talking about music.'

'We will set aside ten minutes for telling each other that it's a fine day but it's going to rain. I'll call you next time I'm likely to be free for something that might interest us both. You will need to progress beyond Tippett.'

'Oh, I'd love to try, but . . . well, there's something you ought to know . . .'

She hesitated again. Was there any way she could ask him not to tell Mrs Capstone? The big eyebrows had risen, amused, mocking. She floundered.

'I don't want . . . oh . . . you see it looks as if my daughter-in-law is going to be the Labour candidate at the next election.'

He sat silent for an instant, and then burst into a big, raucous, uncontrollable laugh. He rose and slapped his thigh and stretched like a waking dog. He was a peasant in a mired farmyard, bellowing mirth at some rustic mishap.

'And Deborah and Toby are getting on so well . . .' she explained.

'So I am to keep the affair secret from my family and you from yours!' he said. 'And Cherubino is hiding behind the curtain and Falstaff in the laundry basket! Wonderful! But her name is Jones, isn't it? Were you twice married?'

'Janet uses her maiden name. Do you think it matters?'

'Of course not. It's a triviality. Still, I think we will keep our meetings to ourselves, perhaps. Are you likely to meet any of your acquaintances at concerts of modern music?'

'Good heavens, no.'

'Nor I. There's a McCall-Baines recital next Thursday at a church hall in Whitechapel. I have another engagement but I'll see if I can change it. Would you be free?'

Thursday was bridge night. Poppy had already agreed to play. She had never heard of McCall-Baines.

'I'm not doing anything,' she said. 'That would be lovely.'

The call came early, while Poppy was on her first cup of coffee. The voice was unmistakable.

'Go to the nearest call-box and ring me on this number,' he said, and gave her the number. She kept pencil and paper ready.

'Don't ask any questions. Do it.'

'All right,' she said, baffled.

She was still in her dressing-gown but scrabbled on clothes and reached the call-box panting and angry. He answered at the first ring.

'What is this about?' she snapped.

'Were you aware that your flat was being watched?' he said.

'Watched? But . . .'

'You remember I had to park in the next Street? As I was walking round to my car somebody who had been standing in the shadow of that hedge opposite you started to follow me.'

'Are you sure?'

'I know about these things. I walked past my car and on for long enough to make sure. Then I shook him off, went back for the car and drove home. It is just conceivable that somebody had been watching me and that we were followed back to your place from the concert, but if so that part of it had been very skilfully done, whereas the latter part when I left you was not.'

'Did you see his face? Had he got a beard?'

The phone bleeped for more money. She fed it in. 'A beard? Why?'

'Somebody tried to follow us from the play centre the other day. He was, you know, interested in Toby. That sort. He'd got a beard. I've only got one more lot of money left.'

'You want to report this to the police?'

'I think I've got to. Sorry.'

'In that case . . . Can you see that corner from your window? No, that won't do. Will you please report that I told you I saw somebody there who I thought was watching your flat, but not that he tried to follow me?'

'Oh, but . . .'

'I will tell them that I wasn't bothered at the time, but decided later I ought to warn you. If, as seems likely, the man's interest was in you or your grandson, then the police will have been made aware of it, and that is all you need.'

'I suppose so, but . . . You haven't said if he had a beard. If you're going to tell them you only saw him under the hedge, you wouldn't have seen, would you?'

'I didn't, in any case. You don't let your man know you're aware that he's following you. But you can give the police my name and I'll tell them as much as I can. You have our address?'

'Yes.'

'All right. I'll send you a ticket for the Whitechapel concert. We'll meet there.'

'All right.'

She walked back to her flat feeling chilly and sick. The house opposite had a ramshackle garden shed and a shaggy privet hedge at right angles to it, composing that corner of the cul-de-sac. Right in the corner, under the arch of the outward-leaning privet, there were seven or eight scattered cigarette stubs. Sicker still now, beginning to believe, she telephoned the police station and asked for Sergeant Osborne, who had been visiting the play centre regularly since the man had tried to follow her home with Toby. She wasn't on duty yet, so Poppy, flustered now, had to speak to the duty sergeant, who switched with electric suddenness from apathy to attention at Mr Capstone's name. A detective sergeant and a uniformed WPC were round within twenty minutes. She showed them the cigarette butts, and explained rather too emphatically that she and Mr Capstone were no more than acquaintances who had met at a concert and come back for supper so that they could continue to talk about music.

For several mornings after that Poppy inspected the corner for fresh cigarette butts. Before she went to bed at night she switched off the living-room lights, waited till her eyes were used to the dark and peered for any sign of an extra darkness in the shadow under the privet. Twice she took out her flour-dredger and powdered the area over in the dusk, but could see no signs of footprints there in the morning. Sergeant Osborne, visiting the play centre, told her that the cul-de-sac was now on the list for random night-time checks, but these, if they took place at all, must have happened while Poppy was asleep.

McCall-Baines turned out to be an organist, female. She played some Poulenc in the first half, and then a piece which called itself 'Variations on a Theme of Schoenberg's' but whose sections seemed to Poppy quite unrelated to the announced theme or to each other, though some were pleasant to listen to. Mr Capstone liked it more than Poppy. The conversation about the supposed watcher was brief.

'I'm sorry to have alarmed you.'

'It was a bit frightening, but I've got good locks and a chain on the door. I don't think he's come back. What did the police say?'

'Their interest was perfunctory. It suited me to have them believe that the man, if he was not a figment of my imagination . . .'

'Of course he wasn't! There were cigarette butts all over that corner!'

'It's a sheltered spot for a down and out. He may have wanted to beg off me, or mug me if he could follow me to a suitable place.'

'But you seemed so sure at the time!'

'Ah, well, when one has lived by one's wits in a police state . . . Do you think Poulenc overrated?'

NOVEMBER 1989

1

Something was happening by the play centre. Poppy had already been aware of it while they were feeding the ducks, some kind of crowd, a police car, TV crews. Bother, she thought—they're shooting a telly ad and they won't let us in, or more likely they'll expect us to wait around for hours while they set things up so that they can film us for about two minutes. Nell will have gone home, anyway—it's not her sort of thing at all. Poppy wanted to talk to Nell. The *Ethelden Echo* had had a story yesterday about closing a squat in Sabina Road at the weekend. She thought it must be the one where Nell used to live, and wanted to know whether shutting it down affected her at all, but Toby was not to be hurried.

It was a grey day, still vaguely autumnal, but chill. He insisted on the full ritual, the gravel scratching and fence rattling and peep-bo. A fluffy poodle demanded his attention for several minutes. He found a big chestnut leaf and considered the possibility of restoring it to its tree. Poppy began to wonder whether any research had been done on the incidence of constipation among the mothers and minders of toddlers. It wasn't the sort of work that won Nobel prizes, but she did find that the wearying yet unexercising pace had that effect on her, though she treated it with extra bran and striding flat out whenever Toby could be prevailed on to use the push-chair. Not now, so she had plenty of time to study the scene ahead.

It became apparent that it was not what she'd thought. There were too many TV crews, and several men with stills cameras too. Another police car arrived. The crowd was not right up against the fence, but held well back by a barrier of yellow tape on iron poles, patrolled by uniformed police. Attitudes were wrong: too still, too interested. Oh God, she thought, someone's been hurt. Badly.

'Look, darling,' she said. 'Cameras.'

He let her pick him up and carry him, pushing the pushchair with her free hand. Some of the children were running around behind the crowd, apparently unwatched. The crowd itself was larger than she'd thought, eighty or ninety people, most of them unconnected with the play centre. She spotted Big Sue's diabetic bulk with Denny looking tearful on her shoulder.

'Sue. What's up?'

Sue craned round.

'They've been looking for you, Poppy. That woman cop, the one came about the fellow that other time, she's been asking.'

'What's happening?'

Bystanders, hearing what Sue had said, refocused their interest.

'It appears they discovered a dead body in the building this morning,' said a man with a fastidious voice.

'Murdered,' said a woman.

'We have not been told that,' said the first man.

'Ah, come off it,' said another man. 'Haven't been told a bloody thing yet, have we? But look at the bloody cameras—wouldn't get that for a dosser having a heart attack, would you now?'

'You better find her,' said Sue. 'Don't want to get into trouble, do you?'

'All right. Keep an eye on my push-chair, will you?'

Toby was wriggling to get down and go and help the camera crews. She ignored him and marched down behind the line of the crowd towards the entrance path. Two constables and a sergeant were guarding a gap in the tape.

'The play centre is temporarily closed,' said the sergeant for what sounded like the hundredth time. 'Pass along, please.'

'Apparently I'm wanted.'

'Not now, madam. Please will you . . .'

'Sergeant Osborne has been asking for me, I'm told.'

'One moment, madam. Seen Ozzie, Bob?'

'She's around.'

'Get hold of her. No, hold it. What's your name, madam?'

Poppy told him. The moment she'd approached she'd been aware of the click and purr of cameras trained on her, but the centre of their interest had switched again and they were pointing towards the hut.

'Wait here a moment, please,' said the sergeant, and let himself in through the gate. Two men had emerged from the hut and were standing a few yards along the path, talking. One wore a black leather jacket and jeans and the other a brown suit and hat. The sergeant spoke to them and returned.

'This way, madam,' he said. 'Bob, find a WPC to take charge of the little lad. You hang on to him for the moment, madam.'

Thrilled with the nearness of the cameras Toby had been almost uncontrollable, threshing and bucking and reaching out pleading hands. Poppy's arm was aching unendurably.

'I'm going to have to put him down,' she said, not waiting for introductions. 'Can we go over to the climbing frame?'

'Used to take my own kids to a place like this,' said the man in the brown suit. 'Not so much kit those days.'

He walked beside her in silence to the frame where Toby, though still yearning for the cameras, allowed himself to be coaxed into his routine of inspection. Poppy positioned herself to stop him when he made his inevitable break for the gate.

'I'm Detective Inspector Firth,' said the man. 'You're Mrs Tasker, right? Now, a few weeks back you reported a man watching you here . . .'

'Watching Toby, I thought. So did the others. Then a man—I think it was the same one—tried to follow us home.'

'You'd know him again?'

'I think so. My eyesight's not very good, even with specs, but I got a proper look at him when I was in Mrs Jinja's.'

'And if he'd shaved off his beard?'

'Oh, well, yes, I think . . . hang on a mo—I'll have to introduce them.'

A strange WPC had arrived and was trying to make friends with Toby, who was ignoring her advances.

'Hello,' said Poppy. 'Nice to meet you. I'm Poppy and this is my grandson, Toby.'

'I'm Vi,' whispered the girl.

She was as petite as regulations could possibly allow, frail-looking and uncertain, obviously fresh out of whatever training they did.

'Hello, Vi. Can you say Vi, darling?'

Toby had remembered about the cameras. Poppy blocked his path. He glowered. His lower lip protruded. In a couple of seconds he'd yell.

'No, darling, we've got to stay here for a bit. Look, Vi's got a really interesting radio sort of thing. She'll show you how it works. And I expect you've got a whistle too, haven't you, Vi?'

Indeed she had, a whistle on a gleaming chain. She blew hesitantly through it. That was enough to start the friendship. Poppy turned back. Mr Firth was alone now, the other man walking back towards the hut.

'I'm sorry,' she said. 'That'll keep him happy for a bit. They said somebody's dead. Do you want me to look at the body?'

'The sergeant's gone to see if the lab boys have finished lifting the footprints off the floor. Normally we'd leave identification twenty-four hours, but this time the boss thinks it's worth knowing straight off if it's the same chap you saw before . . . Ah . . .'

The sergeant had disappeared through the door of the hut and now returned and waved. Poppy walked up the path beside Mr Firth.

'You feel all right about this, Mrs Tasker?' he said.

'I hope so. It's got to be done. I shan't know till I've tried, shall I?'

'That's the spirit. Now, I don't want to go putting ideas into your mind. Like as not this isn't the fellow you saw, and it's no use to me you saying it is because you think that's what I want, right?'

'Oh, yes. Of course. Jim Bowles got a much better look at him than I did, you know. He's the crossing warden at the Primary, the one in Starveling Lane.'

They had stopped under the projecting roof at the door of the hut.

'Oh, we all know Jim,' said Mr Firth. 'He'll be along to tell us everything he knows, and more. Now listen, Mrs Tasker—you'll see the face is a funny colour. Don't worry about that. And stay on the matting, so you don't go leaving your own prints around. You'll be all right. In my experience women are better at this sort of thing than men.'

He opened the door and led her in. She kept her eyes down, not wishing to look until she had to. A narrow path of canvas matting had been laid towards the kitchen, then turning to cross the room.

She saw the feet of camera tripods and other pieces of apparatus. There were strong lights, an electrical hum, the mutters and movements of intent work. The path stopped just short of the Lego table. The Lego blocks, always ritually tidied back on to the table when the centre was about to close, lay scattered across the floor.

'Ready?' he said.

'You want me to look now?'

'Please.'

The man lay spread-eagled on the table, a green sheet covering his body. As well as the head, a hand protruded. It had been lashed by the wrist to the leg of the table. From the further leg another cord strained up to the invisible ankle. The face . . . without Mr Firth's warning Poppy would have assumed it had been painted, or partly made up, a preliminary shocking cherry-red base laid on to the visible cheek in a great coarse blotch, the lips tomato-red, the mouth-surround, nose and temple seeming white by comparison but in fact pinker than any natural skin. She would have known he was dead. This was never the colour of live flesh.

'Let go, will you?' she whispered. 'I'm all right.'

He released her elbow and she crouched to study the face in profile. The fine, slightly curving nose repeated the line of the brow, but less markedly than she'd remembered. Perhaps that was because there was more to see with the beard gone, a small, rather immature-looking mouth and chin. Even in death, even in the obscene colours of that death, he had the look of a child. Poppy guessed he was in his early twenties. The hair was the right shade.

She rose and accepted his steadying hand on her arm.

'I think that's him,' she whispered. 'I only really saw him in profile. His forehead and nose are right. How tall was he?'

'Five nine.'

'That's about right. Mrs Jinja at the corner shop saw him as well as Jim Bowles. What made you think it might be him?'

'Chap who found him this morning, play-leader here . . .'

'George?'

'George McWatters. He'd seen him that day—was on his way to tell him to clear off, in fact, when he left. He said he thought it might be, but you'd had a better look.'

'Yes. May I go now, please?'

This time she needed his help to cross the room. Outside, the breeze had winter in it. She swayed, pulled herself upright, and shook herself as if waking from an unwanted doze.

'I'm all right,' she said. 'Where's Toby?'

He had dragged his captive over to the Wendy House and was trying to get her to understand the importance of getting the barrel properly jammed in the entrance before they could begin their experiments into the police-whistle-in-Wendy-House-and-barrel phenomenon. Beyond the barrier the ranked cameras jostled. Unlike Toby, the WPC was desperately aware of them.

'Looks like he's busy for a moment,' said Mr Firth, pulling out a notebook. 'Now, if you'll tell me about the time he followed you. I know we've got a report on file, but I'd like the details. Feel up to it now?'

Poppy was glad to have something she must do. There were voices in her mind—Big Sue's and the others'—and her own unspoken wish that the man was dead, six feet under, buried in lime. It was as though their curses, working together like the power of their united stare that had driven him off, had made the wish reality. She drowned the voices by concentrating on the exactness of her memory. Mr Firth made a few notes.

'And you didn't see him again?' he said.

She hesitated.

'No,' she said. 'But, well, I had a guest for supper a few days later, who rang next morning and said that when he left he thought he'd seen someone in the corner opposite my flat, watching. I looked and there were a lot of cigarette ends there. The man who'd followed us seemed to be pretty well chain-smoking. I did report that too, but I don't know how seriously they took it.'

He made another note.

'But you say the man was interested in Toby,' he said. 'Why should he be watching your flat? How do you know it wasn't you he was interested in in the first place?'

'Oh, we get that sort too—eyeing the young mums and the nannies. Sometimes you're not sure. But when you are . . . it's happened twice before since I've been here. It's something about the way they stand, I think. So still. All I can tell you is I knew. We all did.'

'Right. I'll accept that. Now, how did you feel when you first noticed him watching you?'

'Feel? What you'd expect. Shocked. Angry. Sick. Sad.'

'And the other women?'

'Much the same, I expect.'

'Angry?'

'Yes, of course. You can't help it.'

'Did they express their anger in any way?'

'Just the usual things. You know. What ought to be done to people like that. Teaching them a lesson and so on.'

Poppy paused. The image of Big Sue's face came to her, just after the man had left, in the brilliant sunlight, the sense of primal female rage, ungovernable.

'Yes?' he said.

'It was just talk. You know how people's minds work I mean, I'm against capital punishment but I remember thinking . . . I couldn't stop myself . . .'

'There was talk of catching him and teaching him a lesson?'

'Well, yes, but . . .'

'Killing him?'

'I suppose so. I tell you it was only talk.'

'Anything else?'

'What do you mean?'

'You tell me.'

She stared at him and he gazed enquiringly back. His tanned, finely wrinkled face was solemn but unreadable.

'No,' she said. 'I don't remember. I'm not going to say. You can't make me. I know they didn't mean anything. They aren't like that.'

'This is a murder investigation, Mrs Tasker. A man has been killed in a manner that links him to the play centre, and also suggests disapproval of his sexual activities. This is a line of enquiry I am forced to pursue, if only to eliminate it. You understand?'

'Can I go now, please?'

Without waiting for an answer she turned and walked down the path. Jim was there, waiting for his interview, but stood out of her way without a word. Her face seemed to have set like plaster. She could think of nothing but getting away. The WPC's neat bum protruded from the barrel to a fusillade from the cameras. Poppy tapped her on the spine and she backed out, her face pink with the posture and embarrassment and puffing on her whistle.

'Thank you very much,' Poppy managed to mutter. 'You've been a great help. Come on, darling. Home now.'

She tugged the barrel clear. Outraged, Toby seized the other rim and tried to pull it back.

'More eek!' he demanded.

'Not now, darling. Home.'

He clung to the rim, wrestling to free himself as she snatched him up. Then somehow he must have sensed that the rules had altered, felt the tension in her body, perhaps, understood with near-animal instinct that this was a time for stillness, for silence. They must know about danger, children. Deep in their genes there must be mechanisms that can feel the adult terror. Poppy hugged him to her, thankful to have him so close as she headed for the gate.

Sue had the push-chair ready—she must have got someone else to take charge of Denny. She didn't ask any questions.

Men with notebooks and microphones jostled near by, but the police held them back. Toby made no attempt to resist as she strapped him into the push-chair—normally he would have insisted on walking at least as far as the ducks. People were shouting to her, questions, her name, what she'd seen. Their voices were wind in the trees, meaningless. She pushed the pram clear of the crowd but was aware of still being followed. A hand touched her arm.

'Please go away,' she said.

It was Sergeant Osborne.

'Please go away,' she repeated. 'I'll be all right.'

'Inspector says to take you home in a car. You'll be followed everywhere, else.'

Poppy pushed on several more strides before she could take in the sense of it. A car, enclosing glass and steel, refuge. She let herself be guided back past the crowd to the west gate of the park. Several police cars were waiting there. She unstrapped Toby and lifted him clear.

'You'll have to let me show you how the push-chair folds,' she said.

'I'll manage, love,' said the driver. 'Mothercare, isn't it? Got one like that for my own little girl.'

She climbed into the back seat and sat with Toby in her lap. He too seemed to feel the relief of being sealed off from the horror in the park, closed round, safe, and as soon as the car moved off he wanted to explore. Of course he'd seldom been in a moving car before without being strapped into a baby-chair, and now could see no reason why he shouldn't use his freedom to help the driver in his interesting activities. Poppy shoved him up on to her shoulder to watch the road dwindling away behind. That distracted him for the moment. Sergeant Osborne was also looking out of the rear window.

'You're clear, Mike, I think,' she said. 'Back to your daughter-in-law's, Mrs Tasker?'

'Yes, please. Oh. I wonder if we hadn't better go to my flat. I don't want all those people knowing where Toby lives.'

'I'm afraid you're in for that, whatever. This is the kind of case the papers really get hooked on—they'll be at you over and over the next few days. Maybe you'd better have a social worker, help take a bit of the heat off.'

'But surely when they realise I'm not going to say anything . . .'

'Depends what else they're getting.'

'All I know just now is I want to be alone. My daughter-in-law's a social worker—not that sort, but she'll know. I'll talk to her. So don't do anything about it for the moment anyway, please.'

'If that's how you want it.'

The driver chose an indirect route, presumably to discourage anyone else who might be trying to follow them, so the journey home took long enough for Poppy to have pulled herself together and be able to say thank you in a normal voice. Once inside the flat she put a

kettle on, gave herself a slug of gin in a coffee cup while she was waiting for it to boil, made a pot of strong tea and rang Janet.

'You want me to come home?'

'I can manage, I think.'

'I'll be about forty minutes.'

'You're wonderful.'

Toby meanwhile had been trying to interest Elias in building a
ramp of cushions up to the sofa and then rolling down them. Elias
was unresponsive. He had never in any case been able to see the slight-
est reason why Toby should occupy a space in the universe. Poppy's
impulse was to give herself another big slug of gin and then sit on the
sofa hugging Toby to her and rocking to and fro while she wept over
the beastliness of things. Instead she took him into the kitchen, half
filled the washing-up bowl and put it on the floor, and settled down
to play water games with some yoghurt pots, the kitchen funnel and
the bulb-baster until Janet arrived.

2

Poppy was listening to *Rosenkavalier* when the doorbell rang again.
Another reporter, she assumed. She'd had several telephone calls and
then unplugged the cord, and had turned two separate men and a
woman away from the door, telling all of them that she wasn't going
to say anything. She opened the door the couple of inches the chain
allowed.

'Who is that?'

'Jim Bowles. Just come round to see you're all right.'

She opened the door.

'How very kind of you. Come in.'

'More caterwauling,' he remarked as he followed her into the living-room. She spun round.

'Don't be stupid,' she snapped.

'No call taking offence, Poppy. Just my way of saying it's not my type of music.'

'You're still being stupid. Listen! Can't you hear? Her lover's there and she knows she's getting too old for him. She's singing about time. She's telling him how she gets up at night and stops the clocks. Oh, please listen, Jim! For God's sake, you might at least try!'

She turned the volume up and filled the room with the voice and the leaf-fall comments of the orchestra. She stood by the fire with her arm along the mantelpiece and didn't look at him until the aria ended. Then she switched the player off.

'You don't have to say anything,' she said.

'You aren't too old, Poppy. My eye, you're a fetching woman.'

'Thank you, but it isn't about me. Not just me. Everything. It makes you share the sense of everything getting old and worn and lost and forgotten. Names on gravestones nobody will ever be able to read again. Bones under moors. That young man we saw this morning, he was a baby like Toby once. Somebody thought he was the loveliest thing that had ever happened.'

'Maybe. Or maybe they didn't. Or maybe they tried to love him too hard, him turning out how he did.'

'It was the same man, wasn't it? You remember, the one who followed us that day?'

'I'd say so. Tricky without the beard.'

'Do they know who he was yet?'

'Not as I heard. Not local. Nothing on him barring a return ticket to Mitcham.'

'Nothing? No money? No cigarettes? He pretty well chain-smoked.'

'Not a sausage, and the ticket's a plant, like as not. That sort don't buy returns.'

'He'd been castrated.'

Jim looked at her.

'Who told you that?' he said.

'Things the Inspector said. They'd lured him along to the play centre by saying there was a child he could have, and then they'd tied him up and done that to him—and other things. I don't know if they meant to kill him.'

'Ali, now, you mustn't give yourself nightmares. Wasn't that way, hardly at all. First, he'd been gassed—gassed himself most like—in a garage or shed somewhere big enough to hold a car, and then . . .'

'Not in the play centre? How do they know it wasn't in the play centre? What do you mean, gassed?'

'Notice his cheeks at all?'

'Yes, of course. That awful colour. As if he'd been painted.'

'Carbon monoxide, that is. You get it in car exhaust. Does something to your blood, turns it that colour. And about him being moved, you can tell that straight off if he's laid any length of time dead, before they come to move him. Soon as your heart stops pumping the blood around it sinks down in your body and gathers in whichever bit of you's downest, and then after a bit it sticks there, so it looks like a ruddy great bruise all over that part. This fellow it's not blue, like a bruise—it's that red. Down in his feet and legs, and the hams and the bottom of his back. Notice his hand? White, so it must've been up. He couldn't've died where you saw him, with his hand tied down like that. No, he was sitting somehow, with his head hanging forward on to his arm, as it might be on the dashboard of a car. Lot of people do themselves in like that, with car exhaust. There was that MP, only the other day.'

'You keep saying he did it himself.'

'Stands to reason. I don't see him sitting still having that done to him. I wouldn't.'

'But *something* had been done to him, hadn't it? I mean more than just moving him?'

'I was coming to that. Let's take it he did himself in in a car somewhere, and then somebody found him, and—don't ask me why—they moved him out and brought him along to the play centre—hey had to break in—and they stripped him off—his clothes were all folded neat under the table, I forgot to tell you—and they laid him out and tied him down and then—Poppy, you got to believe this—they fastened a bouquet of flowers round his cock. That's how they left him.'

'Flowers?'

'Smelly little ones you get from florists.'

'Freesias?'

'That's them. Used a couple of elastic bands.'

Poppy stared at him. Relief streamed through her like an injected drug.

'The feminine touch,' he said.

'What do you mean?'

'Don't take it serious. Just something one of my mates at the station came up with.'

'But it isn't a joke, Jim. They think it's something to do with the girls at the play centre, don't they? I don't believe they really think it was suicide. They're saying we somehow lured him into a car and gassed him and then we took him along to the play centre and decorated his penis with flowers and left him on the Lego table?'

'No one's saying it was you, Poppy.'

'I tell you, it can't have been any of us! You simply don't under-stand what the play centre means to us, what a help it is, what a com-munity! I tell you it's absolutely inconceivable that any of us would choose to desecrate it by doing something like this. Can't they see? I mean even supposing we'd caught him and killed him we simply wouldn't have dreamed of then taking the body along there. None of us. It's quite impossible. I can't prove it, but I absolutely know. You'll just have to take it from me.'

'You've got it wrong, Poppy love. Police work's not like that. You don't start off saying "This is what must've happened" and then trying to prove it. You look into all the possibilities, such as the girls being involved, some of them, for instance.'

'Well, I'm not going to help them, or you, or anyone else, look into this one. You haven't told me what you thought about the music.'

He studied her in silence. She could feel his disappointment. How he must long to show the youngsters at the police station that he could still be some use to them. Perhaps he'd even persuaded the Inspector to let him try his luck with Poppy.

'I'm sorry, Jim,' she said.

'If that's how you see it. I respect that. All right, let's give the lady another listen. Some of this modern stuff they set for comps, you've got to play it and play it before you even begin to see what the bloke might be at. Got any gin?'

'Good idea.'

She couldn't have kept the eagerness out of her voice. 'Like that is it sometimes?' he asked.

'I had one when the police car brought me back. That was against the rules, because it was the middle of the afternoon and I had Toby with me. Anyway, there was just enough for another good slug as soon as the clock struck six. I've got a fresh bottle but another rule is I don't start one on the same day I finish an old one, but since you're here . . .'

'You need that many rules?'

'Only on bad days. I know they're stupid, but they do help.'

She fixed the drinks and started to run the tape back. 'That class of singers,' he said. 'Trouble is you can never hear what they're saying.'

'It's all in German anyway, I'm afraid.'

'Ah.'

'I've got the text. I could translate for you as we go along if that would help.'

'You do that.'

So that she didn't need to shout across the room they sat side by side on the sofa with Poppy murmuring the lines. The gin and the music, relief at what Jim had told her about the man's death, Jim's closeness, Hofmannsthal's words, the whole complex of sensuality and of time rushing away from the day when the body first wakens to its possibilities until the day when flesh goes cold, made her skin crawl. Her tongue chose the English it needed. She was electrically aware of the solidity of walls and furniture. When the aria ended she rose and switched the tape off and stood by the mantelpiece again.

'I sort of get what you're on about,' said Jim. 'Like the Last Post, Armistice Day. Know what that can do to you?'

'Do I not.'

'Way I see it, you can have too much of that type of thing. In its right place, like I say Armistice Day, it says stuff you can't say any other how, not with words, know what I mean? But mostly what you want music for is make you feel good.'

'Hallelujah Chorus all day long?'

'Didn't say that. You got to have a bit of variety for a start. More the better, my case.'

'That's not what I meant—I wasn't fair, putting it like that. I suppose it depends on what you mean by feeling good. When I was about, oh, fifteen I suppose, I spent most of my time mooning around imagining romantic ways of dying for the man I loved—you know, he'd marry this other girl and be happy with her and have everything he wanted and never know it was my sacrifice had made it all possible.'

'Morbid.'

'Lovely, for me, then. It really made me feel good. I can laugh at myself now, but I'm still glad it happened. What we've just been listening to makes me feel good too, a little bit in the same way, I suppose, but it's infinitely richer and deeper and stronger because it's about real life, not childish moonings. She's younger than I am, but she knows what it's like.'

'You've got a bit of time yet, Poppy.'

'I hope so.'

She looked down at him. He was sitting on the edge of the sofa, cradling his glass, beaming up at her, bright-eyed, so doggy that she only just stopped herself from saying 'Rats!' to him. Or was she reading into his normal look of interest what Mrs Jinja had told her about his dealings with the young mothers who came to the school? He didn't seem to sense the sudden discomfort she was aware of, but she felt a need to change the subject and did so, awkwardly.

'You help a lot of people, don't you?' she said.

'Do my best.'

'Mrs Jinja said you were wonderful about her daughter.'

'Mind like a sewer, that woman. Fuss she made coming to see me that time. Brought her auntie along, little old lady like a dried mushroom, couldn't speak a word of English. Suppose she thought I might have a go at her out there in the street. Gah, it would've been like climbing Mount Everest!'

He was clowning it, deliberately. Had he read her thought? Was she as transparent as she thought him? And he, perhaps, not? She laughed, and he laughed with her.

'That's more like it,' he said. 'That mood, I could really go for you, Poppy.'

Laughing still she shook her head. He could take her blushing how he chose.

'Let's stick to music,' she said.

'If that's how you want it.'

She'd hurt him now. Not good enough for you, then, his look said.

'I didn't mean that, Jim. I like you. I admire you. I'm glad I got to know you. But, well, we've really been talking about this already when we were talking about the kind of music we liked. Music is fun—I agree with you about that—but it isn't just fun for me. It's something deeply involving, something I can give my whole self to. It can be tragic, it can be almost incomprehensible, it can even be tedious in a special kind of way, but still . . . I want it all, not just the fun.'

'And what have you got? A lot of tapes and books in a basement, and a ruddy great cat, and one little kid to watch after till he's old enough to do without you?'

'Yes, that's fair. I've got myself into a rut. All I know is this isn't the way out of it.'

He swilled his gin round in his glass, sniffed it luxuriously and drank.

'All right,' he said, 'I'll accept that. Let's talk about something else. Those girls at the play centre. Ever strike you, Poppy, what a nice little set-up for blackmail someone might have there?'

'What do you mean?'

'Classy old families some of them work for. And I bet you they gab around among themselves when they're watching the kids. You'd just have to have one of them listening extra careful, and passing it on to her bloke, maybe.'

'Jim, they're my friends.'

'You think about it. Could have something to do with what happened to the chap on the table. He could've been trying something in that line.'

'You're wrong about the girls—I'm sure you are . . . Did you actually see him, Jim? Naked, I mean, without the sheet on him? Saw that he hadn't been mutilated or hurt?'

'No, it's just what they're saying, but I bet it's right. Why'd they go making something like that up?'

'And his beard? Had they shaved it off after he was dead, or had it been done before?'

'Have to wait for the lab tests for that, but to my eye it had been done recent. Sort of a dead fish look round his mouth, didn't you think, spite of the pink bits? Why d'you want to know?'

'I can't help wondering about him. I mean if he'd tried following us again, perhaps when I hadn't got Toby with me. I think he was watching outside here one night. Perhaps I did see him, but I didn't recognise him because he'd taken his beard off. Suppose I'd stopped and talked to him. Suppose he'd just needed help . . . Oh, what was he like? What kind of a life had he had, what kind of a childhood? Somebody must have loved him once. He mattered. And now he's nothing. There won't even be a wreath on his grave. Don't you think that's awful?'

'He's not the only one. You're working yourself up, Poppy. Getting morbid. You better snap out of it.'

'Oh, if you say so. How about another gin, and I'll find you the Hallelujah Chorus.'

'Wouldn't say no to either.'

When he'd gone, late, with the gin bottle half empty, Poppy lay in the bath and reeled the evening through her mind, seeing it all with the illusory clarity of the half-seas-over. He had made her a friendly offer and she had said no, rejected him, clumsily, rudely. Why? Snobbery, a little. Timidity, a bit more, maybe, though there was nothing to be afraid of. He would have made the whole thing so easy, an uninvolving romp like a game of squash or a twirl with a fresh partner in a Highland reel. He'd have been good, too, she guessed—better than Alex or Derek. Pity. Perhaps, after all . . . But no. It wasn't what she wanted. At least she'd been right about that. She couldn't live Jim's life nor he hers. He'd simply have been another piece of furniture in the rut, along with the tapes and the bridge and Elias. What she did want, though? She tended to ask herself this question most evenings, after a couple of gins, but seldom when as woozy as she felt now. The usual answer was that she wanted someone's life to share, to grow into, to become part of, while he grew into and became part of hers, as the nerve ends grow and branch into the brain of a child. She needed, desperately at times, physical, sensual love, but it had to be love. Alex had taught her that lesson, at least. But now, as she eased her body to and fro, setting up currents of water to caress her tingling skin, she found herself released from that body and able to float away, to perch in spirit on the glass shelf beside the toothbrush rack and look down at her drowsing self. A common case. The left-over half of a smashed marriage. For twenty-six years she had let herself be moulded to one functional shape, to be baked in the slow kiln of the years till the shape was fixed, one half of a clumsy jar. Then smash, and she was left lying useless, a shard on a rubbish tip. What chance was there that somewhere else on the tip, close by, there should be lying another similar shard which, with only a bit of filling along the crack, would fit on to hers so that together they could once again hold water? It was even more of a fantasy than the furry lover. The Poppy on the glass shelf folded its arms, crossed its dangling legs and gazed sardonically down at the pink shape in the Badedas-yellow water. (She must be really dreaming now, she knew in a corner of her mind, for the dichotomy to be so clear, so embodied.) You look soft enough, she told it. Floppy, to be blunt. But you're still baked hard. Hard, broken edges, still shaped to your lost other half. Dead. If you want a living life to share you've got to have a living life to offer, flexible, self-sufficient. What are you afraid of? She glided down from the shelf and into the pink, comfortable flesh. It's a pivotal moment, said some still wakeful corner of her mind. No it isn't, answered another. It's just gin.

Elias woke her, swearing at one of his enemies under the window. She was dead—laid out in some kind of preserving fluid in the chill, white mortuary. No she wasn't. She was lying in a less than tepid bath, drunker than she'd been for months, but not ashamed. Giggling she rose and towelled her rubbery flesh, did her teeth and made swayingly for the bedroom. There was something she'd got to do. Start living? Something else, first, something important. She remembered as she was reaching to turn the light out. She got up again and staggered into the kitchen where she scrawled a memo to herself and used the magnetic ladybird to fix it to the fridge door.

'Order wreath.'

3

'Your Toby's in all the papers,' said Mrs Jinja.

Poppy was late today, having slept badly in the first half of the
night and then overslept, still without real rest. She'd snatched her
Guardian from the rack outside and rushed in with the money ready.
Mrs Jinja showed her a Daily Mail. There he was, unmistakable on
the front page, with his head peering out of the Wendy House over
the top of the barrel while the WPC knelt at the other end as if pros-
trating herself before some masculine altar. RITUAL DEATH AT
LONDON PLAYGROUND shouted the headline. The caption had
his name and age right. One of the girls must have told them. The
Mirror and the *Sun* had almost the same picture. Mrs Jinja showed
her the centre spread of *Today*, which had several—that one, and one
of the hut with Inspector Firth at the door and another of Poppy herself pushing the chair, with Sergeant Osborne and a policeman (she'd
never noticed him at the time) walking beside her as if she'd already
been arrested for the crime. Her face looked set with shock and grief.
It could have been her own son she'd left splayed on the Lego table.
The caption gave her name as Polly Tasker.

'Not that good of you, is it?' said Mrs Jinja. 'You look a lot
younger than that, mostly.'

'Horrible. Horrible. They all want to know about the time when
that man was following us—you remember?'

'Of course I do. Was it the same man?'

'I don't know. Probably. But please don't talk to them about it.'

'Oh, of course not. You can trust me,' said Mrs Jinja, pursing her
lips as though no gossip had ever been known to pass between them.

• • •

Janet had found the picture in her *Guardian* and read the news story too.

'I simply don't believe it,' she said, 'if that's what they're hinting at. I suppose it might happen in some really primitive culture.'

'You should see the gutter papers,' said Poppy. 'But they've all got it wrong, I'm glad to say.'

She explained about the freesias, and the car exhaust.

'My friend Jim—you remember, the lollipop man at the school who helped me that time—he says they'll find out more in the postmortem. He used to be a policeman.'

Typically it didn't enter Janet's head to wonder how Poppy had come to hold such a conversation.

'That just makes it incredible in a different way,' she said.

'But it's easier to think about somehow,' said Poppy. 'I don't understand why it should be, but it is.'

'They'll close the play centre, for several days I should think. What are you going to do?'

'Get together in different people's houses, I expect. I hope someone remembers to ask us.'

'Of course they will—they'll want to know all about it. But are you sure you're all right, Poppy? I could take Toby if you're not up to it.'

'Oh, I'm all right now. I was terribly grateful to you for coming home yesterday, but I'll be OK today. The girls can be really supportive when you need them.'

'Well, if you're sure. I've got a meeting this morning when I've really got to fight my corner. I could take Toby, but it gives the others an unfair advantage being nice to me about him, and me not being able to concentrate.'

'Off you go. Don't forget the scythe-blades on your bike wheels.'

Janet grinned. That was how she saw herself, Poppy thought,

charioted, helmed, bronze-bodiced, hurtling into the reeling male legions with her red hair streaming behind her. It would be interesting to see how she got on with Nell, who lived by a more contemporary sort of myth, urban terrorist in the gender war.

Janet left and Poppy took Toby up to dress. Recently this had become a bit of a struggle, since he'd worked out in the play-group that big kids don't wear nappies, but had for once failed to make the connections that would allow the same to be true for him. Poppy had potty-trained her own babies from day one and was convinced that Toby could have been persuaded to use a pot without fuss or trauma by exploiting his experimental bent, but Janet, characteristically, had been unable to consider the possibility that Poppy could be right about any point on which they disagreed. The upshot was that Toby would now only consent to the indignity of having nappies put on him when he'd been allowed to do the same for his favourite cuddly toys. The polar bear fitted snugly, with an odd hint of kinky sex in the result, but nappy design and natural selection had not come together for the giraffe. Poppy had Toby halfway into his overalls when the telephone rang.

'Mrs Tasker? Sergeant Caesar here. Detective Inspector Firth would like to see you, soon as poss. Can you nip along to the station? Know where it is?'

'I've got my grandson with me all day.'

'No one you can leave him with?'

'No, but he'll be sleeping, almost certainly, between about half past ten and twelve. If Mr Firth could come here then . . .'

'No can do. There's statements to be taken et cetera et cetera. Want me to send a car?'

'Don't bother. If I've got to come I might as well walk. It's not that far. I could be with you in about half an hour. Try not to keep us waiting. Once he gets restless . . .'

'See you soon, then.'

She finished dressing Toby, packed his changing bag, added a few toys and books, set the answerphone and started out. It was a windy dry morning with dead plane leaves rattling along the gutters, but there was a smell of rain in the air. Toby struggled with the straps, demanding to get out and walk, so she pacified him with his mug of juice and pushed on. I'll tell the Inspector anything he wants to know about me, she thought, but not about anyone else. Not about Big Sue, or how upset Nell seemed to be. And I won't let on that Jim told me anything about the body. That might get him into trouble. I wish he hadn't said that about blackmail.

Instantly her mind was back in the repetitive, useless swirl of ideas and images that had kept her awake last night, more manageable now because less distorted by the delusions of the half-awake mind, but still troubling enough, because true. She could easily call up memories of groups of girls, sitting, particularly on the bench against the wall behind the painting area, and talking among themselves, chit-chat, telly-babble, pop-dross, but here and there more titillating kinds of small talk—their own lives, of course, and their boyfriends' vagaries, and sometimes too their employers'. No doubt they were more discreet in Poppy's company than they were among their closer cronies, but even in the last few weeks she'd learnt that Lucinda's teenage stepbrother had what sounded like a serious drug problem, and who Serena's father probably was, which the nominal father seemed not to know. If you were one of the cronies, or if you were clever at eavesdropping . . .

Poppy couldn't banish from her mind the image of one of them— but who? Who? Because all of them were already elsewhere in the dream picture, recognisable, innocently chatting away, while there was still this shadowy other, listening, remembering . . .

The police station was a baleful Victorian building in a quiet avenue south of the Uxbridge Road. A group of what must be journalists
waited by the steps in macs and anoraks. Two of them photographed
her as she heaved the push-chair up the steps, but none took the
ice-breaking opportunity of giving her a hand. She knew the form,
having had to report a stolen handbag last spring. Gone were the days
when you walked right in and told your woes to a fatherly sergeant at
a long mahogany counter and he fetched out a St Peter-sized ledger
and wrote in it in slow copperplate. Most of the old Station Office
had been sealed off. Only a short section of the counter remained,
and that had to be reached through a double set of swing doors, the
inner set being electrically locked so that only one caller at a time
need be admitted through to the counter. Between the two sets of
doors there were three metal chairs for people waiting their turn.

Poppy had hit a quiet moment and was let straight through, only
to be told that Mr Firth had been delayed somewhere, and she would
have to wait. Crossly she returned through the inner doors and settled down to read Toby *But Martin*. It was this week's favourite book,
but with new surroundings to explore he was only slightly interested
and the moment a newcomer pushed through the outer doors he was
lost. It was the door mechanism that did it. When opened and then
let go the two leaves hurtled towards their closed position, only to
slow mysteriously and sigh shut over the last few inches. They per-
formed this magic in both directions. The phenomenon cried out for
investigation.

Poppy had hated swing doors since Hugo had crushed a finger
in one at the age of three. If there'd been anywhere to go she'd have
taken Toby away. She turned him round, but there was the other set
of doors, with the counter beyond. *But Martin* had no charms, nor
any of the other books, nor the glove-puppet wombat. He flung the

plastic post van across the lobby. In desperation she gave him her handbag, normally forbidden, and let him unzip the compartments, but of course all the best things in it were forbidden too—the lipstick with its amazing combination of removable cap, protrudable stick and smear potential, the purse with its change. In Toby's economy what you did with change was slot it through cracks in floorboards (Janet kept a pot of foreign coins for this purpose, to the confusion of future archaeologists), but this floor was solid.

The doors swung again as a woman buttocked her way in dragging a double push-chair. She had that grey, pulpy, used look you sometimes see on young mothers trapped in the prison of child-care, with their men out all day, no help, no contact with friends, each dragging hour a desert. Why didn't more of them come to the play centre? They and their children were the ones who really needed it, not the Tobys and Deborahs and Dennys. Some did, of course, but far too few.

The push-chair held a sleeping baby and a boy a little older than Toby. As soon as his straps were undone the boy rushed to the outer door, shouting with excitement, shoved it open and let it swing back. The mother was lighting a cigarette and made no move to warn or stop him. Poppy managed to catch Toby as he flung himself off her lap. He squirmed in her grasp like a fresh-caught fish.

'No, darling, not you,' she said.

He threshed. He yearned with his arms for the door. It was his, a piece of apparatus he first of all mankind had discovered, and now this interloper . . . He yelled, full throat.

'Ah, go on, love,' said the woman. 'Let him have a go.'

'My son smashed his hand in a swing door,' snapped Poppy. 'That was thirty years ago and it's still not right.'

The woman shrugged. There was no hope of fixing Toby into his push-chair in this state so Poppy slung him up on her shoulder, shovelled her belongings one-handed into the changing bag and turned towards the inner door. The previous caller was still at the counter, but one of the policemen was coming round, presumably to restore order in the lobby.

'We can't wait here,' said Poppy as he came through the door. 'Tell Mr Firth I'll be back in ten minutes. He'd better be ready.'

'You'd much better wait . . .' he began but Poppy had already turned away, dragging the push-chair with her free hand. The boy had the door conveniently open so she strode through, the mixture of angers in her expressing themselves in an extra forcefulness of movement. Unfortunately Toby responded to the insult of passing so close to his rival with a sudden heave and wallow and she almost dropped him, letting go of the push-chair and unbalancing herself at the top of the steps as she struggled to hold on. She had to take the steps at a run, and would have fallen at the bottom if a man hadn't caught her and held her steady. It was Mr Firth.

'Morning, Mrs Tasker,' he said. 'Sorry to keep you. What's up with the little lad?'

'He wanted to play with the door. There was another child . . .'

They looked up the steps. The policeman was speaking to the boy, who pouted, let go of the door and went inside.

'There's still a few do what a copper tells them,' said Mr Firth. 'Couple of years older and it mightn't have worked. I'll get your pram.'

He nipped up and fetched the push-chair, then wheeled it empty along the pavement. Poppy followed with Toby still screaming and struggling in her grasp. The photographers had their cameras up but she spoilt their sport by leaving too large a gap for her and Mr Firth to appear in the same shot. He nodded cheerfully to them as he passed and turned down an alley beside the police station. Following, Poppy found him pressing numbered keys to open a side door, an activity in which Toby would normally have demanded to join but was now too engrossed in his tantrum even to notice. He didn't seem to notice the lift controls. Upstairs was a corridor with windows on to a central well on one side and labelled doors on the other. A few chairs stood against the inner wall. Mr Firth turned two corners and paused at a door.

'Just got one call to make,' he said. 'And I'll lay on a WPC to look after Toby.'

'Oh, please not. She wouldn't have a hope with him in this state, and I certainly wouldn't be able to concentrate. He'll be asleep in half an hour.'

He went in, but emerged almost at once.

'I'm sorry, Mrs Tasker. Something's come up. I'll have to ask you to wait a bit more, I'm afraid. At least it sounds like he might be quieting down.'

Indeed Toby's yells were modulating into sobs.

'Oh, all right,' said Poppy.

'Thanks a million.'

She put Toby down on one of the chairs and began to organise for another session with *But Martin*. She was re-stowing the changing bag when she heard the sigh of a door.

Toby was off his chair in an instant and charging down the corridor. A WPC with an armful of files had just come through a fire door half-way along the corridor. It did exactly the same trick as the ones below, hurtling towards closure and then slowing for the last few inches. The WPC stood out of Toby's way but lost control of her files as she was trying to do the same for Poppy, and they collided. Files slithered to the floor.

'Sorry,' muttered Poppy and dashed on, but he had reached the door. Oh, all right, she thought, and softened her defeat by turning it into a lesson on the swing-door menace, crouching by the jamb, pretending to get her hand trapped, miming agony. Toby, his face still swollen and smeared with his tantrum, ignored her and sternly adhered to the course of his experiment. At least his approach was gratifyingly different from that of the child downstairs, who had simply exulted in the physical effort of shoving the door open and letting it swish shut. Toby did that a few times, but then became fascinated by the invisible barrier which stopped the door from slamming. He experimented with opening it only a few inches, and then with trying to hurry it past the deceleration point. He held it part open with one hand and felt at the space in front of it with the other, to see if the air was somehow thicker there. From time to time people came past. He held the door for them and then returned to his exploration.

Poppy hovered by the jamb, waiting for the moment when he'd trap his fingers, but he justified her anxiety only once, at the point when he'd finished his investigations and needed a fresh audience to demonstrate to. Behind her in the corridor footsteps squeaked on lino. Toby turned to the newcomer and held out a summoning arm. As the door closed towards his other hand Poppy snatched it clear and held it till the danger was past. At that point she became aware that his stance had changed, to one of disappointment. The footsteps, two sets now, were no longer approaching but receding. She glanced over her shoulder and saw a man and a woman turning the far corner and moving out of sight. She caught only a glimpse of the woman—brown tweed coat, thick stockings—because she was largely screened by the man—blond hair, dark grey suit. For an instant she thought it had been Laura, but immediately became uncertain. She hadn't seen enough. But whoever it was had started to approach, stopped and turned back.

'Sorry about that,' said Mr Firth's voice from beyond the door. 'Where . . . ? Ah, there you are. Calmed down now, have we? Come in.'

His office was a functional, cramped mess, less decrepit than Poppy had expected. Stacked files, shelves of books and pamphlets, charts, organisation diagrams. Another door opened into a larger room, where several people seemed to be working. Mr Firth dug around in the drawers of his desk and found Toby a stapler, a fancy key-ring and a ruler with rollers in it. He settled Poppy into a chair opposite his desk and gave her a couple of sheets of paper.

'Anything like, d'you think?' he said.

Dismally Poppy stared at the drawings. Likeness or not they were so infinitely other than the living flesh that comparison seemed impossible.

'I don't think his beard was quite like that,' she said. 'Longer, and not so thick. And it had a sort of silky look—you know, as if it had never been cut. I'm not sure. I only got one good look at him, across the street. Otherwise I think it's quite like.'

'Thanks. We'll see what Jim Bowles says.'

'What's going to happen now?'

'We'll wait for Bob Caesar to come back. I like him here from the start, so he knows what line to follow while he's taking your statement. Then I'll ask you to tell me what happened and maybe question you about it, and then Bob will take you next door and get it down in detail.'

'How long will it take?'

'Two or three hours, if you're lucky.'

'Oh, God. He'll sleep some of that, but then he'll be wanting his lunch.'

'We'll be as quick as we can. He's a nice little lad. Two yet?'

'Not till after Christmas.'

'Talking much?'

'He seems to get a new word every day.'

'It's a great age.'

Mr Firth looked down at Toby, who was slithering the ruler across the carpet like a snowplough, pushing the stapler in front of it. He shook his head, inwardly rejecting a thought. The movement, with its speaking humanity, made Poppy look at him more closely. In the shock of events in the playground she had been aware of Firth mainly as a bearable presence, almost sympathetic, autumnal with his brown suit and tanned and time-marked face, appropriate to the presence of death. Sitting in his office, without his hat, he was still like that, superficially, but she was aware of an inward energy, a sense of purpose, or perhaps of dedication, not subject to the shift of seasons. If he'd been an actor there'd have been a tendency to typecast him as a priest. He was younger than she was, by several years she guessed, but was already bald right across the top, an effect enhanced by the dense, short, dark brown hair at the sides of his head.

'How old are yours?' said Poppy.

'In their teens. Two girls. I don't see much of them these days. I split up with my wife when they were nine and eight and she's taken them to live in Scotland.'

'I'm sorry.'

'Yes, I miss them. It was the job did it, really. It's a lot to ask of a woman . . . Here's Bob.'

A man's voice, macho-mocking, said something to a WPC in the inner room. When he came through he was the one Poppy had seen in the corridor, large, blond, grey-suited. So Laura, if it was Laura, had already been here when Mr Firth had arrived. He hadn't expected her, and had had to ask Poppy to wait. Sergeant Caesar had then taken her out through the further room and the other door and she'd then turned the wrong way, but almost at once turned back. Realised her mistake? Recognised not Poppy, crouched by the door and facing away, but Toby, manifest and commanding attention? If so, it had to be Laura. It wasn't any of the others

'Right,' said Mr Firth. 'I'd best explain that I'm not in charge of this case. That's Detective Superintendent Collins from the Area Major Investigation Team. I'm the local officer working with him. We'll start with the occasion when a man who may have been the deceased seemed to be following you. September the tenth, according to the report. About three o'clock in the afternoon something took place. Will you tell me in your own words about that?'

Poppy told the story yet again, unemotionally, as if explaining the plot of a serial episode to somebody who'd missed it. She stressed her unwillingness to swear that the man who started following her out of the park was the same as the one who'd been watching from under the trees. Mr Firth interrupted once to clarify a point.

'Excellent,' he said. 'Clear and concise. There's just one aspect I'd like you to expand on, Mrs Tasker. When you saw this man watching you, you say you and the other adults in the playground stared deliberately at him until he went away. What did you do then?'

'Let Toby go on playing for a bit, then started to take him home. It was a bit early, but the atmosphere wasn't happy. We were all upset.'

'And angry?'

'Yes, of course, and frightened and shocked and everything else you'd expect.'

'And did people express their anger?'

'I suppose so . . . I know what you're trying to get me to say, and I'm not going to. It was just talk, just a gut reaction. You can't really believe that a group of ordinary women, in this day and age . . . I mean . . . and anyway, how did they find him, how did they know who he was? Do you know who he was?'

'I can't tell you that at the moment. Look, Mrs Tasker, I understand what you're saying. That's what I think, too. At least, suppose I had to bet on it, I'd lay about twenty to one against any of your girls getting together and killing this man. Maybe I'd lay better odds against one of them telling her boyfriend, and him and some pals doing it, or at least setting out to teach him a lesson and it going wrong. But those are still possibilities I've got to look into. You follow?'

Poppy shook her head. She'd never met Big Sue's Trevor, a crass-sounding, beer-swilling, football-going van driver for a builders' merchant, by Sue's account. He sounded just the sort to get a group of his mates together for a lynching, and what's more he wouldn't understand the importance of the play centre to the women. He'd desecrate it without a thought.

'You're an intelligent woman . . .' began Mr Firth.

'I'm not saying anything.'

'Don't you see that by refusing to tell me what was in fact said, and by whom, you are reinforcing the suspicion that much more was in fact said than would be normal on such an occasion? That you have, in fact, something to hide?'

'I've nothing to hide. I just don't want to tell you. You'll have to ask the others, that's all. I'll tell you that I didn't say anything along those lines myself, but I certainly felt it. I tried not to, but I did.'

'Very well. Put a note in, Bob, to the effect that Mrs Tasker is unwilling to say at this juncture what was said among those present after the man had left the playground. Now, Mrs Tasker, a point you've already raised—how would anyone know where to find the man? Did any of those present say or do anything to show they might have recognised him?'

'No. I'll tell you that much.'

'Are you sure? You answered very quickly.'

'I'd already been thinking about it.'

'You had? So the possibility of a connection was already in your mind?'

'I didn't sleep much. And you'd pretty well asked me yesterday, hadn't you? I mean, just by suggesting some of us . . .'

'All right. Now we'll move on to yesterday. I took you into the hut and asked you if you recognised the deceased. Carry on in your own words.'

It didn't take long. There wasn't a lot to say. By now Toby had exhausted the possibilities of the ruler and was attracted to the word-processor console on the table beside which Sergeant Caesar was sitting. Sergeant Caesar didn't notice his approach till he began to climb into his lap.

'My do it,' said Toby.

'Not now, sonny.'

'My do it,' said Toby, slowly and loudly, like an English tourist coping with the stupidity of foreigners. The sergeant mimed helplessness.

'Wait till you've got some of your own, Bob,' said Mr Firth, getting out a sheet of paper and a felt-tipped pen. 'Bring him over here, Mrs Tasker, and we'll see if the trick still works. What's this, Toby?'

Already he'd started to draw. Poppy picked Toby up and carried him across to watch.

'What's this, Toby?' he said again.

Towards one edge of the page he had drawn a small, half-open book with a mouse on the cover.

'Tory,' said Toby, wriggling, not interested.

'Ah, but what's this?'

A cat had appeared, reading the book.

'Miaow,' said Toby.

'Aha! But what's this?'

A few quick lines turned the picture into the cover of another book, and then almost as rapidly a pig appeared, reading that book, only to recede into the cover of a still larger book, perused by an elephant, filling the page. The pictures had humour and fantasy, unsuspected in Firth's manner. But the trick wasn't over. He folded the paper in half, and in half again, several times, down to a book-like shape with the original book on its front cover. He turned it over and drew a quick cartoon of a small boy.

'That's Toby,' he said. 'And this is Toby's book.'

Poppy laughed aloud. Toby took the book, and finding that he couldn't turn the pages, carefully unfolded it. Mr Firth helped him fold it back into book shape again, letting him feel he was doing the work himself. He must have been a lovely father, Poppy thought. When the job allowed.

Toby studied the pictures on the front and back.

'Mine,' he said, and tucked the book carefully into the pocket in the bib of his overalls. The telephone rang. Mr Firth answered, then put his hand over the mouthpiece.

'Right,' he said. 'Now Bob will take you next door and take a detailed statement from you. He'll check it with me, and then if we're all happy you can sign it. OK?'

They went next door and settled at a desk in the corner of the room. Toby gave signs of wanting to assist the police in all their activities, but he was tired now and consented to sit in Poppy's lap and let her read snatches of *But Martin* to him while Sergeant Caesar was writing whatever she'd just said in slow long hand. He had his rusk, then orange juice, stimuli to which at this time of day he had acquired an almost Pavlovian response. At one moment he was sucking at his mug and pointing with his free hand at a detail of the pictures, and the next he had plunged into sleep. She strapped the inert lump into the push-chair and was able to give her full attention to Sergeant Caesar.

He wanted to know everything—who else had been at the entrance to the park, for instance, and the exact time of day, and how had she known and whether anyone else had used the crossing. She learnt not to leave things out—it took longer that way. Mercifully Toby, exhausted by his tantrum, slept almost two hours and woke only as Poppy wheeled him into Mr Firth's office. He had crapped in his nappy while waking, a recent habit, so she laid him out on the carpet and cleaned and changed him while Mr Firth was reading the statement through. The homely pungency she released was pleasing to her in that world of paperwork. Out of the corner of her eye she saw Sergeant Caesar wrinkling his nose and averting his gaze with absurd male squeamishness, especially considering the really obscene horrors his work must sometimes confront him with. Mr Firth glanced up, repressed a smile, and went on reading. When he had finished Poppy initialled each page and signed the final sheet.

'Well done,' he said. 'I think that's all. I'm sorry it always has to take so long.'

'There's just one thing,' said Poppy. 'I don't know how it works, or who to ask, only when the poor man's buried I'd like to send a wreath. How do I . . . ?'

She stopped. Mr Firth and the Sergeant had glanced at each other and changed, their faces becoming professional, withdrawn.

'It's all right,' she said hurriedly. 'It doesn't mean anything. Only I was thinking last night, because of Toby, about him having been a baby once too, and being loved, and now no one even knowing or caring what's happened to him. It wouldn't be a wreath for him really. It would be for me, for all of us . . . I know it sounds silly . . .'

The weird moment had passed.

'Not at all,' said Mr Firth, relaxing. 'Just make a note, Bob, to see Mrs Tasker knows about the burial arrangements. Now, Mrs Tasker, what about a spot of instant lunch? There's a place just up the road if you've time?'

'Oh,' said Poppy, startled, suddenly unable to think. She knew the place he was talking about, a tolerable-looking burger bar. Toby would adore the forbidden food. 'Well, I mean yes, if you . . .'

'Even policemen need to eat.'

He led the way out through the other room, pausing to check work progress with a WPC at a word-processor, and then on into the corridor using the door through which the woman who might have been Laura had come. They turned on, round the far corner, as she had done, so perhaps it was just routine, and she hadn't recognised Toby at all, had been a stranger . . .

Outside it was raining now. Rather than struggle with the push-chair cover for so short a distance Mr Firth held Poppy's brolly over Toby. The photographers, luckily, had taken shelter. The eatery was too noisy and crowded for talk, and Toby, thrilled by the adventure, made himself the centre of attention, studying how Mr Firth dealt with his hamburger and trying to copy him. Poppy had a toler-able cheese salad. Eating together is a way of communicating, she thought—safer than speech in some ways. They had a moment of privacy outside as she fixed the push-chair cover under the shelter of the awning.

'I want to put one thing into your mind,' said Mr Firth. 'We have very good reason to think that whoever was responsible for the body in the play centre must have known about the man's previous appearance there. This isn't simply because it may be the same man. There are other strong indications.'

Poppy nodded. The freesias, she thought.

'So somebody must have told them,' he said.

'Perhaps he told them himself.'

'You think that's likely?'

'I don't know.'

'Well, if you have any further thoughts I hope you'll let me know. Ring me on this number.'

'All right.'

Poppy pushed home beside the swishing traffic thinking not about anything to do with the young man's death but about Mr Firth's lost daughters.

4

There was a message on Janet's answerphone: 'Hi, Poppy, if you're in. Big Sue, this is. Play centre's closed, of course, but some of us are meeting at Little Sue's after dinner if you'd like to come along. Nine, Linen Walk, that is. See you soon.'

By the time Poppy was ready to move again the rain was really teeming down, so she borrowed Janet's rock-climbing cagoule, which reached almost to her knees, and battled her way south. Toby discovered a new game in the watery environment. He would watch the pool of water forming on the top of the push-chair cover and when it was full he'd reach up and punch the bottom of its sag, producing an effect like an elfin depth charge. His first effort sluiced straight into Poppy's face, under the hood of the cagoule, but after that she learnt to watch for the moment of impact and turn her head away. This kept him happy for most of the journey but by the time they reached Linen Walk he was restless for new amusements.

Linen Walk ran east/west beside the Metropolitan Line viaduct. It was said to occupy a strip of land which had been used a hundred and fifty years ago by the local washerwomen to lay out their sheets to air. Now it was a terrace of pretty but jerry-built 1880ish houses with front gardens and a pedestrian passage between them and the blackened arches of the viaduct. In the front rooms every ornament, every piece of crockery on every shelf, trembled to the passing trains. You got used to them in no time, Sue said. During the last rail strike she'd kept waking up wondering what was wrong, and little Peter, who'd been sleeping right through, had started crying in the night again.

With the railway so close the houses might have been near-slums, a dingy blotch on the gentrification and prettification of the area, but they too had their coats of ice-cream-coloured paint, with the ornamental details picked out in white, and French-style number-plates by the doors. They changed hands frequently. There was always a 'For Sale' notice or two on show. Young couples bought them because they were cheap, and moved on as soon as their salaries would support a higher mortgage. Apart from the railway, they looked decidedly attractive. No traffic ran past their front doors, and there was another advantage, hidden from the street. Behind each house a strip of garden ran north, the far wall being also the wall of the park, with a door directly through. A previous owner of number 9 had altered this arrangement by building a studio across the end of the garden, which Pete's three elder brothers used as a playroom during the school holidays. In term-time Peter, an afterthought by some years—his first name provided the P of the initials P.S.—had it to himself while his siblings were at boarding-school. It wasn't as large or well equipped as the hut in the play centre, but much better on a wet day than anyone else's house could have provided. Pete had largely absentee parents. They kept a yacht in a Turkish marina and seemed to spend most of their time there. Poppy couldn't imagine what they did for a living that would pay for that and keep several children at boarding-school.

Little Sue was a live-in nanny, small and brisk, with an East End accent she made no attempt to gentilify. The bond between her and Pete seemed to Poppy quite as strong as motherhood. She'd often arrive at the play centre not having bothered to bring the push-chair that short distance, carrying him on her hip and looking with her gamine build just like a figure in a Phil May low-life cartoon, eldest sister minding baby while mum went out to char. It was an old-fashioned nanny-child relationship, doomed to the traditional emotion-stunting traumas when in a few years' time Pete, in his turn, would be wrenched away to prep school.

The door was opened not by Sue but by an unknown woman who looked at her and snapped, 'You're supposed to be coming in through the park.'

'I'm so sorry,' began Poppy. 'I didn't . . .'

At this point Toby, impatient for release, flailed again at the pool on the plastic cover. The water shot straight into Poppy's face. Perhaps it was that that did it. Perhaps it was Poppy's obviously cut-above-mere-nanny accent. At any rate the woman, now dimly seen through soaked spectacles, relented. It would have been a longish walk round to the back, the last part a squelch across sodden turf.

'You might as well come through now,' she said.

'Oh, thank you so much.'

The woman was presumably the normally absent Mrs Simpson, Pete's mother. She had a shock of coarse, leonine hair, a Mediterranean tan, snub nose, tough little chin and pouting mouth. Discontent looked to be second nature to her, but she waited patiently enough while Poppy tilted the excess water off the push-chair and then wheeled it down the tiled hail, through the kitchen and out into the garden.

The TV was on in the playroom, with a video of *Ghostbusters* cartoons, absolutely forbidden at home by Janet's stern code. But in the Nafia you accepted the customs of the household, except where sweets were concerned, so as soon as Toby was out of his straps and coat he ran across and settled down with the other children to be zombified. The roof was leaking into a bucket in one corner, and the nannies had built a barrier of push-chairs round it to keep the children away, so Poppy added hers and at last, thankfully, stripped off the overwhelming cagoule.

'Great you could come,' said Little Sue.

'I'm afraid I didn't realise we were supposed to use the park door. Mrs Simpson let me in, but she didn't seem too pleased about it.'

'Doesn't matter. Big Sue must of forgot to say. Cup of tea?'

'Those answer gadgets, they always faze me,' said Big Sue. 'Shove up, Fran—there's room on here for three, even if one of them's me, and Poppy can tell us the news.'

As well as the Sues, Laura was there, and Nell, Fran, and Gina, a jolly and intelligent Mauritian who appeared to be disgracefully exploited by her employers but was unable to complain because she hadn't got a work permit. They had pushed the sofas and chairs into a semicircle so that they could watch the children while they talked.

'Tea's just what I need,' said Poppy. 'But I'm afraid I don't know any more than's in the papers.'

'Lovely pictures of you,' said Big Sue.

'I thought they were horrible,' said Poppy.

'Didn't mean it like that. Course it must of felt horrible.'

'Looked like you might of been going to faint when you came out of the hut,' said Fran.

'I expect I did,' said Poppy.

'Got you to look at him, didn't they?' said Big Sue, determined not to miss anything. Then, realising that this wasn't the occasion for the simple gusto of the uninvolved, she added, 'That's a bit rough on you.'

'I suppose somebody's got to,' said Poppy.

'Was it him, Poppy?' said Fran. 'The fellow who tried to follow you that other time?'

'I think so,' said Poppy. 'I hadn't seen him that close, and he'd got a beard then. I don't know if he'd shaved it himself, or . . .'

'No, they done that,' said Little Sue. 'Least, that's what it says here . . . where was it? . . . hold on . . .'

She scuffled among the scatter of papers on the floor. Poppy glimpsed pictures of herself, of Toby, the WPC, the hut.

'Not all they did to him, either,' said Big Sue meaningfully.

'That's not right,' said Poppy. 'I mean, if it actually says . . .'

'Not straight out, it doesn't. They aren't allowed, are they? But they tell you, good as . . .'

They were all looking at her now, even Laura. This was more than nosiness and prurience—they too felt the nightmare. And anyway, what gave her the right to know the truth, and them not?

'Don't pass this on,' she said. 'I got it from Jim Bowles—you know, the crossing warden—and I don't want to get him into trouble. He used to be a policeman and he's still got friends in the police station. He says they think the man didn't die in the hut. He'd been gassed somewhere, with carbon monoxide, apparently—you know, you get it in car exhaust—and then they'd brought him along to the play centre and stripped him—his clothes were neatly folded under the Lego table—and laid him out naked on the table and decorated his penis with freesias. That's all.'

The silence of disbelief.

'Freesias?' said three of them together.

'That's right,' said Poppy. 'Jim says they'd fastened them on with elastic bands.'

Someone began to laugh, and in a moment as the tension ravelled away the studio was filled with their whooping. Poppy felt the hysteria rise inside her like the uprush of a wave in a cliff cleft, uncontrollable, bursting up into a fountain of sound. It was as though the affronted spirit of the play centre had embodied itself into a force, a pagan godling, local, earth-powerful, and had possessed them into this communal release, selves lost in the summoned presence. Something was shaking her knee. She looked down and saw Toby there, trying to attract her attention, his face full of puzzled alarm. She caught him up and hugged him, rocking to and fro in the dance of laughter. A soft thing nuzzled at her lips. Toby had managed to wriggle an arm free and was holding his hand across her mouth, trying to seal the maenad cry back in. She mastered the uprush, held herself still and with her free hand straightened her specs over her streaming eyes. Around her the laughter of the others dwindled as the god withdrew.

'No,' said Toby. 'Go way. No.'

He stared at her with masculine command, Pentheus confronting the Bacchae, and put his hand back over her mouth in case the laughter should erupt once more.

'It's all right,' she mumbled. 'I've stopped. I won't do it again.'

'All gone,' he confirmed, then slithered down and stumped back to the idiocies of the cartoon. The women adjusted themselves into their workaday sanities with eye-dabs and sighings and shakes of the head. They glanced at each other, half-shamed, half-pleased. Gina had hiccups. Big Sue was bright red, her whole body heaving. Little Sue was giggling, her eyes darting around and her face full of mischief. Laura had her head turned away, and Nell, sitting cross-legged on the floor, was talking to Nelson, who like Toby must have felt the wild-wood female revel as some kind of threat and run to her for reassurance. The fall of her pale hair hid her face, and as usual Poppy was struck by the way the bond between mother and son seemed automatically to constrain their poses into an aesthetically satisfying group, so that, skill-less though she was at any kind of art work, she felt that if she'd at that moment had charcoal and paper to hand she could have sketched her own Mother and Child. Could Nell really have made the transition from that wildness to this serenity in so short a space?

Laura turned, her face stiff and angry. She clearly had not been caught in the godling's grip.

'It's not decent,' she said. 'He's dead. He's dead. Please.'

'Course it's not, love,' said Big Sue. 'But oh dear. Elastic bands. That's just perfect.'

Her body quivered with an after-tremor of the eruption. Nell looked up. No, she had not been laughing either.

All that clamour had come from just five throats.

'They're trying to make it look as if it was us,' she said.

'The cops, you mean?' said Fran.

'All of them,' said Nell. 'If Poppy's right, if Bowles is telling the truth—did he say he saw the flowers, Poppy?'

'I don't think so. I think it was something he was told.'

'They could've been pulling his leg,' said Little Sue. 'Jim takes himself so serious, you know.'

'It doesn't make that much difference,' said Nell. 'Whoever set this up wanted to make it look as if it was us, and if it suits the police to go along with that they will.'

'Last evening,' said Fran, 'they came round, a couple of them, and they were on at me to say how we'd talked about finding the bastard that day he was at the play centre, and what we'd do with him when we'd found him.'

'Me too,' said Little Sue.

There were murmurs from the others.

'Yes,' said Poppy. 'Inspector Firth was asking me about that again this morning.'

'What did you tell him?' said Nell.

'I said we were naturally shocked and angry, and some of us expressed our anger in the way you'd expect, but it was just talk, it didn't mean anything. I refused to tell him any details, what was said, or who'd said it. I tried to persuade him that it was absolutely impossible that any of us could have done something like that in the play centre. It means too much.'

'How'd he take that?' said Big Sue.

'Well of course he took the line that he had to explore all possibilities . . .'

'Gah!' said Little Sue.

'It's how men think,' said Nell.

'My Trev was on about it half the night,' said Big Sue. 'Couldn't let it alone. Didn't know it was only flowers then, of course. There'd been talk going round in the crowd, and when I told Trev . . . Like picking a scab it was. Over and over and over.'

'Tell him he's got a castration complex,' said Nell.

'I wouldn't dare! Do you think he has?'

'I wouldn't be surprised—they mostly seem to. Anyway, given half a chance that's the line the police will take.'

Poppy remembered the book Mr Firth had made for Toby, and felt she had to make at least a token defence of him.

'I think you're wrong,' she said. 'At any rate this time. Mr Firth told me he himself thought the odds were about twenty to one against it being any of us.'

'You don't know them like I do,' said Fran. 'OK, they aren't all sods, and there's some of them doing their best, the way they see it. But good or bad they'll put words into your mouth, soon as look at you. Not just to do you down, not always. Some of them are like that, but mostly all they want is to make life easier for themselves, cutting a few corners. They think they know what's happened, and they'll do anything they can to prove it.'

'It's more than that,' said Nell. 'OK, men aren't all bastards, but there's a bastard in all of them, and the ones who took it into their heads they wanted to become policemen are good as telling you what kind of bastard they're likely to be. Best thing you can do is tell them nothing.'

'I don't agree,' said Poppy. 'That just makes it look as if we've got something to hide, and if we all refuse to say anything then they'll think it's a conspiracy, and if we can conspire to keep silent then we can conspire to do other things. I think we should admit we talked a bit about finding the man and teaching him a lesson, but it was just talk, and we knew it was.'

'Trouble is,' said Fran, 'they treat you different, Poppy. Voice like yours, they're going to be nice to you unless they think they've really got something on you. Someone like me, though, they'll keep on and on at till they've worn me down and I start saying things just to be shot of them.'

'It's the system,' said Nell. 'It's happening all the time. It's how they get confessions out of innocent people.'

'That's right,' said Sue. 'Like when my Trev had his van nicked.'

She embarked on her favourite story, about Trevor's van, loaded with plumbing supplies, being stolen from outside a transport café. He'd had a conviction for shop-lifting when he was a teenager, but he'd gone adequately straight since then. At first his main concern was not to let Sue know he'd been in bed with the manageress in her caravan behind the café at the time of the theft, so he'd blustered and lied. Then, as Trevor's kind of luck would have it, the police got an anonymous telephone call from a man (the manageress's regular lover, insane with jealousy—often Sue was unable to continue for laughter by the time she reached this point) and searched the caravan and found getting on for a kilo of hard drugs in a compartment under the floor. Trevor had spent several weeks on remand, charged for the time being with connivance in the theft of his own van, but then that was picked up somewhere up north being driven by a pair of runaway lovers who'd clearly got nothing to do with Trevor but had been selling off the contents of the van piecemeal to finance their escapade, and the manageress in revenge implicated the lover and thus, casually, exonerated Trevor.

Poppy only half listened, having heard most of the story before. She was concerned about Nell. After the abortive closure of the Sabina Road squat Nell, good as her word, had stayed only a couple of nights in the flat and then moved on. It had all been perfectly amicable, and Nell had continued to bring Nelson to the play centre, but now there seemed to be a definite constraint between her and Poppy. Poppy felt she mustn't expect, let alone ask for, any increase of friendship on the strength of the brief and not very demanding help she'd given Nell, and she guessed that Nell, though grateful for Nelson's sake, would not want to be drawn at all into Poppy's world and interests and values, and in fact positively needed to re-establish the barrier between them. This didn't stop Poppy continuing to like and admire Nell, and wish for her friendship, but her tentative moves in that direction had been set gently aside.

Was Nell happy, she wondered, in anything more than her love for her son? Was she actually as in control of her life as she liked to seem? There'd been that time, for instance, when the man had first come to watch the play centre and they'd driven him away with their stares. She had reacted differently from the others. Poppy wouldn't have expected her to join them in their primitive revenge fantasies, but it was surprising that she hadn't taken the obvious opportunity for one of her bitter little harangues on the destructive impulses of the male. Instead she had seemed to be running away, protecting Nelson, presumably, though he'd been up by the slide, well away from the man's focus of interest.

She was looking more drawn these days, Poppy felt, sadder, disillusioned. The decision to leave Sabina Road must have been a wrench

The reverie was interrupted by Laura, bursting into Sue's epic.

'You don't have to go on!' she snapped. 'They're all like that, all of them! I could tell you things!'

They looked at her, startled. Just as clearly as Poppy she didn't belong to the culture which finds itself being harried by the police. You'd have thought her main experience of them was having the traffic held up so that she could push her pram across the road. She faced their stares undaunted.

'Once they've decided to pick on you you've not got a hope,' she said.

They waited.

'That's all. I'm not saying any more. Take it from me! And that's enough of that rubbish for the children. We don't want them getting square-eyed, do we?'

Without waiting for assent she rose and switched the TV off, leaving the video running. There were cries of protest from the children—even those whose vocabulary was still at the 'More' and 'No' stage contributed their vehement monosyllables. She faced them down with the full authority of the Victorian nursery.

'That's enough of that,' she snapped. 'One hour a day is all you get. You know what will happen otherwise? Your brains will go soft and your willies will fall off.'

Four of the nine infants were girls, but the tone of the threat was enough to quell the rebellion. Grumblingly they began to disperse to other amusements. The adults glanced at each other. There was something uncontrolled about Laura's behaviour, quite different from the release into wild laughter earlier. Was she drunk, Poppy wondered? On the verge of a breakdown? Didn't she, in this day and age, understand what she might be doing, saying things like that? Poor little Nick watching his favourite programmes, desperately clutching his crotch as he did so to keep everything in place? Had Toby understood? If so, would his fear of the event outweigh his interest in observing the phenomenon? Perhaps one worried too much.

The rain became heavier, and the drip increased to a thin stream into the bucket, which needed emptying every ten minutes, an activity that attracted the children's attention—indoor water-games—so that conversation became impossible until fresh rules were evolved and understood. During this process Mrs Simpson appeared, all charm and laughter.

'Oh, dear,' she said, gazing at the leak from the ceiling, 'I thought it was supposed to have been fixed.'

She gave a lively little shrug, like a comedy actress, and turned to the children. At least she was able to recognise her own son, though Pete seemed in some doubt about who she might be. Mostly the children ignored her advances but Sophie, Laura's older charge, responded gravely to her questions. Poppy caught a snatch of the conversation.

'. . . a theatre designer! How fascinating! And does Mummy take you to a lot of lovely plays?'

'Not a lot.'

It was a bit like a royal visit. Though the nannies didn't actually line up to curtsy and shake hands the introductions had some of that stiffness and unreality, as though Mrs Simpson, with her yacht and her winter tan, belonged to a world too alien for the others to contemplate. Laura, indeed, glared at her hostess as though she was about to burst out with some wild rambling grievance, like one of those eccentrics who believe that a few words from the monarch will right their own ancient and intolerable wrongs. Mercifully she managed to hold her peace.

Still smiling, but now concerned and sympathetic, Mrs Simpson turned to Poppy.

'And you're the one this silly man tried to follow?' she said. 'I wonder if you'd mind coming and having a few words with my husband. He's a bit worried. And with us being here so little . . .'

'Of course. I'll just explain to Toby.'

They crossed the garden under Mrs Simpson's umbrella, which she managed to share in such a way that drips from its rim fell on Poppy's shoulder. She led the way upstairs, and opened a door. From higher still Poppy caught the plop of leakage into yet another bucket. A man was standing at the window, staring out over the roof of the playroom at the sodden park beyond.

'This is Mrs Tasker, darling,' said Mrs Simpson. 'She's the one Sue was telling us about at breakfast.'

He turned. You would have known he was a sailor, Poppy thought, wherever you'd met him and whatever he was wearing. It wasn't just the weathered face and under-the-chin beard (no shaving the tricky bits with the boat heaving around). There was also something about the stance, and the strong, half-contemptuous look. He was older than she'd expected, fiftyish, so a dozen or more years older than his wife. Bald on top, the scalp sun-mottled. Plump, wearing an old grey jersey, slacks, sandals on sockless feet.

'Lovely climate,' he said.

'The playroom roof's leaking too, I'm afraid,' said Mrs Simpson.

'I'll get up there if I've got time. Hello. And what can you tell us?'

'You're worried about Pete, Mrs Simpson says.'

'If she says so then I am. She's the boss.'

'I don't think you need be. Sue is an absolutely first-class girl—she's really fond of him and very responsible . . .'

'Wouldn't have hired her, otherwise.'

'And, well, men who are interested in small children—I'm afraid you're never going to stop that, and of course they turn up at the playground from time to time. As soon as it's clear that's what they are the play-leader rings the police, who get someone along almost at once. It's upsetting, of course, but . . .'

'One of them tried to follow you home.'

'Yes. I admit that was rather more disturbing, but it's only happened once, and now he's . . .'

'Not in a position to do it again. Good riddance. OK, begin at the beginning. There you all were, and the fellow turned up. What next?'

He stared intently at Poppy while she explained, grunting impatient understanding every third sentence.

'Right,' he said. 'That bit's clear. So you didn't see him again till yesterday. Then what?

'Well, I only think it was him . . .'

Again she explained what she'd seen, but this time not what Jim had told her. It was no business of his, and she resented his manner, his lifestyle, his neglect of his children. She'd already told Sue. She would explain again about it being confidential, and leave it to Sue whether to pass on the rest. What did it have to do with any possible threat to Pete?

'And what are the cops making of it?' he said.

'They don't tell you. They just ask questions.'

'Haven't got a clue themselves, of course. What did he look like, then? White? Yellow? Green? Any sign of drugs? I ask myself, you see, who'd do a thing like that? It's not how I'd dispose of a body, nor you, neither. But a group of young layabouts on a high, and one of them takes an overdose and the rest are all pooped out of their minds, they might take it into their heads to ferry him along there. You follow?'

'I wouldn't know about drugs. He had bright red blotches on his cheeks.'

'Did he now? Did he now? Then that's something else. That's a faulty water heater, maybe. Or maybe he did himself in with vehicle exhaust. Then you've got someone who doesn't want him found where he is—drugs again, maybe, or some other reason . . .'

He rasped his fingers through his beard, meditating possibilities.

'Oh, that would make it all so much better,' said Mrs Simpson. 'I mean if it was an accident . . .'

Reluctant though she was to agree with her about anything, Poppy felt the same. How long does it take to disinfect a horror? A murder on that very spot, with deliberate cruelty—decades at least, your own whole lifetime, maybe. A suicide in the place—a year or two, perhaps. An accident elsewhere, with the body brought to the play centre only as a kind of clownish aftermath to a life that could never have had much to offer . . . perhaps in a few weeks' time she would be able to sit in the hut, oblivious among the clamour of lives just begun.

'There's still someone around with a nasty sense of humour,' said Mr Simpson. 'If the papers have got it right, what they're hinting at.'

'Oh, no,' said Poppy, involuntarily forthcoming in her relief.

'Not so?' he said softly, staring her in the eyes.

'Well . . . no . . . I don't believe so.'

He didn't press her any further, apart from continuing to stare at her with a pleased, meditative hum.

'And they still don't know who he was?' said Mrs Simpson.

'Not as far as I know. I'm afraid that's all I've got to tell you, and I really ought to go back and look after Toby. Look, shall I give you my telephone number? Then if you're worried about anything while you're away . . .'

'Oh, that's very kind of you,' said Mrs Simpson, 'but it's all right. My mother's only too pleased to have an excuse for a trip to London. Thank you so much for being so helpful. Can you find your own way down? Goodbye.'

Poppy was glad to leave, if not to be so perfunctorily dismissed. She used the umbrella to get herself across the garden, and found only Laura and Little Sue and the four relevant children still in the playroom. Nick was in tears, Toby having apparently tempted him into a jumping-off-sofa competition and then jumped on top of him, but Laura was brusque and uncomforting with him. It was still comparatively early, but Poppy felt, as the others seemed to have done, that in this filthy weather it would be best to get home, dry off and snug down. Toby had other ideas, and by the time Poppy had cajoled him into his all-in-one and then into the push-chair Laura had her two ready. She herself seemed to have come in nothing but a head-scarf and light tweed coat, both still sopping from the outward trip, but Sue had found her a plastic mac with a hood. Sue opened the door out into the park and together Laura and Poppy made for the nearest stretch of tarmac path. The squelching turf was so soft that they had to turn and drag the push-chairs through it, with Sophie, in yellow sou'wester and scarlet boots, picking her way disdainfully between the puddles behind. It was hard work, but it didn't stop Laura now, after almost unbroken silence in the playroom apart from her outburst about the police, suddenly wanting to talk.

'What did they want, Mrs Tasker? What did they want with you?'

'Just to find out if I knew anything. It's their job, after all.'

'Their job, indeed! They haven't got a job! Not unless you count sailing around in that stupid boat.'

'Oh, the Simpsons, you mean. I thought . . . Well, Mrs Simpson seemed a bit worried about Peter . . .'

'Stuff and nonsense. She isn't worried about anyone. Herself's the only person she thinks about. They're all like that. None of them care for anyone but themselves!'

She spoke with savagery. Poppy was not as startled as she might have been, having read that Laura's employer, the theatre designer Mary Pitalski, was far from easy to deal with. Many nannies, finding themselves expected, in addition to their practical duties, to become a stop-gap and dispensable substitute love figure for the children of under-involved parents, must have felt much the same kind of rage at times. To change the subject Poppy gestured with her head towards the play centre, now over to their right. A caped figure guarded the gate, the only sign of human life in the sodden park. Nothing seemed to be happening around the hut.

'I wonder how long before we can have it back,' she said.

'I'm not going there. Never again. Never,' said Laura.

Poppy glanced at her. The normally solemn face was like stone. Her hood had half blown back and the rain streamed down her face unheeded. This wasn't anger at her employer, Poppy realised, or squeamishness at the idea of closeness to a stranger's death; and after all he should have meant even less to Laura than he had to the others—he hadn't been there on the day he'd come to the play centre. Still, unmistakably, and accounting for the rest of her behaviour that afternoon, this was grief.

Laura straightened and shook the water from her face, like a queen turning from the body of her murdered lover to resume the dreadful destiny of empire.

'I shall take the children to Holland Park,' she announced.

NOVEMBER 1989

1

The concert was sub-minimalist, slithering chords and plangent or spiky half-phrases dropped into reaches of silence. A cough from among the sparse audience was both blasphemy and relief. At the interval the stir and shuffle of release from stillness was the most satisfactory sound Poppy had heard for an hour. Mr Capstone glanced at her with a look of ferocious amusement.

'Enjoying this?'

'Not much.'

'Let's go.'

Most of the rest of the audience seemed to be making the same decision. A large woman about Poppy's age had fallen asleep—the composer's mother? she wondered. Would her snores mitigate the silences in the second half? It wasn't worth staying to see.

The hall was in an unfamiliar bit of North Islington. They came out into a dark side-street. Late though it was in the year Poppy still couldn't smell the coming winter. 'Not a lot to say about that,' said Mr Capstone.

'I thought he was just teasing.'

'His earlier work was more interesting. I saw a pizza place in the main road.'

'There's some food at home, if you'd prefer. I'm fairly sure no one's been watching. I think it was probably that poor young man they found in the play centre, and he's dead now.'

'I have to meet someone in central London later.'

'Then I'd love a pizza. *You* haven't seen him again?'

'Who?'

'The man who tried to follow you.'

'Wouldn't recognise him if I had. Some drifter. Probably wanting to beg off me. I was more worried for you.'

'That's nice of you,' said Poppy, though this had been far from her impression at the time.

The restaurant was busy. It would clearly be a while before anyone came for their order.

'You had to identify the body, I gather,' he said.

'Not exactly identify. They still don't know who he was, I believe. His beard had been shaved, to make it harder, I suppose. But I'm fairly sure it was the man who'd followed us. How's Deborah? Toby's been asking for her.'

'You haven't seen her?'

'Well, we've rung a couple of times, but . . . this is a bit awkward, I'm afraid. I'm probably just imagining things. I got the impression that your wife didn't want to be involved with anyone from the play centre for the moment. Because of the publicity, I suppose. It's quite understandable. I'm sure my daughter-in-law would feel the same.'

'You're mistaken. At least I know Deborah was asked to play with some children in Barnsley Square, because we picked her and the girl up from there yesterday on my way home. A house with a ridiculous, inappropriate mural on its garage door.'

'That's Mary Pitalski's. You know, the theatre designer.'

Poppy felt a twitch of irritable jealousy on Toby's behalf. Deborah had nothing in common with Nick or Sophie, and Mrs Capstone's brush-off on the telephone, though polite, had been unmistakable.

He seemed to have read her thought.

'Deborah has been going to the Holland Park play group,' he said.

'Oh, well, they'll have met there. I know Laura was planning to go.'

'Do you want me to intervene on your grandson's behalf? I wouldn't normally do so.'

'Oh, no. I'll try again when this has died down.'

He nodded, apparently relieved, and changed the subject.

'I've cheated you of your Polish conversation.'

'Let's leave it till next time. I'm not up to conversation yet. I can rattle away in German, though. That's really coming back to me.'

'You would outpace me then. I no more than get along in German.'

'How many languages do you speak?'

'Speak well? English, Romanian, Polish, Italian. Tolerably, French and Russian, and maybe German. I smatter a few others—Hungarian, Greek . . .'

'What's Romanian like?'

'Latin-based. You wouldn't find it difficult. You seem to have chosen a good time to learn Polish.'

'Haven't I? It's getting even more exciting what's happening there.'

'In so far as anything extremely dangerous is likely to be exciting.'

'I didn't mean like that. I meant thrilling, wonderful. All those East Germans flooding across the borders. And the Czechs demonstrating like that. And even the Bulgarians, I saw. It's like ice-floes breaking in the spring.'

'Or like the groan of an avalanche about to loose itself from a frozen mountain.'

'You don't think it's going to be all right?'

'Politically, I agree with you. The sense of human freedom, human responsibility. But economically I fear the worst. The economies of all those countries are in a far worse state than even the most pessimistic official figures allow for. They are like starving men, and we are offering them the banquet of the West. They will never be able to digest it. I don't know how this will affect your prospects—or have you already found yourself employment?'

'Oh, I'm not looking yet. At my age I've got to have something other people can't offer.'

'How old are you?'

'Fifty. I was born on the day war broke out.'

'And then?'

'You want my life history?'

'Why not? This looks like a long wait.'

'It's not very interesting. My father was a spice importer—it was a family firm. I had two elder brothers. Twins.'

'Still alive?'

'Yes, of course. They're several years older than me, so I never knew them well. One of them teaches in a Jesuit seminary in Wisconsin and the other one manufactures petrol pumps in Middlesbrough. He's got five daughters—I know their names but I doubt I'd recognise them if I met them.'

'What happened to the spice business?'

'My father was killed on the retreat to Dunkirk, and the firm went bust in the war. My mother's still alive. She's an extraordinary woman. We'd been quite well off till the war, living in Wimbledon with four or five servants in the house, and she'd been just an idle, rather sickly beauty, doting on my father, letting him do everything. His sister told me that, so it may be a bit partisan. I don't think she wanted to have me, but—this is just something she once said—he knew the war was coming and he had a premonition he was going to be killed, so he wanted to leave as much as he could behind. That was me. Anyway, he'd set up trusts for my brothers' education, but I was a girl and the war was starting.

'Because of the bombing my mother took me away to live on a farm in Shropshire, and by sheer willpower she stopped being sickly and became tough. She still farms, on the same farm—we were just lodgers at first, but she used the last of the family money to buy it. She's over eighty. If you were interested in pigs . . .'

'I am.'

'Then you'll know the name. The McEwen herd.'

'My interest doesn't extend to British pigs.'

'Oh, well. My mother knows more about Gloucester Old Spots than anyone else in the world. She is the authority. She is totally dedicated. She only consented to come to my wedding if I arranged for it to take place during the Smithfield Show, in a lull in the pig-judging. You should have seen her hat.'

'How did you meet your husband?'

'Oh, at a party, the way one used to. I'd been to the local grammar school. I was quite a clever girl and they wanted me to go on to university but my mother was determined I had to start earning my living. I didn't mind. All I wanted to do was get away from the farm, and she wanted that too. She's incredibly superstitious. She mates her pigs according to their horoscopes and she persuaded herself my stars were having a bad influence on them. Really, of course, she wanted me out of her life—I should never have been there in the first place. She gave me an allowance so that I could come to London and learn to type and so on, though I was terrible at it and didn't take it at all seriously, but I loved scraping by on my pittance. I lived at one of those *Girls of Slender Means* places and I met Derek at a party given by a brother of one of the other girls. He'd come with a spare ticket for a concert hoping to pick someone up, and it was me. I adored the concert. That's when I discovered I could have been musical. Anyway, one thing led to another. The only men who'd shown any interest in me before were farmers' sons, and I couldn't reciprocate. I'm sorry to hear you're interested in pigs.'

'It is a blemish on my character. How does your husband earn his living?'

'It's a very technical sort of ship-broking, to do with difficult cargoes. I expect you know every country's got different rules. I used to try and get him to explain, but I could only understand the really simple things. Like, for instance, did you know there's a Central American country—I can't remember which one—which has rules about the import of step-ladders? The president's brother died when he fell off an imported step-ladder, so now they won't let them in if the rungs are the wrong distance apart. But there's no control over single ladders, so the trick is to import short single ladders and assemble them into step-ladders when you get there. Derek's firm specialises in knowing that sort of thing. He finds it unspeakably boring but he's very good at it.'

'Then he is only pretending to find it boring. Go on.'

'Oh. There isn't much else. We had two children, a girl and a boy. Anna trained as a nurse and married a doctor from New Zealand, who took her back there. She's got two children. There's a vague sort of agreement I'll go and visit them next year, so I'm saving for the air fare. My son, Hugo, works for a firm of law publishers, and I look after his son, Toby. That's about it.'

'When did you divorce?'

'Three years ago. I don't talk about it. It's water under the bridge.'

'But you think about it still?'

'I try not to. Look . . .'

He was looking already, directly into her eyes. His face had its mask look, withdrawn, judgmental. The dark eyes told her nothing. But she was aware that if she withheld there would be no more invitations to outlandish concerts, no more of his alarming company. She had been looking forward to this evening for days. She had laid in the calculated makings of an apparently improvised supper. That he should seem to want to see her made her feel and think better of herself than she had for years.

'All right,' she said. 'I think about it all the time. Do you want the bedroom details?'

'No.'

'I tell people he found himself another woman. She's quite different from me, not just because she's younger, I mean. She looks slinky-sophisticated, but I doubt if she's got much in the way of brains. I can't stand her. But that isn't really it—Derek and I had been coming apart for years. In the end it was only music kept our marriage going at all.'

'You've left out what you did between the time when your children started going to school and the break-up of your marriage.'

'Nothing.'

'Really?'

'Well, almost. Silly little bits of good works—the Oxfam shop, the local conservation committee. We had a cottage near Banbury—I made quite a good little garden there. I would have joined a choir if my voice had been good enough. I started to learn the flute . . .'

'And stopped?'

'I lost heart. Look, it's difficult for me to be fair to Derek. If you could understand us both from outside you might get a quite different picture, but from my side I slowly began to realise that he couldn't bear the idea of me being interested in anything except through him. Even music. He felt he had given me that, but by learning an instrument I was making myself independent of him. I'd joined a quartet, very amateur but we were having fun in our simple way until he started arranging theatre nights and things on the only evenings the others could do, holidays at times when they were all in town . . .'

'You didn't object?'

'Not enough. Not in time. For instance it would be a play I really wanted to see, and there'd be a reason why it had to be that evening. He's a clever man, very amusing to talk to and be with provided he's in control. It was the same in a different way with the cottage . . . Yes, of course I should have understood what was happening years ago, fought harder to be myself . . . I'm not really a fighter, I'm afraid.'

'You had stopped living together before your divorce?'

'He moved in with Veronica. I took in lodgers for a bit in our house, and then we sold it—very well, actually. I was determined to get my share but at the same time not to give him a chance to say I owed him anything, so I got him to agree to almost all of it going straight to the children. We made a settlement on Hugo's marriage which saved a lot of tax. Then I found my flat and got a job, the first real job of my life, with a company organising coach-tours of historic buildings. I enjoyed that, you know, getting all the details right, coping with dotty little crises without panicking, smoothing people down, all that. Unfortunately the boss had rather grand ideas. He longed to have his own airline to fly the customers in. He never got that far, but he set up a New York office and started trying to cover the whole of Europe, which we didn't know how to do, and he'd borrowed a lot of money just before the interest rates went up, and soon he was running up a down escalator and of course he went bust. That was a bit over a year ago. I was going through a bad patch for personal reasons—a love affair that wasn't working, if you must know—and I didn't feel like looking for a new job. I'd got really depressed, applying and applying and applying, before I landed the other one, and that was only the fluke of actually being in the office for my interview when they needed someone to answer a German telephone call. So when Toby's nanny left I said I'd do that for a bit. Janet pays me the proper wages. But it isn't good for me. I can feel myself shrinking. I simply have to find myself a real job or I'll become like my mother might have been if she'd never got interested in pigs. Now it's your turn. You can tell me why you are interested in pigs.'

'I made my first money in pigs.'

'Begin at the beginning. Where were you born?'

He had not apparently expected this. There was a jerk of the head and a shrug, peasant-like, self-exculpatory. She watched him, keeping her face stiff, returning his original look, saying with her eyes that she too wasn't interested in continuing to meet him unless he gave her a glimpse, if not behind the mask, at least of the processes that had moulded it. The waitress came and took their order. He did not, as Derek would have, use the interruption to escape the challenge, but instead resumed the eye contact. The silence lasted at least as long as any of those between the snatches of music at the concert, but full of tensions which the composer had failed to achieve.

'I am two or three years younger than you,' he said. 'I am a Pole by birth, but I was born in Romania, almost certainly in 1942. The Nazis had shipped a group of workers down to Romania for their own obscure, bureaucratic reasons, and my mother, who was already pregnant, had disguised herself as a man in order to remain with her brother. I know nothing about my father. When my mother's sex was discovered she was allowed to have her baby but I was then taken away and put into a Romanian orphanage. Being Germans, they provided me with documentation. That is how, in the attempts at repatriation after the war, I was sent back to Poland, to another orphanage, on the theory that efforts would then be made to trace relatives who might take care of me. Of course nothing was done.

'The orphanage was a terrible place, heartless and incompetent. It was ruled by the oldest children, brutally. So I learnt to fight. The orphanage in Romania, though the food was scant and the blankets thin, had been run by kindly monks. I yearned for it. When I was about twelve I was big and strong enough for the boys who ruled in the Polish orphanage to decide they had to break my will. I was not prepared to have my will broken, and their other option would have been to kill me, so I escaped and started to make my way back to what I regarded as my native Romania.'

'At twelve? Did you have any money? Any help?'

'No money. No papers. No help. I stole. I cheated and lied. I had reached Slovakia when a man attempted to rape me. I stabbed him with his own knife, and was arrested. I answered all questions in Romanian and gave the name of a boy I had known at the first orphanage—if I'd given my own obviously Polish name they'd have sent me back to Poland. The man I had stabbed had a record of attacks on children. It was obvious I had been acting in self-defence. I was simply a trivial problem to the Slovak authorities, which they solved in the obvious way by transferring me to Romania.'

'Hurrah. Some things work out all right.'

'Not yet. I didn't even know the address of my orphanage. I had imagined it could be traced through the church authorities, but all such enquiries now had to be made through the communist apparatus, and they were not interested. At twelve, I was old enough to work. I was given identity papers in my new name and sent to a collective. A pig farm. We have this in common—like you I knew in the depths of my being that my future was not in a pig farm. As soon as I could I left, illegally of course, and made my way to Bucharest. I had by now given up hope of returning to my orphanage. That was the past.

'In Bucharest I learnt to live in the cracks of the system. All systems have these places, and the less flexible the system the more cracks. Eventually such systems are bound to collapse. This is what we are seeing happen now, in these very days, in Eastern Europe. They are like the crust of the earth, these countries, with the various bureaucratic elements in them floating like huge, inflexible plates on the mass of the people below. They grind against each other, causing tensions and crumplings, which must eventually build to a point where the whole system erupts and the people burst through. This is what is happening now. But until that point of eruption, inevitable but unpredictable, there are these interstices between the plates in which it is possible to survive. The system positively depends on them, because they provide the lubrication which allows any movement to take place at all.'

'They're saying Romania's the one place where there isn't going to be a revolution. What's-his-name has got it all buttoned up.'

'Ceausescu. They are wrong. It will erupt, with worse violence than we have seen elsewhere, very soon. There will most likely be a full-scale civil war. Take it from me. I have very good information.'

'Sorry. I didn't mean to interrupt. Please go on. You were lubricating the system. With pigs, somehow? You said that's how you made your first money.'

'Yes. At the collective I had of course heard all the grumblings about the system, and seen how everyone who had any authority used it as far as they could to feather their own nests. Because Romania had an extremely inflexible system it positively demanded corruption at every level to make it work at all. So the managers would falsify the numbers of pigs and have some slaughtered on the collective instead of being sent to the state abattoir. They would sell some of the meat on the black market, keep some for themselves, and use the rest to bribe the inspectors who came to see that they were not doing any such thing. The state abattoir was so inefficiently run that many animals died before slaughter, often of starvation waiting to go through the sheds, or else meat would wait for transport until it was unfit to eat because the refrigeration system had broken down or the generator fuel had been sold on the black market. It was extremely easy to write off imaginary carcasses. But all this cheating was unsystematic, small beer. Those who tried to operate on a larger scale were too stupid and greedy not to get caught, and shot. By the time I was sixteen I had set up an organisation, at first with a single collective and a single abattoir but later with a whole network, under which they co-operated to their mutual benefit. I ran the distribution, which was much the most difficult part. I found that I understood what was necessary without having to be shown or taught. I knew, as if by instinct, that I had to have a lot of small outlets and also had to maintain a balance of supply and demand so that my customers were satisfied, but at the same time I kept the price of pork as high as the market would stand.'

'It sounds absolutely hair-raising. What would have happened if you'd been caught?'

'If I'd been officially caught, and so unable to bribe my way free, I would have been shot. I was a criminal, an enemy of the state. I say this with no shame—in fact I say it with pride. You see, I and my friends and others like us were the only honest operators in the country. The official system and the people in it were totally dishonest, corrupt beyond belief. Truth was alien to their beings. But we kept our word. We had to. Everything depended on that. At the very simplest level my customers knew that they were getting clean, fresh meat from me, whereas if they bought from the state there was every chance that it would be diseased, rotten and underweight. You must also understand that in a system like that everybody accepts the necessity of lubrication. Everybody is on your side. The chief danger was in attracting the awareness of the secret police, the Securitate. They knew, of course, that a black market existed, and were happy provided they got their rake-off. What I had to keep from them for as long as possible was that a single organisation was now controlling the illicit pork trade. As soon as they learnt that they would move in and take the machinery over, for their own profit. I operated under fifteen different names. I kept myself as far as I could in the background. I became a Securitate informer and was then able to buy information about the Securitate itself . . .'

'Did you inform against anyone?'

'About one in five Romanians is an informer. I informed against other informers, against customers who tried to cheat me, and people like that. One has at that age and in such a milieu a very hazy concept of moral priorities. Yes, certainly I did things which I would now much rather not have done. Be that as may be, I judged my time and got out, carrying a suitcase full of dollars. I was about nineteen.'

He shook his head, rueful, nostalgic, almost like an Old Boy looking back on the irrecoverable months of sixth-form fame. Poppy thought he would now stop. He'd told her more than enough to repay her own mild self-revelations, but he was in a mood to remember.

'I didn't go far—only as far as the student quarter,' he said. 'I knew I intended to come West in the end, but I wasn't ready and nor were the times, so I decided to learn English. I had fresh, good papers, and bought myself a job as cleaner at the university, where I paid a professor for lessons. She was half-French and had married an Englishman before the war. She and her husband had been with the partisans. They were both communists, but the Russians immediately deported him and from then on denied his existence. Now the climate in Russia has changed and I am having fresh enquiries made.'

'He can't still be alive.'

'Highly unlikely, but I wish to know. As I told you, I had barely any contact with my mother and not even knowledge of my father, so at the age of nineteen I chose my own parents. Natalie I came to know well. She played me music, lent me books, talked about the world, and also things which may exist beyond the world. She had no faith in any religion, but you felt when you were with her that there were concerns of immense importance, eternal matters to which we give names such as truth and beauty and justice, without which we would indeed have been what the regime in that country was organised to make us, automata, ants in a nest, will-less and blind to any objective beyond the survival of the nest. She inhabited her own cavities in the system, different in kind from mine, crystal caves. But we recognised each other all the same as allies.'

'She sounds absolutely marvellous.'

'You remind me a little of her.'

'Oh. I'm afraid I'm not like that.'

'No? Then perhaps it is only that she lived in a basement with a giant cat.'

Poppy laughed and he watched her.

'And her laughter, like yours, said yes to the world,' he said.

'Does it? I suppose it does, in spite of everything. I'm afraid I don't pay as much attention to the world as I ought to—I seem to have shrunk into myself, somehow.'

'You don't need a state apparatus to achieve repression. Perhaps you have made your husband into a Stalin, and you are now in your Brezhnev era.'

'Oh, I hope not! Is Natalie still alive?'

'She died eighteen months ago, still in her basement. She'd had a stroke four years earlier which left her speechless, though when I visited her I was able to persuade myself that she knew who I was. And I was able to see that she was cared for to the end.'

'You didn't bring her back to England?'

'The authorities wouldn't permit it. They had their reasons. Even in a country like Romania there are some things money can't buy. And besides, she would have refused to come while she still had the understanding to choose. She was a Marxist, of the sort they are now trying to tell us were the norm before Stalin. She wasn't an active dissident. Her nature was to be, rather than to do. Her faith was in the people. One day, she used to say, they will find their voice, and then nothing will stop them. She believed that the Revolution had not been perverted, but that it had never come. She would often when things were bad quote Gramsci—pessimism of the intellect, optimism of the will. And the West would have had no attraction for her at all. Here's our food, at last.'

Certainly he knew how to operate systems. The restaurant was part of a chain, with identical decor, identical menus, all prescribed by HQ. Tepid milk didn't figure in HQ's concept of the pizza paradise; there was no price for it, no way of recording it at the till, but he had asked for it and it came. He ate, as before, in silence.

While she was sipping her coffee she said, 'What happened about your pig system, after you left?'

'What you would expect. The Securitate moved in and took it over. They charged higher prices for worse meat and at the same time flooded the market in their greed. The market collapsed, so they arrested a few people at random and had them shot for corruption, and the system reverted to what it had been before I came, but worse. That has been the history of Romania over forty years. It is difficult to convey the feel of such a society, the effect of more than a generation of inefficiency, corruption and brutal but aimless totalitarianism.'

'But you still have dealings with them? You got Natalie looked after.'

'I am useful to them. Without channels to the West, official and unofficial, President Ceausescu's cousins would not be able to buy their Gucci shoes.'

'Do they trust you?'

'Of course not. Shall we go?'

They came out into a warmish drizzle. He took a collapsible umbrella from his briefcase, snapped it open and held it over her. She put her arm in his while she peered this way and that, trying to get her bearings so that she could walk to the Tube station. The neon of the shops and the lights of passing cars glistened off the wet tarmac, sheeny-slick with road oil after the long drought. She felt quite lost. London was her warren, her context, but she couldn't for the moment locate this road into it. It must run north from the City, but was she on the east side, or the west? She could have been anywhere, in any city in the world, isolated under the shelter of his brolly.

'I've changed my mind,' he said. 'I'd like to come home with you.'

'I thought . . .'

'My appointment's not until after midnight.'

He was looking at her, his eyes mere gleams in the dimness. Unlike his earlier challenge, this time his voice seemed to be telling her she could say no and still not alter their friendship. This wasn't anything she'd expected, or hoped for, or imagined she'd wanted, but her feelings about it, about him, about herself, seemed unfocused, the blur of the world without her spectacles. In those large general terms, where anything more than a couple of feet away becomes mere bulk and hue and only what is almost on your nose has shape, she knew what she wanted, now.

'All right,' she said.

His wrist-watch snickered its alarm. He was asleep, she was not. He didn't stir to the sound, so she stroked his shoulder-blade to wake him. He had a very solid-seeming body, meaty muscles, big bones.

'Your alarm's gone,' she said.

'I heard it. Put some milk on, please.'

She rose and groped her way to the kitchen. From force of habit, as if it had been her normal rising time of half-past-seven, she turned the radio on. It was The Trojans, final act, live from Covent Garden, she guessed. She wondered if Derek was there. The Dido had a voice, all right, but she didn't recognise who it was. He liked them good and plump.

Mr Capstone, as she still thought of him, came in buttoning a shirt-cuff.

'That's where my man is,' he said.

'He was lucky to get tickets.'

'No trouble. He's on a trade delegation.'

'I wonder if he has any idea where you are.'

He took the question seriously.

'Probably not. But if I call you at any time, will you be careful what you say?'

'Heavens. Yes, of course, if it's like that.'

He drank his milk in silence. She wondered whether he was going to say anything. He had his mask firmly in place. She had no idea of his feelings beyond a sense that the past two hours had been for him time out, a space, an island of escape from the treacherous pressures against which he'd erected his defences. Raining though it was, he had paid off the taxi several streets away and made her walk home ahead. It was like that, and for the moment she fulfilled a need, someone who was no threat to him at all, chance-met, with a laugh like Natalie's. Perhaps in his mind he had been making love as much to Natalie as to her. It didn't matter, in fact it meant she need have no bad conscience at all about his being a married man with a child. This was part of a different life.

Elias came in from one of his night prowls neatly flicking his tail clear of the closing cat-flap. His fur was seed-pearled with the drizzle. She picked him up and held him against her, letting his purr throb through her body. Mr Capstone looked at the pair of them and smiled. She smiled back.

'What colour was Natalie's cat?' she said.

'Ginger. My next free evening is Thursday.'

'Oh. I've got to go to Janet's adoption meeting—he needs every vote she can get. It should be over by half-past nine.'

'May I come round at ten?'

'That would be nice. Would you like something to eat?'

'A snack. I must go.'

'Is your phone really tapped?'

'Probably. I have to assume so.'

'And are they watching you?'

'Some of the time.'

'Your chauffeur, Constantin, is he a Romanian?'

'Why do you ask?'

'He feels like a policeman, somehow.'

'Very likely. Don't worry. It'll happen any time now. In a few more weeks all that will be over.'

Next morning, while Poppy was in the bath, the telephone rang. She reached the instrument, dripping. A voice, muffled, but probably female she later decided, said, 'What's it feel like to know your lover's a murderer?'

'What did you say?'

'What's it feel like to know your lover's a murderer?'

'Who is that?'

But the caller had rung off.

2

Thursday was a dry night, with a chilly, gusty wind which made standing around waiting for the doors to open thoroughly unpleasant. Poppy told herself that it was necessary for the sake of democracy, but the edge was taken off her sense of virtue because earlier she'd been watching the news and seen shots of a demonstration in East Germany, immense, unanimous, disciplined, excited masses of people cramming a square and the surrounding thoroughfares, a primal force like the pressure of oceans, such as John Capstone had talked about in the pizza restaurant. She looked round at the forty or fifty citizens waiting with her on the pavement and tried to imagine them being stirred to a similar joint passion. None of them looked like a breaker of nations.

None of them looked as if they had a lover to go home to either, but nor, no doubt, did she.

'Membership cards,' a voice bawled. 'Please have membership cards ready.'

The doors of the church hall had opened. The crowd, larger now, jostled towards the lit rectangle. 'It only seats a hundred and twenty,'

Janet had said. 'Don't be late.' The stewards at the door were checking every card, slowing the in-flow. Pressures behind built up, quite unnecessarily as there was still plenty of time, but groups of people as if for the fun of it were forming wedges and trying to barge their way in towards the door between others like Poppy who had been waiting longer. She found herself shoved sideways into the back of a woman with a sleepy child on her shoulder, almost knocking her over. The child, startled, looked up and Poppy at once recognised the large-eyed, dark face under the peaked blue hood.

'Hello, Nelson,' she said. 'It's all right. It's only me.'

Nell twisted her head with a brief 'Hi' as he snuggled back into her shoulder, then turned away again. Poppy managed to follow her closely through the door because an altercation between some would-be voters and the steward on the other side had slowed the stream to single file.

'Shall we sit together?' she said. 'Or do you want to be with your friends?'

'That's all right,' said Nell, not very welcomingly. Poppy hadn't seen her in the week and a half since the meeting at Linen Walk, and had been worrying at times about her. With the play centre still out of action the Nafia had fragmented, small groups meeting in different houses and either arranging then and there for next time or using the telephone. Nell hadn't come, and had left no number, but she could easily have made contact if she'd wanted.

They found seats near the end of a row about half-way down the hall. Nell didn't sit at once; she stood looking round as if for people she knew, but gave no smiles or waves of recognition.

'Are you all right?' said Poppy when at last she settled. 'I see they manage to close the commune down last week. You hadn't gone back, though, had you? I hope you've found somewhere nice to live.'

'We're fine,' said Nell, not answering the rest of the question. 'How's Elias?'

'Large and lazy and moulting everywhere. You must bring Nelson to see him.'

'He'd like that. Have you been a member long?'

She was too honest at heart, Poppy thought, to make the question ring natural.

'About fifteen months,' she said. 'I used to vote Liberal, but they made such asses of themselves after the last election that I lost patience.'

'Most people wouldn't bother to join.'

'I didn't want to have to vote for someone I hadn't helped choose.'

Poppy had had that admirable sentiment ready, in case she was asked, and though it was partly true she disliked herself for bringing it out for Nell. Nell looked almost pityingly at her and adjusted Nelson down on to her lap. He had fallen asleep now, in that impervious stupor so expressive of the needs and vulnerabilities of childhood. This time Poppy spoke without thought.

'I love to see you with him,' she said.

Nell glanced at her again, more sharply.

'Don't,' she muttered. 'It's different.'

'Yes, I know.'

They fell silent, awkward with the constraint of thought between them, and the conspiracy of feeling. Was it possible, Poppy wondered, that any creed, any bunch of fellow-believers, could be so austere in their fanaticism that they should want to take even this away if they understood it was there? Wasn't it the touchstone of any programme that this should be among its chief aims, in some form, for everyone, the possibility of personal love? She liked to think well of people, to believe that most of those she disagreed with had good, if mistaken, motives. Indeed, knowing the half-heartedness of most of her own impulses, she tended to be cynical about the moral honesty of middle-of-the-roaders like herself, and to envy the braying certainties of those on the wings.

Almost all the seats were full now but people were still crowding in. The candidates and officials took their places behind a trestle table on a platform at the end of the room, Janet at the extreme left of the row. In the past few weeks Poppy had been dutifully reading the *Ethelden Echo* so that she could keep up to date with the party infighting, so she recognised some of the faces. Trevor Evans, the left-wing candidate, a large shambling man with a long nose and neatly trimmed beard, sat one away from Janet, so between them must be Bob Stavoli, a pinkly bouncy middle-aged man in a blue suit.

Of the three it was Janet who caught and held the eye. She wasn't wearing her usual outfit of polo-neck and jeans, but a dark grey trouser suit, a white blouse with a floppy red bow at the neck and, of all things, a pair of dangling gold earrings. The Labour Party had held a seminar for women would-be candidates, and apparently this was the recommended style for getting men to take you seriously. Janet and Poppy had worked themselves into near hysterics trying out variations in front of the mirror at home, while Toby had stumped around like a disgruntled putto in *The Robing of Minerva*, trying to persuade his mother to put on recognisable clothes again. Now, of course, she wore the result with total confidence. Even the lipstick and eye-shadow looked right.

Next to Evans was a stranger, a youngish-looking Asian, and then the chairman, Alasdair Meakin, stooped, anxious, with a kneaded, deep-lined face but beautiful white hair combed into sculpted waves and jelled into place. Then, presumably, the rest of the executive committee, most recognisably a fat disorganised-looking woman in a caftan. Lucy something, according to the *Echo* the mouthpiece of Militant on the committee.

'Trish says it's going to be all right,' Janet had said. 'The local party's been pretty thoroughly Kinnockised, apart from Trevor and Lucy, and Walworth Road's determined to have someone who can stand up to Capstone. Bob's on the short list to keep the gays happy—he'll get a few of the ballot votes but nothing from the unions. I'll be second choice on most of those. Trish thinks she's got most of the union votes sewn up for me, so if I do well enough tonight I might just about get in on the first count. It's lucky Trevor's such a shit, such an obvious rat.'

'Why does anyone vote for him at all?'

'Don't be naïve, Poppy.'

'Will there be any public rows? I shan't enjoy that.'

'Nothing serious. They've all been in the committee. But I'd better warn you there's bound to be a tedious ritual at the beginning when the left try to hold things up by challenging people's right to vote. The idea is that the good old sober citizens who've come along out of a sense of duty will get bored and bewildered and disgusted enough to go home, leaving the hard core to vote Trevor in. It used to work, sometimes, but we're ready for it now. Your job is to stick it out. Just remember, you might be the one who makes my 51 per cent.'

'For your sake, darling.'

And sure enough, no sooner had Mr Meakin banged his gavel enough to produce a shuffling kind of silence than a young woman was on her feet near the front of the hall. Poppy felt Nell stir beside her.

'Point of order,' called the woman.

'No points of order while the chair is speaking,' said Mr Meakin in a calmly weary voice, signalling his confidence in his procedural rectitude. 'Will you please stay in your places while the stewards check numbers present against those registered as having come in with valid credentials. The register will be available for scrutiny at the back of the hall after the counting is complete. I will then accept points of order. All challenges of rights to vote will be taken at that point and none thereafter. Now the purpose of this meeting . . .'

He explained the procedure in the driest possible tones, and the counting followed, very thorough, two stewards checking each row separately and confirming their count with each other. Poppy gazed around. The room was a parish hall, apparently used at times for some kind of school activity. Children's paintings on the theme of St George and the dragon had been Blu-tacked to the walls. Close enough for her to study in detail was one of a charmingly pudgy princess lashed to a palm-tree and weeping immense tears on to her ballooning breasts while a tiny knight and dragon battled it out in the distance. It's all a matter of perspective, she thought. Standpoint. John Capstone—but for this meeting she would have been with him now, watching him finish his tepid milk, perhaps, and feeling pleased that she'd managed to supply him with that odd little satisfaction. His presence, the prospect of soon undressing and lying naked beside him in her candle-lit bedroom and feeling his hard, deliberate hands moving over her body, would then have filled her whole mindscape. As it was, he had become a figure in the middle distance, moving away and dwindling as the activities in the hall more and more filled her foreground. All the questions about him—whether she loved, or liked, or trusted him; what his feelings might be for her, and for his wife and daughter; what shape the hidden parts of his life might take, so sinisterly signalled by his prevarications over whether he had been followed, and then by the shock of that first anonymous telephone call. (There'd been two more, but at least she'd been partly ready for them. The first one, though, how had they known he was there? And if they had been right about that, did the rest of the message represent a truth? And should she tell him? Before, or after?). All these were for the moment curiosities, vaguely seen at the edges of her perception. As she walked home to wait for him they would begin to loom again. Meanwhile the foreground was filled with this event, so deliberately boring that it acquired a sort of fascination.

The counting ended and the gavel banged again. This time the silence was almost attentive. A moment of mini-crisis had come. Would the numbers tally?

'We have a discrepancy of one,' said Mr Meakin.

A sigh of failed hope. An hour of tedium while the snark was hunted.

'However,' said Mr Meakin with no change of voice, 'Charlie Grubier who was in charge of the stewards at the entrance informs me that one person did enter without proving a valid twelve-month membership. There was a disturbance at the door, apparently intentional, during which a man pushed past without showing his card. Charlie Grubier followed him into the hall and observed where he sat. It was you, sir, there. Yes, you. Will you please stand?'

Heads craned. Poppy turned with the others to see the man, thirtyish, cockily defiant. She heard a faint groan of bored recognition.

'Sure, that was me,' he said. 'And sure, nobody bothered to check my card. I'm a member all right, and you know I am, but if I got in without proving it it shows there's others as aren't members could do the same. You're going to have to check everyone against that list again, Alasdair mate, no matter what.'

Mr Meakin gestured towards the young Asian on his left.

'This is Mr Simeon Kumar,' he said. 'He is ARO—Assistant

Regional Organiser—and is here to supervise the ballot and see that party procedure is correctly followed. Mr Kumar?'

Mr Kumar put his fingertips judicially together and spoke in so soft a voice that people at the back shouted 'Can't hear!'

He tried again.

'I observed the procedures at the entrance. I am satisfied that the discrepancy of one is accounted for by the gentleman who has just spoken, and that there are no other discrepancies.'

'All right,' said Mr Meakin. 'So will you please show your credentials to the stewards. I will accept no further points based on discrepancy of numbers. We will now take other points of order, including challenges to rights to vote. Copies of the register of members, with names of those attending this evening marked, are available at the back of the hall for inspection. I will allow half an hour for points of order, including challenges, and accept no more after that. I will accept only particular challenges of named individuals.'

More points of order from various parts of the hall, dull and confusing statements repetitively challenging the chair's right to make the ruling, all ruled out of order and confirmed with a nod from Mr Kumar. Poppy did her best not to become angry, but her mind's eye was filled with the scenes she'd been watching on television, the will of a people expressed directly on the streets, honourable and glorious, despite the risk of getting truncheoned or shot or flattened by a tank. These people, these protesters, were on the other side, the side of the tanks and the truncheons, or in their case the lies and the manipulations. They had all the insolence of autocracy, in their own petty way, in the obvious wasting of time, in the not caring whether anyone believed what they were saying because they didn't either, until the half-hour was almost gone and then they'd start to produce whatever genuine objections they might have, trying to force the chair either to weaken its authority by extending the deadline or risk the validity of the vote by accepting challengeable memberships.

It was twenty minutes before an actual name was mentioned, something to do with an unpaid subscription, an actually genuine case apparently, as after a brief consultation with Mr Kumar the chair ruled that the offender, a baffled-looking old man, could remain at the meeting but must not vote. Then . . .

'What about Jones's ma-in-law?' called a woman's voice.

'Is that a challenge?' asked the chair.

'Jones put her ma-in-law on. She pays her to mind the baby. Told her to come and vote. Or else.'

'For a challenge I must have a name.'

Poppy was on her feet, barely able to control her voice for fury.

'My name is Poppy Tasker. It is true that I am Ms Jones's mother-in-law and look after her son. I joined the party fifteen months ago out of my own free will and paid the subscription myself. I renewed it this August. I showed my card at the door.'

Poppy sat down. It wasn't just the insult, it was the hidden irrational threat that somehow Toby was going to be dragged into this filthy rigmarole of public exposure. Nell was looking at her.

'Did you tell them?' Poppy muttered.

'You never told me,' said Nell, equally accusingly.

'I didn't tell anyone. I didn't want Mrs Capstone finding out from Peony.'

Nell thought about it and nodded. In the different, decent world of the play centre it was an acceptable reason.

'She's your daughter-in-law? Jones?'

'That's right. It doesn't . . .'

'Shh!' from behind, and a warning tap on the shoulder. Someone was making another tedious and jargon-ridden general objection.

Poppy's anger subsided, leaving her shaky and sad. She looked at Nell, who was sitting tense in her chair, unapproachable. How had they known, if Nell hadn't told them? And Nell hadn't known about Janet. Had she been lying? Why should she? And her reaction to Poppy's explanation—if she'd been lying, surely . . . How had they known?

A bang from the gavel.

'Out of order,' said Mr Meakin. 'I will take one more point. Yes?'

'You've got a Simon Venable of 40 Sabina Road down as come in tonight. Can't be him. He's dead.'

The man's voice was confident, with street-cred vowels, but precise. Unlike earlier challenges it carried the sense that here was something real, something that was expected to have a concrete effect, more than irritation and time-wasting. For the first time Mr Meakin seemed off balance.

'Er . . . the secretary will check the list,' he said, and bent to confer with Mr Kumar, and then to look at a page which one of the officials passed to him, with a finger pointing at an entry.

'Is Mr Venable in the room?' he asked. 'Mr Simon Venable of 40 Sabina Road?'

'No S,' said the challenger. 'Just Venable.'

Poppy could see him now. He was fortyish, balding, with a clipped fringe of grey beard and outdoor complexion. Either he was a concerned and earnest citizen or he knew how to seem one.

Silence. Poppy made a mental picture of Sabina Road. She knew the name because that was where the squat had been which the Council had at last managed to close, but it was beyond her usual lonely-stroll range, south-west of the park in Ormiston, and she couldn't place it exactly. One of those streets of large, late-nineteenth-century houses, she thought, elaborately stuccoed, looking as if they'd never, even when new, attracted the frock-coated bankers and surgeons for whom they'd been built, and so from the first had tended to look a little seedy. Then their paint began to peel and stucco to crumble, and gardens to fill with split mattresses and upturned wheel-less prams among the willow-herb and brambles.

'I tell you he can't be here,' said the challenger. 'He's dead. You've all read about him. It was him they found in the kiddies' place in the park last week.'

Poppy felt her mouth fall open. Instantly, without thought, she turned to Nell. Unlike almost everyone else in the hall, Nell hadn't turned to look at the challenger and was still facing the platform, apparently barely interested until this moment in what was being said. But now the neat, determined face had gone white, the mouth was an O, the eyes wide with shock. The tremor must have communicated itself to Nelson, who woke as if from a nightmare, screwed up his eyes and wailed. At once Nell had him up on her shoulder and was rocking to and fro, murmuring comforts for both of them. She had known something was going to happen, Poppy realised, but not this, not this.

Nelson's dwindling wail was drowned in the general gasp and uproar. Mr Meakin was banging his gavel and shouting for order. Two women, evidently reporters, one with a notebook and one with a microphone, were struggling towards the challenger from opposite ends of the row where he sat. The others in the row were obstructing their passage, deliberately it seemed. Elsewhere in the hall people were on their feet, shouting comments and questions. Janet might have thought that her side had the meeting all sewn up, but now an unlikely seam was unravelling fast.

Nell had coaxed Nelson back to sleep, but was still rocking to and fro, staring at nothing, her face pale and hard.

'Are you all right?' whispered Poppy.

Nell nodded. She looked as if she might faint. The event was shocking, horrible, but even to Poppy, who had actually seen the body, it didn't seem quite of that order. If you'd known the man, though, if you'd recognised him that first time he'd come to the play centre . . . Poppy remembered how Nell had left that day, her anger as strong as the others' but different, her furious determined stride. She'd been going somewhere, to do something definite. She could do that because she knew who he was. They both lived in Sabina Road . . .

And Laura had known him too! That extraordinary outburst of grief as she and Poppy had been pushing across the sodden park, the day after his death. His death. Grief for him, someone known and loved . . . And if Laura had known him, she could have told him about Poppy and Janet, because Poppy had told her, and he could have passed it to these sinister manipulators . . .

She didn't want to think about it. She pushed the whole horrible business out of her mind and concentrated on Mr Meakin belting the table with his gavel and bellowing for order. At last he had some effect. The uproar dwindled. The reporters had been forced back to the edges of the hall, where they stood poised for another try. The challenger was still standing patiently in his place, unruffled. A tense, inquisitive silence settled on the hall.

'You have not been to the police with this information?' asked Mr Meakin.

'Some of us haven't been that lucky in our doings with the police,' said the man. 'I don't see it signifies for these proceedings. Just you've got someone here personating a dead man. If there's one, could be others.'

'May we have your name and address, please?'

'Mark Giraldi. You'll have Sabina Road as my address, but that's been shut down.'

The man sat and the reporters started to struggle towards him again. This time their attempts were even more actively resisted by those around him. The one with the notebook had it snatched away and thrown across the room. As the stewards closed in towards the disturbance they too were resisted. The scuffles escalated to fighting. Everyone in the hall, except Nell, seemed to be standing now and Poppy couldn't see what was happening. A rhythmic chant of 'Meakin out! Meakin out!' arose. Mr Meakin was shouting for order. At the end of her row, Poppy glimpsed several tough-looking men moving towards the back of the hall. Nell at last rose.

'I've got to go now,' she said.

'You're not going to stay and vote?'

'What's the point? It's all fixed.'

'Listen. I've got to talk to you. About the young man who died. Please.'

Nell looked at her and shook her head.

'I've got to go,' she said again.

'Hadn't you better wait till . . .'

'It's all right. They're going. See you soon.'

She pushed past with Nelson inert on her shoulder. Poppy realised that the uproar at the back of the hall had changed its nature, becoming organised into a chant of 'Out! Out! Out!', and was at the same time receding. Elsewhere people, not very many, were shoving their way along rows and making for the exit. The shouts, clatter and stampings dwindled into the street and died almost to silence when the doors were closed. An angry calm settled on the hall as chairs were put straight and places found for some of those who before had been standing, though there still weren't enough to go round, which showed how few in number the disrupters must have been. A woman and a man were attending to one of the reporters, who had a nosebleed. It was like the programmed gathering of healing corpuscles round a wound in the body, Poppy thought, the way all those remaining, even when they could do nothing much to help, at least willed the re-establishment of order. Mr Meakin waited for silence and then merely tapped the gavel down.

'You aren't going on, Alasdair, surely?' said the woman Poppy thought was called Lucy. Her voice was a disdainful twitter, like a Harrods customer complaining at a street-market stall.

'I see no reason not to,' said Mr Meakin.

'A substantial group of perfectly valid electors has been forcibly ejected by your stewards after making well-supported allegations of electoral fraud.'

Her tone managed to condescend in three different modes at once, implying that Mr Meakin lacked the manners, intelligence and moral sense to behave correctly. Something, at any rate, stung him out of his hard-won monotony of delivery.

'Lucy, that's a bloody libel!' he snapped.

'It's not even a slander, Alasdair, but if you expect me to co-operate any further in this travesty of democracy you are mistaken. Trevor?'

She rose and tittupped off the platform with prissy little steps, loose areas of flab wobbling at each movement. Trevor Evans, who had watched the whole disturbance with his fingertips pressed together in front of his mouth, gave a start. Poppy saw Janet glance sideways at him and smile. His thought processes must be transparent to everyone in the hall. The Lucy woman had clearly known what was going to happen, but he'd been taken by surprise. He coughed, half rose, sat again, and finally stood and cleared his throat.

'Brothers and sisters in our great movement,' he said. 'You all know me. You all know I'm not one to refuse a fight. No doubt there's some here would like to see Trevor Evans running off with his tail between his legs, so they can fix everything up nice and quiet, how they want it. All I can say is, they don't know Trevor Evans. Trevor Evans is going to tough this one out.'

There was a surprising number of cheers, not, as far as Poppy could tell, ironic. It made you almost despair of democracy, Poppy thought, that anybody could bring themselves to support such a creature, such blatant, smarmy, calculating self-interest. He had a wife and three daughters, according to the Echo, so somebody had gone to bed with him, kissed and been kissed, made love . . . even that was somehow more imaginable than bringing oneself to go into a polling booth and put a cross opposite his name.

Mr Meakin explained the procedure again, and the candidates drew lots for who should speak first. It was Trevor Evans. He was less dreadful than he might have been, though he thumped out clichés and kept referring to himself in the third person, like a footballer. He didn't mention the episode just finished. He used his big voice with practised timing and variation of tone, and got a lot of perhaps rather forced applause when he sat down.

Janet rose next, to a shout of 'Pink Thatcher!' from the back of the hall. Immediately her head went back and her eyes flashed with the joy of battle.

'The only thing I have in common with Thatcher is that I am determined to see my party running this country,' she cried. 'Unlike the self-destructive idiots whose antics we've just had to put up with, I believe we can and will win the election, and that I can and will win this constituency for Labour!'

She went into her prepared speech, making it sound just as impromptu, saying all the right things as if she meant them—though

Poppy, knowing her so well, didn't find her totally convincing when she spoke of Labour being the party that cared. She finished to applause, too, plenty of robust cheers as well as good old bourgeois claps and murmurs.

Bob Stavoli was drab-voiced and earnest. He said straight out that he was a homosexual, and that he trusted people to accept that it didn't matter any more than did Janet being a woman or Trevor a man. Otherwise he said much the same as Janet—the poll tax, Europe, schools, the National Health Service, Labour's great chance, need for unity and pragmatism, etc.—but making it all so grey and parochial that he might, Poppy thought, have been a woodlouse addressing a convention of woodlice and affiliated beetles and millipedes about the dilapidated state of the bark they lived under. He was clearly a nice man, though. It was a secret ballot and she was tempted to vote for him, telling herself he must be a conscientious worker and very good on committees, but really for the secret joy of voting against Janet. Pink Thatcher? Not bad, not bad at all. The intelligence, the arrogance, the drive and ruthlessness, the indefinable sense of values somewhere deeply, and perhaps badly wrong, the surface fire, the coldness at the heart . . .

Dutifully, however, she put a 1 against Janet's name and a 2 against Bob Stavoli's. While the ballots were being collected the hall became like any other gathering during a lull between excitements: chat, scraping of chairs, coughs, a queue for the inadequate loo. Poppy thought about the dead man. There was something about his face which reminded her of someone else; not a family likeness, more a sort of style, the vulnerability and need. At first the memory file wouldn't function, but then, as Mr Kumar gathered and checked the ballot papers and sealed them into an envelope, and Mr Meakin rose to bang his gavel yet again, the image leapt clear: little Nick with his sun-bleached hair patting sand into a bucket; Laura gazing at him; 'That's the pity of it, Mrs Tasker. That's just the pity of it.'

Yes, Laura. Poppy didn't hear a word of Mr Meakin's closing speech or notice how the meeting ended. She found herself standing near the doors, looking vaguely round. Janet was up at the other end, surrounded by an excited group. The votes wouldn't be counted till tomorrow, and the union block vote added by some arcane formula, and then the result would come shambling out in a typical Labour Party manner, but already the mood of congratulation around Janet was obvious. Poppy wanted no part of it. Janet could triumph through the constituency like Joan of Arc, calling on the peasants of Ethelden to rise up and drive out the alien forces of Capstonism and Thatcherism from their beloved motherborough, and they would follow her as if to a crusade, starry-eyed, while only Poppy stood apart, a crone by the wayside watching through rheumy eyes and mumbling unheard forebodings.

She walked slowly home, trying to sort herself out to be ready for John Capstone's visit. Contented physicality, combined with intellectual zip. Never had she felt less like either. She would have to tell him about the telephone calls. Not the moment he was through the door, but as soon as he was settled. She would demonstrate by touch and voice that she was glad to see him, get his supper on to the table, and perhaps then . . .

She needn't have bothered. He never came.

3

Systematically Poppy chopped the cold chicken-breast into cat-sized chunks, and mixed them in with some of the cooked rice and a dollop of cream and parsley sauce to make it all cohere. Elias, normally alerted to the concept of food by the click of the opener on the

Whiskas can, came lethargically down from the dresser and gazed at the pale mess in his bowl.

'Go on, you silly beast,' said Poppy. 'It's an adventure in living. Somebody might as well enjoy it.'

He might have phoned, she thought. This morning if he couldn't last night. There'd be a perfectly good reason why he hadn't, and she'd accept it without question, but for the moment her resentment demanded its head. Though when she'd got home last night she'd been too nervous to know whether she really wanted him to come, at eleven o'clock, having decided he wasn't going to, she'd lain in her bath and wept. She left Elias purring over the lickings of his bowl.

It was a bright, early-winter morning after the long late autumn. As she turned the corner out of her cul-de-sac she saw Nell striding towards her with Nelson in the push-chair, wrapped like a Michelin man against the cold and clutching his tortoise.

'Hello,' she said. 'Were you coming to look for me? Or Elias? I've got to go and take care of Toby. You got home all right?'

There was a wariness between them, a shared knowledge of a web to be mended which a clumsy move might tatter irretrievably.

'No problem,' said Nell. 'We'll walk round with you.'

'Lovely, and then Nelson could play with Toby. If you've got time, of course . . . I mean . . . Oh, dear, I wish I'd told you before about Janet, Nell.'

'Forget it. She's going to win, easy.'

'I expect so. We'll know this evening. Did some of your friends see you home?'

'You've got it wrong, Poppy. I'm not with them any more. I came because I've got a vote still, and I met Buzz on the pavement and he told me to get ready for a walk-out. That's all.'

A pause while they waited at the Channing Avenue zebra.

'That explains it,' said Poppy as they reached the far pavement. 'I didn't really believe you knew what they were going to do. Do you want to talk about it?'

'I don't know. Will she be there—your daughter-in-law?'

'Whirling off on her bike the moment we get in. It's all right, she won't eat you . . . I didn't mean that . . . I'm sure you'd give as good as you got . . . I'm making it worse, aren't I?'

Poppy had never seen Nell laugh, but her quick grin made her face for a moment innocently wicked, Pan-like, before good and evil.

'Do you spend all your time worrying about personal relations, Poppy?'

'Of course not. Well. Quite a bit, I suppose. Not exactly worrying, but . . . Are you teasing me? Hang on a mo—this is where I buy my paper, then it's just a couple of streets.'

Janet in fact had already left. Hugo was waiting in the living-room with his overcoat on, reading his *FT*. He eyed Nell briefly as he rose.

'Hi,' he said. 'The great white queen's gone to rally the nation. I couldn't make it last night. Were you there?'

'She was terribly good,' said Poppy. 'She had them eating out of her hand in the end.'

'No doubt. She says there was some sort of hoo-ha put on by the loony left—something to do with that chap they found in the park.'

'That's right. Where's Toby?'

Hugo looked round the room, miming vague surprise at his son's absence.

'I think I heard him going downstairs,' he said.

'I'd better look. This way, Nell, and we'll make a pot of tea.'

She scurried down the stairs, muttering under her breath. He was so like Derek sometimes, just as egocentric, just as coldly determined to prove he couldn't be trusted with responsibilities he regarded as a nuisance. Toby had dragged a chair out of the kitchen, put it against the forbidden door of the utility room, climbed up, opened the door, dragged the chair on into the room and used it to climb on to the top of the washing-machine. He was now filling the detergent dispenser with a mixture from the packets and bottles on the shelf behind. The dispenser had begun to fizz interestingly. Pinkish foam was welling out of it and drooling down the front of the machine. The air reeked of ozone.

'Do wash,' he said earnestly.

Poppy snatched him up before he could paw his hands into the rapidly reacting solvents. She heard the front door bang as Hugo left.

'No darling,' she said. 'Nasty. Hot. Not ordinary hot, but ouch! There's acids there, you see. Or alkalis, or something.'

'Do wash!'

'Not now. Look, Nelson's come to play with you.'

This was sufficient distraction, so he made only a token struggle and then let her carry him into the kitchen. Nell was still bringing Nelson one step at a time down the stairs.

'Men!' snarled Poppy, and took Toby to the sink to sponge off any of the chemicals that might have got on to clothes or skin, but he seemed to have been characteristically deft and there was only what seemed to be ordinary Persil in one shoe. Nell started to unparcel Nelson. Poppy gave Toby a wooden spoon and the most resonant of the saucepan lids and went back to the utility room to clear up. Wearing rubber gloves, she used a yoghurt pot to scoop what she could of the now quiescent pink goo into a bucket, which she filled with water and tipped down the sink. She sponged the overspill off with plenty more water, took the dirty clothes out of the machine and ran it. And if the mixture clogs its intestines, she thought, or rots its seals, or the whole thing explodes, Hugo can bloody well explain to Janet. It's not my fault. But if I can get Hugo alone I'll tell him what I think of him—not that it'll do a blind bit of good.

By now Toby's peremptory voice was coming from the kitchen, cries of 'No!' and 'Mine!' mixed with Nell's placating murmurs. The machine embarked on its cycle with a contented-sounding chunter, so Poppy went back to help. For the last few weeks Toby had been into tower construction with any materials that came to hand. He'd become quite expert in judging the moment of ultimate teeter, and would knock his edifices over with maximum mess and clatter just before they collapsed of their own accord. Nelson had a more primitive view of the delights of demolition. One brick on top of another was worth his attention, so there was a conflict of interest.

'Let's have some tea and take them upstairs,' said Poppy. 'There's more toys there. Honestly, my son!'

She let her anger, overtly with Hugo but in fact as much with John, stream out as she made the tea. By the time she'd finished her tirade she was half-way up the stairs, mug in one hand and Toby (far too grand to be carried when there were strangers watching) gripping her other forefinger.

'There's a way out of all that,' said Nell behind her. 'You don't have a man. And you don't have a washing-machine.'

She spoke in her usual dry voice, so there was no way of knowing how much it was a joke. Poppy stopped, turned and looked down.

'You know the worst thing about splitting up with Derek?' she said. 'It was knowing that from now on perhaps no one would ever love me again.'

'You can get by without.'

'I can't.'

Toby was in an unusually show-off mood. He got out all his soft toys and arranged them in a wide semicircle on the floor to form an audience. Nelson got the idea and contributed his tortoise, then climbed contentedly into Nell's lap to watch, with his thumb in his mouth. Toby made Poppy move up close to Nell so that there was room on the sofa for the blue elephant. These preparations took some time and kept him fully occupied, while Nelson seemed happy to do nothing.

'I've been thinking about what you said about personal relations,' said Poppy. 'You're right—there really isn't anything else I know or care about. All the rest, I mean all the other ways of dealing with people, politics and so on—they're such an impossible mixture of rights and wrongs. Have you ever tried sorting out a bag of old knitting wools which have come unrolled? You have to tease them apart, humour them, and then if you're patient you may be able to ease the one you want out and roll it up into a ball you can use, but if you try and tug it out all you do is make a lot of tight knots you'll never untangle. Not without scissors, anyway. That's what people who know they're right keep doing. They don't seem able to see how their rights are all mixed up with their wrongs, and everyone else's rights and wrongs as well.'

Nell shrugged, not totally dismissively.

'People who know they're right do dreadful things,' said Poppy. 'They shoot boy soldiers in the back, they make tired old men and women sleep out in the streets, they let villages starve because they want to topple a government. They can't see that all they're doing is adding to the wrongs on their own side so that in the end, even if they were right when they started, the balance tips over the other way. It makes me weep.'

'That's men.'

'I bet you, women would have been just as bad if they'd been given the chance.'

'Are you talking about last night?'

'Partly. But I'm not getting at you, Nell. If you don't want to talk about it . . .'

'I don't know. I really don't know.'

'Would it help if I guessed, and then you could tell me if I'm wrong. Yes, darling?'

Toby, having arranged his audience to his satisfaction, had been gazing round the room as if in imitation of his father's absent-minded puzzlement, seeming by now to have forgotten the subject of the demonstration he had intended to lay on. He'd resolved his problem by coming and thumping Poppy on the knee.

'Gamma do it,' he said.

'I'm too big, darling,' she said. 'Shall I get it out for you and you can show us?'

She fetched the spare bit of bookshelf from the slot beside the tallboy and the cylindrical log Janet had brought up from the cottage to use as a doorstop. This may not have been the equipment he'd intended to use, but it was something he'd invented a few weeks back and it satisfied him now. He laid the log on its side in the middle of the floor and balanced the shelf across it to make a simple, low-level see-saw. After making sure that Nell and Poppy were watching he edged up the ramp, waited posed and tense at the point of balance until you could all but hear the imaginary drum-roll, tilted the shelf over and charged down the far incline, deliberately falling flat on his face when he reached the carpet. Repetition kept him happy for a while, and then he taught the polar bear and tiger and Kermit the trick. By then Nelson was sufficiently sure of his new surroundings to want to join in, though he seemed to get enough excitement out of a simple charge and tumble, without going through the palaver with the see-saw. This meant that Nell and Poppy could talk almost coherently in the intervals between applauding.

'Well,' said Poppy, 'I'd better start by saying I was very relieved by what you've just told me. I really couldn't believe you'd have come last night if you'd known what your friends at Sabina Road were up to.'

'I don't know. No, I don't think I would.'

'What's more, I think you must have been even more shocked than the rest of us when his body was found in the play centre. You knew him, didn't you? And you knew who'd put him there.'

Nell shook her head.

'It wasn't like that,' she said. 'I knew him, of course, living in the same house, but I didn't know it was the same man they found. I wasn't living there any more, remember, and the drawings in the papers weren't that good. It wasn't till we were talking at Little Sue's next day. And I still don't know it was Mark and the others put him there.'

'Oh, I think it must have been. Whoever it was didn't do it just for a joke. They wanted to distract attention from themselves by using the fact that he'd come to the play centre and we'd all got pretty angry and upset. That means somebody must have told them about that. That was you, wasn't it? I remember you didn't react like the rest of us. You were just as angry, but you were going somewhere, to do something about it. I expect you went and told your friends they'd got to get rid of him.'

'He'd been hanging around Nelson already. I said either he went or I went. Mark said they'd talk to him. They called me in that evening and said he'd given them an explanation which they accepted; I blew my top.'

'I can imagine! What on earth kind of explanation . . . ?' Nell shrugged.

'Doesn't mean there was one,' she said. 'Mark's Mark. Dirwana gets a kick out of making people do things they don't want. Proofs of loyalty, she calls it. And Buzz had brought Jonathan in in the first place. He . . .'

'Don't you mean Simon?'

Nell hesitated.

'Look,' she said. 'I may have split with them, but it's not going to be me who lands them in the shit. I'd still go along with them in most things, in the political line and such. It's just the way they do it . . . Hell!'

Some kind of social security fraud, thought Poppy. Buzz had 'brought him in'. You house and feed a number of the harmless hopeless, help claim their social security, perhaps under more than one name, dole them out pocket money and keep the rest . . . it would be a good reason for not wanting the police all over the place investigating a suicide.

'Don't worry,' she said. 'Let's call him Simon, so we know who we're talking about. You didn't leave at once?'

'It wasn't like that. I mean Dirwana wanted me out, but she wasn't going to make it easy, and the others don't like people going. I'd been there a good time. It wasn't easy for me, either, Poppy. I just don't want this kind of life.'

Nell gestured with her head towards the rollicking children, the fitted carpet, the walnut tallboy, the music centre.

'All right,' said Poppy. 'Let's talk about Simon. Did they make him shave off his beard, do you know?'

'Not before I left. Dirwana wanted that, I'd heard. Proof of loyalty again, see? But he was sticking out.'

Poppy nodded. She could too easily imagine the rigid little tyrannies embedded in the apparent democracy of the commune. Dirwana had wanted Nell out, because Nelson had been a loyalty beyond her sphere. The poor, sad young man had been proud of his beard. Perhaps it was the only thing in his life he had ever achieved for himself. Had he killed himself because Dirwana had won? Or had they shaved it after he'd died, so that he wouldn't be recognised? Did it matter, now?

'There must have been a car or something,' she said. 'Buzz ran an old pick-up.'

'Could Simon have got the keys?'

'No keys. The door locks were bust. Buzz started it by clipping a pair of wires together.'

'What was he like, Simon?'

'A no-hoper. You were sorry for him, at first. Very quiet. He'd a bit of an American accent, but he'd picked that up. Underneath it was Eton or somewhere. Always wanting to prove himself, but as soon as he started on anything he came running to you for help. Pathetic.'

'I don't suppose he had a job.'

'No chance.'

'He must have had some money though. He pretty well chain-smoked.'

'Not in the community, he didn't. Mark wouldn't have it. He'd have drawn four quid a week from the pool.'

'His clothes looked quite good.'

'Right. There was one time he'd got himself new jeans, and Buzz wanted to know where he'd found them. If you got money from somewhere you'd got to put it into the pool.'

Yes. A picture formed in Poppy's mind. That roasting summer. The path just inside the play-centre gate. Laura, grim with mysterious outrage. (Deborah beyond her shoulder, cornering the market in trikes.) 'There's some of them will rob you blind.'

'Laura,' she said.

'Laura?'

'Something she said—I think it must have been about that. I'm fairly sure she knew Simon . . . oh, several things. For instance, do you remember her suddenly having that outburst against the police, that afternoon at Little Sue's . . . ?'

'He hadn't got a record. Buzz was always very careful about that.'

'That doesn't mean he hadn't been in trouble with them, some time. And another thing, when you came and stayed here that time you told me a bit about Mr Capstone. How did you know that?'

'Mark kept dossiers on people—anything he thought we could use. He'd tell us at council meetings.'

'But they knew about me being Janet's mother-in-law, and you didn't?'

'Must have been something that came up after they'd voted me off the council. When I said I was leaving, that was.'

'That makes sense. You see, I suppose someone might have been able to work out about Janet being my daughter-in-law, but I never said anything to anyone about her making me join the Labour Party, except Laura. I didn't mean to, it wasn't even true, really, but I was babbling a bit because . . . oh, how extraordinary! And *that's* what Simon must have told your friends!'

She sat motionless, staring at the back window, not seeing the winter sunlight on the mottled ivy that clothed the garden wall. Links formed, a proliferating network. The furry lover in the sea cave. Miss Poppy! Laura had assumed Poppy had an actual lover, and told Simon. He'd persuaded Mark and his friends he'd got a reason for watching the play centre. To back it up he'd started watching outside Poppy's flat. Mark kept dossiers . . . And Laura needed extra money, and Simon had smoked and bought new jeans . . . and he'd come on the one day she wasn't at the play centre but taking Sophie to the dentist, and . . . ah . . . 'Why must they grow up so quickly?' 'That's the pity of it, Mrs Tasker. That's just the pity of it.'

'I'm sorry . . .' she began, but at that moment Nelson, excited now into wilder and wilder tumbles, completely missed the big cushion Nell had put down for him, sprawled sideways and banged his head on the corner of the log-box. His yells filled the room. While Nell tried to comfort him Poppy fetched his mug of Ribena out of his changing bag. Toby meanwhile had exhausted his interest in using the shelf and log as a see-saw and had instead devised a sort of pro-jectile system, resting the shelf on the log, aiming it in the general direction of his cuddly menagerie and then whooshing it forward to skittle the animals over. It was a lethal device, but far from accurate. Poppy, concentrating on Nelson's plight, wasn't aware of it until she was handing Nell the mug and the shelf cracked into the back of her ankle.

'Ouch!' she cried. 'No, Toby, no! That hurt! Poor Poppy! No!'

It had hurt, too. She sat down with her good foot firmly on the plank and rubbed the battered ankle. Miming angelic repentance Toby came and kissed it better, then immediately tried to prise the plank free, to begin again.

'No,' she said firmly. 'Tell you what—let's go and see if the machine's finished. Then we can do the wash. You can put the soap in. No. That game's over. Finished. Good boy.'

They were in the utility room waiting for the machine's final chunter so that Poppy could open the door and load the clothes in when an unconsidered area of the network expanded in her mind, cancer-like, in fresh linkages. Simon had been watching outside the flat. He had tried to follow John. There had been a picture of John, instantly recognisable, on the notice-board at the commune. And then John had been angry, panicky. But later still, indifferent—it was only Simon, and not . . . who? Of course, John didn't know that Mark was keeping dossiers. Why hadn't they brought all that up last night? Tory candidate's husband sleeping with Labour candidate's mother-in-law. Ah, God!

They'd be keeping it for the actual election, of course.

I've got to talk to Laura.

4

Barnsley Square was south-east of the park, over the border into Ormiston, so Poppy took a taxi. It was probably the best address in the borough. The houses here would have cost you, at the height of the boom, £200,000 more than you'd have paid for similar space around Poppy's area. They were detached, and pretty in an almost Mediterranean way, with wide eaves and shutters, but not grand, a half-basement and then a couple of storeys above. Sometimes camera crews would spend a morning there to film an actor emerging from a door and so give the following scene the gloss of obvious wealth. The other main intrusion on the peace of the square came from driving instructors taking beginners through the early spasms of clutch-control.

It was now late morning, Poppy having timed her visit so that Laura should be back from collecting Sophie from school. She hadn't been able to ring and see if she was in as the number wasn't in the book, or if it was it was under the husband's name, which she didn't know. He was some kind of international banker, she seemed to remember from a colour-supplement piece about Sophie and Nick's mother, the stage designer Mary Pitalski. She didn't know the house number either but would recognise it from the time she'd brought Toby to tea—it would be the only one with a *trompe-l'oeil* grotto on the garage door at the bottom of the ramp by the steps. Number 17, it turned out. As she climbed the steps her mind was still a muddle of imagined conversations—with Laura, broaching the subject, with John, warning him what was going to happen, if it was. ('I've got to see you . . .' No.)

The door was opened by a beaky blonde woman in an orange silk trouser suit. She was exactly like her photographs.

'Oh, thank the kind angels!' she cried. 'I'm at my wits' end!'

Poppy's blank look must have answered.

'You're not from the agency?'

'I'm afraid . . .'

'Holy Saint Boniface, I can't stand it! Send me a nanny or I'll go mad! Just listen to that child!'

She paused, and Poppy heard Nick's characteristic whining wail coming from somewhere inside.

'What's happened to Laura?'

'If only I knew. I'd told her I'd pick up Sophie . . .'

A fresh wail interrupted her, but somehow different, urgent, in need.

'I could come in for half an hour,' said Poppy. 'Just until whoever you're expecting does turn up. He knows me from the play group. My name's . . .'

Ms Pitalski was in no mood for references or identification.

'Oh, that would be divine of you!' she said. 'Of course they'll come. Kids are downstairs. You'll have to excuse me, I'm hours late already.'

'One moment . . .'

'I'm sure you'll manage,' said Ms Pitalski, as she bent in the hall-way and flung magazines, papers and sandwiches out of a briefcase. 'And if she doesn't come the agency number's on that pad. If anyone calls tell them I'm on my way. Not if it's my mother, of course. And thank you, thank you. Mother of heaven's, what has he done with the keys?'

She had crammed a fresh lot of papers into the case and was roo-tling in a drawer. Now she gave up and made for the door, pausing to press a switch beside it. Poppy tried to bar her way on to the steps, saying, 'Please listen to me . . .' but she pushed past.

'I really haven't time. Later, later . . . Mother of God, the car's on fire!'

The switch must have activated the garage door, which had tilted and was now whining up out of sight. Bluish fumes poured out of the opening. The smell reeked into the clean winter air. Not fire, exhaust.

Ms Pitalski rushed down the steps, round and into the garage. Now Poppy could hear the purr of a large engine, idling. Her heart hammered with dread and foreknowledge. She was at the bottom of the steps when Ms Pitalski emerged, having held her breath as long as she could and now gasping for air.

'Go down to the kitchen and get two tea-cloths,' she panted. 'Wet them well and bring them back.'

Her voice was urgent, but steady. She strode up the steps and into a room beside the hall. As Poppy scurried for the stairs she heard the bip of telephone keys. The stairway was decorated as she remembered from her previous visit, with businessmen, horned and tailed, on a down escalator, but the kitchen had changed and was now an under-water scene, with everything in it shades of greeny blue. Sophie was drawing at the blue table, absorbed, her nose close against the paper.

From somewhere in the far corner, behind the blue-green laundry basket, rose Nick's quiet sobs. A litter of toys covered that corner of the floor. Poppy found two seaweed-patterned cloths, soaked them under the taps and wrung them out. As she came up the stairs she heard Ms Pitalski's voice, emphatic but controlled.

'. . . Barnsley Square. Right. Be quick—she may be alive.'

She came at a brisk, competent stride into the hall. Poppy followed her down the steps. A taxi was driving away and a woman coming through the garden gate.

'You're from the agency?' said Ms Pitalski. 'The kids are downstairs. Sophie and Nick. Do what you can. We've had an accident.'

She paused at the garage door to tie one of the wet cloths across her face, speaking as she did so.

'Don't come in with me,' she said. 'Stand clear. I'll get the car out if I can. As soon as it's out, open the doors your side.'

She drew a deep breath and walked into the hazed cave. Poppy heard the thunk of a car door and the blast of a horn, and then the car shot backwards up the ramp and stopped in the open. Its interior was full of fog. Poppy ran forward and pulled the doors wide. Ms Pitalski was out of the driver's seat, gasping, holding the top of the door to steady herself. Poppy ran round behind and opened the far passenger door. A vacuum cleaner hose was wedged into the window, its length running down to the exhaust pipe. Now she could see Laura, in her day clothes, lying on the broad back seat with her knees drawn up. Her cheeks were blotched with the same unnatural scarlet as Simon's had been.

Ms Pitalski came and looked too.

'I know how to do mouth to mouth,' said Poppy.

Ms Pitalski reached in and laid her twenty-ringed fingers against Laura's cheek.

'No good,' she said. 'The ambulance will be here in a minute. Holy St Agatha!'

The invocation was like a spell to reinvest her with her wilder personality, laid aside in the urgency of serious need. She flung her arms to heaven and rushed into the house. Poppy moved clear of the car and waited on the steps. From inside she could hear Ms Pitalski on the telephone, a virtuoso aria of self-dramatisation which lasted until the ambulance came heeling into the square, followed almost at once by a police car, which set down a single uniformed constable and whisked away. Ms Pitalski flung herself on the men, posturing and cackling like some great, gaudy forest bird flopping around in a fig-tree. Laura was dead. If there had been any chance of saving her Ms Pitalski would have been steady, quick and brave—as indeed she had been. She was like the Parkinsonian patients in a book Poppy had been reading, who, confronted with certain urgencies, completely lost their flailings and shudderings but with those needs gone reverted into the grip of their ailment. Poppy took the chance to go into the house and telephone Nell.

'Sure you're all right?' she finished. 'He'll be wanting his rest any moment now. The apple juice is in the fridge and he has it out of the yellow mug. Put him on your lap and read him a story while he's drinking it and he'll zonk out . . . Yes, absolutely dreadful . . . I don't know—I'll be back as soon as they'll let me . . . You're marvellous.'

Ms Pitalski was still in full torrent so she found the number in the telephone book, rang the police station and asked to speak to Inspector Firth. His line was busy, so she asked for Sergeant Caesar. While she waited to be connected she looked round the room. She'd seen photographs of it in magazines, but hadn't believed them. They were true. It was a room in a Pall Mall club, gone infinite. On all four walls diners and waiters and bishops dozing in leather armchairs and uniformed pages and card-players receded down pillared perspectives, and the real furniture in the room was in keeping . . .

'Sergeant Caesar.'

'Oh, this is Poppy Tasker. I'm at 17 Barnsley Square. The police are here, but I thought Inspector Firth ought to know as soon as possible that one of the play-centre nannies has gassed herself with car exhaust. I'm almost certain from things she said that she knew the young man who was found at the play centre.'

'Barnsley Square? Which of the lassies would that be . . . ?'

'Laura. I don't know her surname. Older than the others.'

'Oh, her . . . Right, I'll tell the boss. Thanks for calling in.'

He made no attempt to disguise the shift from definite interest to routine tedium. As Poppy put the phone down, frowning, a renewed burst of wailing, urgent, painful, came from below. Thinking she might be able to reassure Nick with a known face she made her way downstairs and found the agency nanny crouched by the laundry basket, talking into the dark slot between that and a dresser whose shelves, festooned with imitation corals, held brightly lit plates and dishes patterned with exotic fish. Sophie was still drawing, oblivious, shutting the world out.

'He won't let me touch him,' said the nanny. 'It's like there's something in the room.'

'He knows me. I'll see what I can do. Perhaps if you went outside for a moment.'

Poppy sat on the floor. The moment she began to shift the laundry-basket so that Nick could see her his screams redoubled, so she moved it only a few inches until she could see him cowering in the corner. She could smell that he'd filled his nappy. Not looking at him she started to tidy the toys into their Davy Jones sea-chest, waiting for the frenzy to fade to whining sobs.

'Hello, Nick. What's the matter? Come and tell Poppy.'

At once the wail rose, but faltered. She could feel his need to declare his terror fighting with his yearning for comfort. Any move towards him and he'd scream again.

'Poor Nick. But it's all right. It's all right now.'

For some minutes he took no notice, but she continued to coax him, murmuring the old, worn spells of home and love, edging occasionally closer and closer until she was right against the basket, and at last, still shuddering with sobs, he rose and tumbled into her embrace. The pose was awkward, but as soon as she tried to move his body went rigid, so she stayed where she was, rocking him gently to and fro, making gradual adjustments to her posture and discovering as she did so that what she had to do was use her body to shield him from the rest of the room. Now he seemed to grasp that she had understood his need and allowed her slowly to rise on to her knees and then her feet and then, still shielding him with her body from the unseen terror, to edge round the kitchen towards the door. Over her shoulder she tried to see what might have so alarmed him, but there was nothing obvious—in fact that side of the room was much more everyday than the rest, as there is not a lot a designer can do to make work surfaces, hobs and outsize electric ovens look anything except what they are.

'That's better,' said Sophie in a bell-like voice behind her. 'Now I can really draw.'

The nanny was sitting at the foot of the stairs. Nick refused to look, hiding his head in Poppy's shoulder as the adults introduced themselves. The nanny was called Tessa.

'I'll take him up and change him, if he'll let me,' said Poppy. 'He's soaked himself through. Why don't you make a pot of tea, and see if Sophie's ready for lunch?'

The front door was open, with sounds of activity outside. From the living-room came the murmur of a man's questions and the swoops and crescendi of Ms Pitalski's replies. Nick must have heard, but he gave no sign of believing his mother could supply the comfort he needed. He had stopped crying as they climbed the stairs and now began to look cautiously around through his tear-blubbered eyes, as if checking that his known and daylight world was still in place, gazing with a sense of acceptance and relief at the frieze on the stairway wall where whimsically erotic angels beckoned a variety of citizens—portraits of friends, Poppy had read, and indeed she recognised a couple of actors—up the heavenward escalator. Doors opened around a central landing, lit by a large skylight. Poppy headed towards the rear of the house, chose a door at random and found herself in what must be the nursery bathroom, a tropical lake scene with crazy-coloured animals along the shore. The bath was a yellow hippo with purple spots, the loo a green baboon. Next door was Sophie's room. Here bird-headed human figures took apes for walks across a pink, fantastic landscape, Bosch without the horrors. Then Nick's room, with a cot and ordinary Early Learning Centre toys in a cool forest where weird but friendly-looking beasts dozed in the glades.

Poppy found dry clothes and a nappy, but as soon as she tried to lay him down to change Nick's whimpers rose into sobs and his limbs went tense for fresh struggles. To calm him with his own known world she carried him out and explored the rest of the rooms. In the master bedroom masked but otherwise naked men, more than life size, pranced along a flame-coloured wall. A silver bathroom, its light fittings crystal stalactites, its bath a swan. A man's dressing-room, done as an old-fashioned ironmonger's shop, but with real chisels and saws on the painted racks. A night-blue spare room, its ceiling filled with a flying owl whose pitiless yellow eyes stared down on the bed.

Then a perfectly ordinary bathroom, white and cream, untouched by any fantasy, and completing the circuit a plain bed-sitting-room with TV and electric kettle, fawn carpet, cream walls, chintz chair and curtains—Laura's room, presumably, but so impersonal it might have been a hotel bedroom.

Here at last Nick pushed himself up on to Poppy's arm and gazed around. He stared for a while at the mantelpiece, and then at the table beside the easy chair, and then at the chest of drawers. He drew his breath for what Poppy thought was going to be another burst of sobbing, but instead loosed it into a thin and fading wail. With a final shudder he plunged into sleep. Poppy carried him back next door to his own room, gently undressed him, cleaned and changed him and eased him down into his cot, surrounding him with soft toys. The baby alarm was the same model as Janet's; she switched it on and went downstairs.

Voices came from outside but the house was silent. Hoping to ring Nell again, Poppy put her head into the living-room and saw Ms Pitalski standing stock still in the middle of her subfusc masculine elysium, with her ringed hands covering her face.

'I've got him to sleep,' she whispered.

'Thank heavens. Oh, poor kid. Why did she have to do it? I got back this morning and . . . Oh, God, children are not my scene. I do my best, I really do.'

'I enjoyed their rooms.'

'That's something I can do. I thought she loved him. Why . . . ?'

'Listen, I really must go and look after my grandson. I'll give you my number and if Tessa can't cope with him I'll bring Toby up here this afternoon.'

'Oh, thank you, thank you. You're an angel . . .'

'Perhaps you'd better see that Tessa's got the doctor's number. Nick may need a sedative.'

'Yes, yes. And I must take Sophie to school. I must . . . Holy St Agatha . . .'

Like an addict to a fix she stumbled to the telephone and jabbed at the keys. Poppy wrote her own name and Janet's number on a pad and took a note of the Barnsley Square number. As she stole away she was aware of Ms Pitalski miming continued thanks with hands and arms while she cradled the telephone into her shoulder poised for another explosion of woe as soon as her call was answered.

Inspector Firth was at the bottom of the steps talking to another man while they watched the activity round the car.

'I've got to go,' said Poppy. 'I didn't see much. I got here just before Ms Pitalski opened the garage door.'

'This is Sergeant Levison from the Ormiston Division,' said Mr Firth. 'Mrs Tasker is a witness in the case I was telling you about, Sergeant.'

He spoke with none of the warmth she had felt when she'd seen him in his office. The men's body signals showed wariness and restraint between them. Poppy remembered something she'd seen in the *Echo*, a formal denial by a police spokesman of a previous story which she'd missed but which must at least have hinted at bad blood between the Ethelden and Ormiston police. The men ignored her after the nods of introduction, continuing their conversation.

'Right, I'll keep in touch,' said Mr Firth.

'Very good, sir,' said Sergeant Levison, and turned to Poppy as Mr Firth left. She explained about Toby and told him briefly what she'd seen. He made a note of her address and likely movements and said he would send somebody along later to take a full statement, then let her go. As she rounded the corner out of the square, making for the main road, a car horn bipped softly beside her.

'Give you a lift home?' said Mr Firth.

'Oh, that would be marvellous. I had to take a taxi to get here.'

She settled thankfully into the passenger seat and the car eased away.

'A taxi?' he said. 'That urgent, was it?'

Instantly the simplicities of need and action lost their hold and confusion engulfed her. In the horror of Laura's death and the urgency of Nick's nightmare she had effectively forgotten her reason for coming to Barnsley Square. Her defences, not on her own behalf but on John's and Nell's, were completely down.

'Well, yes . . . but . . .' she said. 'Oh dear . . . you see, I suddenly realised . . . Did you hear what happened at my daughter-in-law's adoption meeting last night?'

'You've not seen the papers?'

'No . . . not yet . . . Anyway, that young man—Simon Venable, they said, but it wasn't his real name . . .'

'No.'

'I think it was some kind of social security fraud.'

'We'd got that far.'

'Oh . . . You mean . . .'

'I don't imagine the man who calls himself Mark Giraldi would have thrown his bombshell into your meeting if he'd not been aware that their game was up.'

'No. I suppose not. It did seem a bit crazy, but I gather he's like that. I know somebody who used to be in his group who was pretty shocked. You see . . .'

She explained, stumblingly, what she knew, discovering as she did so that it was possible to leave out the bit about John being recognised from the photograph on the notice-board, and then followed. There was no way of leaving Nell out but completely, but as he knew about the squat she could imply, not mentioning Nell by name, that she had simply picked up her own knowledge as part of the play-centre gossip. He seemed to listen with care and drove more slowly than he need have, though now as she pieced her chains of guesswork together they seemed almost too flimsy to bother with. There were so many other possible explanations.

He grunted non-committally as she finished and drove on in silence. Automatically her mind preoccupied itself again with Nick, his terror, his loss, his gesture of desolation in the bare little room which was all that now spoke to him of Laura.

'She would have had pictures of him,' she said.

'Uh?'

'I'm sorry. I was thinking about Laura.'

'You knew her well?'

'No. She wasn't that sort of person. But I'd taken Toby there for tea and of course we saw quite a bit of each other at the play centre.'

'How did her behaviour strike you?'

'Just what you'd expect from an old-fashioned nanny. Strict but conscientious and fundamentally caring. The children she looked after were her life. That's what . . .'

'But responsible? Sane?'

'Oh, yes. She was terribly upset since the young man was found, of course, but . . .'

'I may as well tell you that she came to the station next morning and insisted on seeing someone. At first it seemed she might have information for us, but in fact she refused to tell us anything and launched into a tirade about police persecution and communist murderers. We put her down as paranoid. A nutter. You get a lot of them, cases like this.'

'Oh no . . . well, I don't think so. I mean, she may have thought the people in the squat had killed him—she wouldn't have put anything past them. And if he'd had problems with the police—he'd have told her, making out it was never his fault, of course, and she'd have backed him up and taken his side . . . Just put me down at the corner, then you won't have to back out.'

He pulled in to the side of the road.

'And the pictures?' he said.

'Oh. I looked into her room, you see, while I was trying to get Nick to sleep. You see, nannies like Laura, they keep up with the families they've worked for, some of them, anyway. They have photographs of babies and schoolchildren, and postcards from first trips abroad, and weddings, and the next lot of babies, and little presents and mementoes, a complete clutter, every shelf, every table . . . Laura didn't have anything . . .'

'Did you look in the drawers?'

'No. I suppose she might have . . . or the dustbins . . . or burnt them. Wiping everything out. Nick knew.'

'Uh?'

'The baby. He knew something was badly wrong. I mean, he cried a lot anyway. The neighbours used to complain. They'd had an NSPCC inspector round once. But this was different. I could feel it.'

He was silent again, but as she reached for the door-handle he said 'Hold it.'

She waited.

'You're telling me she was a very dedicated nanny,' he said.

'Oh yes. Most of them are, you know. The girls too.'

'She would have done anything to protect one of her charges?'

'Yes. Pretty well anything.'

'Our chap, the one in the play centre, had a biggish shot of heroin just before he died. Getting on for an overdose. There were other needle scars on his arms, but old. The natural assumption is that he wanted to go out happy.'

'It wasn't that kind of squat. They wouldn't even let them smoke.'

'That's what we heard.'

He picked up his in-car telephone, called a known number and asked for an extension.

'Firth here, sir. I'm afraid I've got a tricky one. It ties in with our man in Rattigan Park. Apparent suicide in Barnsley Square, car exhausts . . . Ormiston, sir . . . no, sir, I just looked in, told Sergeant Levison about the connection, didn't ask any questions . . . Not yet . . . She was the family nanny, but she seems to have known our chap, a possibility that she nursed him when he was a child . . . No, sir, but I'm told a child in the house appears to have been seriously frightened, and that she was a dedicated nanny who would have done anything to protect him. That would have been a way of achieving the same result . . .'

He put his hand over the mouthpiece.

'How old is the kid? Talking yet?'

Poppy shook her head.

'No luck, sir . . . Right, I'll leave it to you . . . I've got some new lines on the Rattigan Park case, if they tie in . . . Right.'

He called off and put the telephone down.

'I needn't tell you that's confidential,' he said.

'I wasn't going to tell anyone.'

'And I'd like to talk to your Sabina Road informant.'

'Oh . . . I don't know . . . I'll try . . . It's better if she comes to you, isn't it?'

'If possible.'

'I'd need to give her some idea how serious it is. She's very left-wing, very anti-police, but that doesn't mean . . .'

He smiled at her confusion. He looked very tired; his job put him under extraordinary pressures, his family life had been taken from him, but he still had time to make space for people to be themselves.

'I leave it to you,' he said.

Both babies were asleep, Nelson in a nest of cushions on the sofa.

'I need some gin,' said Poppy. 'It's absolutely against all my rules but I don't bloody care. What about you?'

'Well, if you're going to . . . Oi! about a quarter of that! Ta! You all right, Poppy? You've had a time!'

'It's worse than you think. Listen, the people at Sabina Road. How far would they go? Would they actually kill someone, do you think?'

Nell stood still, her mouth half open.

'I don't know,' she whispered.

'It's all right,' said Poppy. 'I don't think they did. There'd be no point in faking a suicide and then drawing attention to it by putting the body in the play centre like that.'

'Fake a suicide? How . . . ?'

'You give him a shot of heroin to make him pass out, so you can fix the van up. That makes it look as if he's fixed it himself and then taken the heroin so that he goes out happy.'

'Not Jonathan—Simon. He'd have needed someone to show him how.'

'Listen, Nell. You're not going to like this. I told Inspector Firth what I'd guessed about Laura knowing Simon. I didn't say more than I had to about the commune, but now . . . I mean it's different, isn't it?'

Nell put her gin down and combed her fingers slowly down through her glistening hair.

'What about Laura?' she said. 'Same with her?

'Not the heroin. You'd never get her to—she'd fight, and there'd be marks. But suppose you persuaded her that you were going to do something terrible to Nick . . . Suppose you actually showed her . . .'

'He'd scream and scream.'

'You could . . . Oh, God, I know! You could shut him into the oven and set the timer!'

'No!'

'There was something that really upset him that side of the room. I must ring Tessa and tell her not to take him downstairs . . .'

'But where were the parents, for God's sake? Surely . . .'

'Ms Pitalski said something about getting back this morning. I don't know about the husband. Look, I'm just guessing. All I know is that Nick was absolutely terrified of something in the kitchen, and he knew Laura was gone.'

A long pause.

'OK, I'll tell them,' said Nell. 'Who do I ask for?'

'I'm sure that's the best thing. Oh, Nell, I can imagine what it costs . . .'

'Let's talk about something else. Can I have another gin? What shall we give the kids for dinner?'

Nelson woke drowsy and fractious. Nell had to coax him, spoon by spoon. She was waiting with another mouthful poised when she said, 'Oh, sorry, I forgot. A man phoned. He said his name was John. He wouldn't give his number, but he told me to tell you he was in Geneva.'

'Oh. Thanks . . . I'm afraid I'm going to cry. Don't worry, it doesn't mean anything.'

Woozy with her huge gin, she let the sobs shake her. 'How does it feel to know your lover is a murderer?' But Geneva? It had to be true.

You could prove it with airline tickets and things. Air hostesses would remember a face like that. Thank God, oh thank God!

5

The doorbell woke her. Where was she? Oh yes, sitting in her own armchair with dried drool on the side of her mouth and the rasp of snoring in her throat. The television was on, a Czech or someone in front of a patriotic statue haranguing the camera about democracy. God! Ten past nine!

She'd turned on the TV to see if there was anything about Laura on the Channel Four news, but fallen asleep and woken now nearly two hours later with a sore throat and a filthy face and a hangover

The bell rang again. She lurched into the hall, scrabbled the chain into its slot and opened the door those few inches. 'Who is it?'

'Me. Jim Bowles. Gone to bed, have we?'

Oh, God, what did she want? Peace. Oblivion. Night and no moon. No, she'd better talk to someone, anyone . . . She let him in.

'Hang on a mo,' she said. 'I went and fell asleep. I've got to tidy myself up. And I haven't had supper yet, and nor's Elias.'

She rinsed her face, tugged a comb through her hair, swallowed an aspirin and made for the kitchen. He followed her.

'No room for two,' she said. 'You can have my stool in the passage. OK?'

'Had a rough day, then?'

'Have I not? I've spent half the morning and all the afternoon holding someone else's baby while he had the horrors.'

'Yes, I heard about that. What do you reckon they did with him?'

Poppy told him, and he shook his head slowly and whistled. She opened a tin of sardines, put one in Elias's dish and covered it with Whiskas so that he didn't get to it straight off.

'I'm not going to offer you gin,' she said, 'or I'll want some myself and I've had enough.'

'Cup of coffee, then.'

'In a minute. My need is greater than yours.'

There were some cold cooked potatoes. She chopped an onion, set it to fry, chopped the potatoes and added them, fished the chunks of tomato out of the remains of yesterday's salad, put them in too, and then the sardines, grated stale cheddar over the resultant mess and shoved it under the grill. While it browned she made his coffee.

'Ta,' he said. 'Two sugars. Things some people will eat, though! I'm surprised at you.'

'I'll get it down somehow, I expect. Let's go into the living-room. I don't think I want to listen to music, I know I don't want to have to resist your advances, and I'm not sure I want to talk about this beastly business.'

'Ah. Reckon it'll rain tomorrow, then?'

She laughed and felt better. Elias had found and eaten his buried sardine and, scorning the Whiskas, had followed the smell of hers into the living-room. He settled in front of the gas fire, watching her every mouthful, wide-eyed.

'All right,' she said. 'You can tell me what they're saying at the police station.'

'Don't know that much. Your little friend came round and spilled the beans about Sabina Road. Pity about her. She could've been an eyeful, if only she'd dress right. She a dyke, you reckon?'

'No, and it wouldn't matter if she was.'

'No offence, Poppy.'

'Well, I find it very offensive, and saying "No offence" only makes it worse. I don't know why men have to feel so threatened by women who choose to live their lives as something other than an appendage of the male animal. I mean I do know, and I think it's stupid. It took a lot of courage, and basic honesty and decency, for Nell to overcome all her prejudices and go and see Mr Firth, and if any of your friends tell you any different you can talk to them the way you talked to that young man who tried to follow me. At bottom they're behaving just the same as he was, and with less excuse.'

She hadn't often felt so vehement about anything. The headache and the anger and the knowledge of what had been done to Laura, and perhaps to Nick, bore in on her, creating the pressure. Jim was looking at her, miming innocence of her accusation.

'You'll tell them, won't you?' she said.

'I'll do my best.'

'Good.'

'About this other woman, Poppy . . .'

'Laura?'

'That's right. What sort was she?'

'Well, until a few weeks ago I'd have said she was a very ordinary, old-fashioned, highly responsible nanny. I was surprised how upset she was when the body was found in the play centre, but if she knew the man, and loved him, which I think she did . . . And even then, the day after he was found, do you remember how wet it was? She'd gone out to Linen Walk without proper rain-clothes, and she was very upset and rather strange while we were there, but she was still very careful about Sophie and Nick, seeing they stayed dry and so on. I believe if the world had been ending she'd still have done her best for them . . . In fact, I think that's just what she did. Oh dear. Who'd have thought I'd ever want to cry for Laura?'

'Don't mind me.'

'It's all right. Carry on.'

'Point is, would she have let just anyone in? No sign of forcible entry. Chain on the door, like yours.'

'She was expecting Ms Pitalski back. She mightn't have set it.'

'Still, suppose someone rang, she'd've used it then, wouldn't she, same way you did just now?'

'Yes. Of course she would.'

'So it looks like someone she knew. Any ideas?'

'I know so little about her. She didn't seem to have any friends, any life outside her work. She was going to start looking after Toby on Saturdays—I know she wanted the extra money, but it didn't sound as if she'd got anything else to do with her spare time. But if she was killed, and the young man in the park was killed by the same person . . .'

'Way I look at it is this. Remember what I was saying to you last time, about that being a nice little set-up for blackmail you got there in the play-group, all those girls gossiping round about what they know? And one of them just listening and passing it all on? Now suppose it was Laura doing just that, and telling this young fellow she's fond of. And suppose she puts him on to the kind of thing that really matters to someone, the kind of thing they'd kill to keep quiet. Right?'

'Well . . . as a matter of fact I had noticed that she'd become much less stand-offish since . . . oh, just about since the time when he first tried to follow me.'

'There you are, then. Now she's not stupid, Laura. She knows what she's told the young man. Maybe he's talked to her about how he's getting on. Whoever killed him has tried to make it look like suicide, but from what you're telling me she's not going to wear that . . .'

'The morning after he was found she was trying to tell Mr Firth that it was the people at Sabina Road who'd killed him. I think they just moved him because they didn't want a police enquiry at the squat. They knew about him coming to the play centre before, from Nell. And the one called Mark would have thought of the freesias. I saw him at my daughter-in-law's adoption meeting. He sounded like that kind of joker. But they wouldn't have gone to the trouble of faking a suicide, and then drawn attention to it by moving him, would they?'

'Not unless they were pie-eyed at the time. No. I'm with you there.'

'I'm afraid I told the girls about all that. I thought they had a right to know. Laura was there too. She could have worked it out.'

'And then she starts thinking about who else might've killed her friend. She's told him things and he's told her things which there's several people wouldn't want known about, supposing they're true. And she's not going to the cops, is she? They wouldn't listen to her, time before.'

'She was a bit paranoid about them anyway, I'm afraid.'

'Silly cow. No off . . . I didn't say it! I didn't say it!'

'Go on.'

'So she starts ringing round, accusing them all of this and that. And with one of them she hits the fellow as actually did the young man in. Right? And somehow—don't ask me how—he knows who it is, making these calls. What does he do? He goes round to Barnsley Square. And she lets him in.'

'I suppose he could have had a key. I mean Laura could have told Simon about something in *that* family, a brother or someone. What about the husband—if you can imagine anyone doing that to his own son?'

'Mr Lewis. He's in San Francisco or somewhere, setting up a film. That's cast iron. They're checking on the keys, of course, and if the mum's got a boyfriend on the side—there's nothing you or me can help with there.'

'Well, I can't think of anyone, assuming we're talking about a man. The only people I know that Laura knew at all were the girls at the play centre, and I simply can't imagine any of them . . . They've mostly got boyfriends, of course, and I know quite a bit about them. There's one who's had a spot of trouble with the police, but even he . . . Honestly, no, Jim. I don't believe it. All right, there you are, greedy-guts.'

She put her plate on the floor, for Elias to finish off the sardine tails and backbones and a few other fish-smelling scraps. Of course he pulled them on to the carpet before eating them—some cats would do that if you gave them a dish the size of a cartwheel. Normally she'd have spread a bit of newspaper under the plate, but she was too tired to bother. All she wanted now was bed.

'I'm sorry,' she said. 'I'm going to have to ask you to go. I'll be asleep in about three minutes.'

'OK, OK. Just a thought though. Suppose he came round with someone she did know, someone she'd open the door for. Suppose, for instance, there was a husband having it off with one of the girls, and neither of them wanted the mum knowing . . .'

'No, Jim. Absolutely not. No.'

6

This time there was no waiting. Sergeant Caesar was already at the counter. He watched while she was booked in and took her straight round. The WPC she'd asked for was in the corridor, ready to look after Toby. It was Vi, and he recognised her so there was no trouble about the hand-over. Poppy was sure Mr Firth had remembered and deliberately sent for Vi. It would be typical of him.

'Thank you for coming,' he said. 'Please sit down. I'm afraid that was a very nasty experience you had yesterday.'

'I'm all right,' lied Poppy.

She had been flung into wakefulness at about three that morning, as if by some violent thought propelling her up out of the ocean of sleep on to this terrible but inevitable course, a thinking missile, aware in advance of the ruin of its impact. She had sat till dawn at the kitchen table making notes of what she needed to say, and then writing it in the form of a statement, like the one she'd signed earlier. She had managed to eat some breakfast, but it lay like gravel in her stomach, undigested. Her blood had no heat in it at all. She changed her specs, unfolded the sheets of paper and began to read.

'I'm going to tell you everything I know,' she said, 'because I don't know how much of it is relevant. As you'll see, there are things I'd much rather keep quiet about, but it can't be helped. I can only hope you'll treat anything you don't need as confidential. I have recently started having an affair with John Capstone. It had not in fact begun on the evening when I reported that someone had been watching my flat. We had merely met at a concert, by accident—I had already met him briefly at his home—and he had then had supper with me. Next morning he telephoned me, speaking very urgently, and told me to go out to a call-box and ring him from there. He then said he had been followed away from my house by someone who had been watching it. When I said I would have to report it to the police he insisted that I did so in a manner which made it seem that the man had been interested in me, or perhaps my grandson Toby, and not in him. Later . . .'

She kept her voice dry and level, filling in everything she'd left out, for John's sake or Nell's or her own, in her previous statement—things he'd told her himself about his activities; things she'd realised, such as the fact that he expected them to come to a crisis in the near future, and the nature of Constantin's work; Constantin's apparent relationship with Peony; and then things she hadn't realised earlier might be relevant, mainly to do with Laura, such as her sudden unbending and efforts at friendship with the girls in the last few weeks; what Nell had told her about the commune—briefly, since presumably they'd already got all that from Nell herself; Big Sue's anger when Simon had first come to the park; and so on. She put no construction on any of the facts, apart from the implied one of their possible relevance. The only real guess she allowed herself was about the nature of Nick's terror.

'. . . we'd arranged that he should visit me the night before last, but he didn't come. Nell told me he rang next morning when I was at Barnsley Square, saying he was in Geneva. I don't know whether he had Constantin with him. There was a blank call on my daughter-in-law's answerphone when I got back yesterday evening, but otherwise I haven't heard.'

She looked up. She had been aware of Mr Firth making notes while she spoke. He was studying them now.

'Get someone to check the Geneva passenger-lists, will you, Bob,' he said without looking up. 'He most likely went sudden, or he'd have let Mrs Tasker know.'

He waited for Sergeant Caesar to leave the room, then turned and smiled at her.

'Thank you very much,' he said. 'That's all extremely interesting. What made you decide to tell me?'

'I don't know. I just woke up, knowing I had to. Because it's a murder, I suppose. Because of what I think happened to Nick, even more.

Of course I've asked myself whether it's really subconscious resentment at John letting me down like that. Honestly I don't think so.'

'This man Constantin . . . ?'

'I think he's there to keep an eye on John. John good as told me he was in the Romanian secret police. John does some sort of financial work for the Romanian government—I don't mean for the official government. It sounds like some sort of currency fiddle. He said it meant President . . . oh, Ceausescu, isn't it? . . . his nephews could afford to buy Gucci shoes. There used to be someone he really cared about in Romania, but she died—early last year, it would have been, so they lost their hold over him. At one point he had to go to Trieste in a hurry and insisted that Constantin went with him, which upset Mrs Capstone's arrangements. She wasn't at all pleased.'

He made another note and looked at her again. He was about to speak when the door opened.

'Hang on a moment, Bob,' he said.

The door closed.

'I think you are still not being quite open with me,' he said. 'You've come to a conclusion, which you don't want to tell me. Right? You don't want to accuse someone, so you're leaving it to me to work it out. It's my job, isn't it?'

He waited, but Poppy said nothing.

'One of the girls at the play centre, it's got to be. Someone you mind about, someone Laura knew. Someone she'd let into the house, right? This Peony, for instance. She'd do what Constantin told her, you think?'

'I don't know.'

'She'd been round at Barnsley Square, you say, when Mrs Capstone said she didn't want Deborah having any more to do with the people from the play centre?'

'That's only an impression I got, and Laura and Peony had both been taking the children to the Holland Park play centre. Anyway, Barnsley Square's different, isn't it?'

'Honorary Kensington? Who asked who, do you happen to know?'

'They went to Barnsley Square, so it must have been Laura asked Peony.'

'You'd have expected that?'

'Not really. Neither way round, actually.'

'But if Laura wanted to talk to Peony about Capstone. Venable would have told her about trying to follow him from your house. And you say he would have recognised him, so he may have made contact later. When you met Capstone after Venable's death he was playing the episode down, right?'

Poppy nodded, miserable. She had travelled this path, to and fro, to and fro, in the small hours.

'Then Peony tells Constantin,' said Mr Firth. 'Or perhaps Laura herself begins to make accusations. You won't have been the only one getting anonymous telephone calls, and Peony would know about the parents being away . . . It's all right, Mrs Tasker. He wouldn't have told her what he was going to do. He'd have sent her away the moment she'd got Laura to let him in . . .'

'Do you think it's true?'

'It shouldn't be hard to find out.'

'Be gentle with her.'

'Even fairly simple-minded people have to take the responsibility for their actions in the end, you know. Yes . . . ?'

It was the WPC, Vi, pink-faced, pushing Toby in front of her.

'He's asking for his granny,' she whispered.

Sergeant Caesar appeared behind her, amused, self-pleased,

making it instantly apparent that Toby's demand for Poppy had arisen from Vi not being able to give him her full attention.

'Hello, Toby,' said Mr Firth. 'Have you still got your book? Any joy, Bob?'

A tiny, warning shake of the head. John had not been on the passenger-lists to Geneva.

Sergeant Caesar slid a sheet of paper, a fax by the look of it, on to Mr Firth's desk. He started to look through it but was distracted by Toby trying to open the drawers of his desk.

'Not in there, young man,' he said. 'Let's see what we've got in here. Suppose we tie this bit of string on to . . .'

'My do it.'

'OK, but I'll help you. Have a look through there, Mrs Tasker, and see if any of the names ring a bell.'

She took the page. A letterhead and a list of names and dates. She gazed at it, not registering. If he hadn't been in Geneva . . . He hadn't come round . . . Oh, God . . .

She forced herself to read.

MRS HORTON'S
Quality Nursery Staff Confidential
Re: Miss Laura Evans. Previous Employers:
1967–1974 Hon. Mrs David Ogham-Ferrars
1974–1979 Mrs Wabeloff
1979–1986 Mrs Gally
1988–   Ms Mary Pitalski

'My do it! My do it!'

Toby's voice of unquestionable command. Mr Firth had found a magnet, tied it to a length of string (how had he intuited Toby's fascination with anything that could be looped or threaded?), pulled a drawer right out of the desk and set it to project from the top so that the string could then be run over the drawer-knobs and used as a crane to raise and lower key-rings, chains of paperclips, file-tags and so on. He handed the apparatus over and looked at Poppy.

'He may well have gone out via Paris, or some other way,' he said.

'I suppose so.'

Yes, it could be true, but probably wasn't. She passed the sheet back.

'Stupid names people have,' she said. 'Not that I can talk. I wonder what she was doing in 1987.'

'Getting him off heroin, maybe. He seems to have broken the habit once, and by all accounts he wouldn't have done that without a lot of help. That reminds me. Heroin. There's a fair amount about, but it isn't something you can just go out and buy on a one-off basis. You've got to have contacts. You might think if you've picked up any hint of that anywhere.'

She shook her head. John? This scheme which was coming to its crisis? A consignment of drugs in Romanian diplomatic baggage? That man on the trade delegation, who couldn't be met till after midnight? It didn't feel like that, and anyway Mr Firth would already have thought of it. Big Sue's Trevor . . . reluctantly she explained about the imbroglio at the transport café.

'Better look into it, Bob,' he said. 'Doesn't sound the type for this, though. It's all too fancy.'

'Please . . .' said Poppy, and stopped. What was the point? Trevor would get aggressive, bluster, lie . . . but the missile had already struck, detonated. Now it was only a question of how far, into what innocent lives, the destruction would spread.

'It's got to be done, I'm afraid,' said Mr Firth. 'Well, I think that's all for the moment, and thank you very much. You may have saved us a lot of messing around. Do you want me to have your notes? If you'll just sign them they'll do as a statement. Save you hanging around.'

'I've done that already,' said Poppy and slid the pages she had read from on to the desk.

'Thanks,' he said. 'And no doubt you'd like to keep the magnet, young man.'

'Oh, no, you mustn't,' said Poppy. 'We don't want him getting the idea he can have anything he fancies.'

'Mine?' said Toby, vainly trying to slide the magnet and string into a non-existent pocket in the bib of his overalls.

'Then I'll lend it to you,' said Mr Firth. 'But I'll need it back. It's an essential piece of investigative equipment, Toby.'

'Just a few days,' said Poppy.

'Few days,' said Toby, getting the tone dead right, his word his bond, though his grasp of time and number was still non-existent. Sergeant Caesar accompanied them out. In the lift he grinned at Poppy.

'Thanks for looking in,' he said.

'I hope it was all right. I mean . . .'

'What d'you mean, all right? If you'd seen how the boss perked up when he heard it was you.'

'I expect he misses his daughters, so he enjoys playing with Toby.'

'If that's what you want to think . . .'

They had reached the lobby. He held the door.

'All right now? Be good. See you soon,' he said.

Poppy pushed home through the wintry streets. The threat of Christmas hung in the air, visible already, to Poppy's eye, in the fretful look of passers-by as they readied themselves for the meaningless but necessary rites of false jovialities and ill-considered gifts. She detested Christmas. It was one of the few things on which she saw eye to eye with her mother. They had reduced it to a minimum. You gave, say, a pair of slipper-socks and received a jumper. You lunched off roast chicken and Lyons mince pies, and shared half a bottle of cheap white wine. You listened to the Queen, and then it was over and you could go out and feed the pigs. How had she come to marry a man with Pharaonic expectations of the festival, demanding, even in middle-age, a full stocking of carefully selected knick-knacks, all wrapped in different papers, with gold-papered chocolate coins spilling out at the top and a tangerine in the toe, and then a camel train of larger gifts (yes, he would really have loved it if she'd hired a few camels and had them come jingling down the street to their door, though he'd have expected her somehow to do it out of the housekeeping money), and a monster turkey and flaming pudding and bloody holly everywhere? The one faint lightening of her inner misery was the thought that she would no longer have to worry about a Christmas present for John.

There was a message on Janet's answering machine, the harsh voice unmistakable.

'I will call on you at nine this evening. Please be in.'

7

Do you offer food to one whom you've betrayed? The question bulked ridiculously larger than the rationally more important one of whether she should have rung Mr Firth and told him John was coming. It was, she knew, possible that John had killed two people, in order to close their mouths. It was therefore possible that he would do the same to her. She was certain that the moment he came through the door he would smell her treachery. She was going to have to tell him in any case; she couldn't keep up a whole evening of pretence. She had felt compelled, out of a kind of duty to others—to Nick, to Laura, to the dead young man, to the whole community to which she belonged—to betray him. But now that public necessity was over. Whatever happened between them now was private, their own affair. She had the right to choose, so she chose to trust him. That was that.

She changed her mind several times about food, but in the end ate supper by herself, early, and saw that there was enough for him, unprepared, if he wanted it.

He smelt nothing. He kissed her briefly, not apparently noticing her unresponsiveness, looked at his watch and said, 'Sorry. May we see the headlines?'

She switched the TV on and just caught them. The pound was falling. There had been an enormous protest in Leipzig, and another in Prague. Cecil Parkinson had launched a sale of personalised number-plates. Lord Aldington in the witness-box. As she was about to switch off he said 'No. Please.'

They watched the stuff about the pound in silence, and then the Eastern Bloc protests. The crowds seemed unimaginable, their joint life, their channelled excitement and purpose. The thrill of being alive in these days broke for the moment through Poppy's misery and apprehension. But then Romania. Shots of a grey man ranting, rehearsed ovations. A six-hour speech it said, and a rule of iron still . . .

'Thank you,' he said. 'Amazing. Amazing. People here have no idea what it means. He hasn't a hope. The whole system is going to come apart. All of it.'

The room throbbed with energies. He was part of those crowds on those roaring streets. It seemed to take him time to realise that she wasn't as involved.

'You don't feel it?' he said.

'Yes, of course . . . I'm afraid I've got something to tell you. I don't know if you've heard about the death of one of the nannies. She's called Laura.'

'Yes.'

'It looks as if somebody tried to make it look like suicide, but it wasn't. The same with the young man in the park. Laura knew him. It's all connected. I've told the police everything I know.'

He laid his hands on his thighs and stared for a while at their backs.

'Everything?'

'Yes. About you being followed, and not wanting the police to know, and then pretending it didn't matter. And what you told me about what you were doing. And Constantin.'

He continued to gaze at his hands.

'I'm sorry. I had to,' she said.

'Is there anyone here?'

'What do you mean? No. This is between us. Only . . .'

She hadn't intended to tell him about the anonymous calls, thinking he would misunderstand her reasons. Now she had to.

'. . . So at first I thought that you must have been followed again, or perhaps the flat was bugged. Happening just after you'd been, you see.'

'You've looked?'

'I tried to, but I wouldn't know where. Anyway I'm almost sure now it must have been Laura making a lucky guess. She didn't know you'd been again. Only, if I'm wrong . . .'

'We'll assume you are right. In any case it's too late to matter.'

'Have you had any?'

'Clara normally answers the telephone, and we are ex-directory.'

'Peony would have told the nannies your number.'

'This is all irrelevant. I came this evening to talk to you about what you could safely say about this woman's death, but as I say I was too late. Tell me, do you believe I am a murderer?'

'No. But I think Constantin might be, and you might protect him.'

'Constantin has two younger sisters. His parents are dead and he has the full family responsibility for them. They are under close watch by the Securitate, and he knows what will happen to them if he doesn't obey his orders to the letter. I was in the same position myself, until Natalie died.'

'Would he kill someone if they told him?'

'Probably.'

'Would you have?'

'While Natalie was alive, you mean? No. I knew she would have chosen to suffer herself, rather than that.'

'Were you really in Geneva two nights ago? When Laura died?'

He looked her in the eye. His face had not changed, but she felt, as she had in the pizza restaurant at their last meeting, that he had for the moment removed his mask—not for her sake, of course, but for Natalie's, the dead woman whom she so inadequately resembled.

'I was not in England,' he said.

'Was Constantin with you?'

The doorbell rang.

'Better answer it,' he said, rising.

With a hammering heart Poppy switched on the porch light, slid the chain into place and opened the door the few inches it allowed.

The threat was not any of those she had imagined. Mrs Capstone stood on the doormat, holding her face to the light so that she could be recognised. Every glistening wave of her hair was in place.

'May I come in?' she said.

What do you do? Slam the door? Go out and confront her on the doorstep? Have hysterics? Poppy fumbled the chain free and let her in.

'Is my husband here?' said Mrs Capstone, chilly but formal—the chair of some local committee calling on a disruptive member to persuade her to resign, for the good of the cause.

'Yes. Come in.'

Poppy opened the living-room door for her. John was standing by the mantelpiece with his hands in his jacket pockets. He was armoured again, formidable but not perturbed. Amused, if anything.

'Hello, my dear,' he said. 'Mrs Tasker has just accused me of being a murderer.'

Mrs Capstone swung to Poppy, her anger now in the open.

'Then it is you who have been making these stupid calls,' she said.

'What calls? . . . Oh . . . You've been having them too? No. Really . . .'

Her voice trailed off under the glare of disbelief. 'And you and my husband are lovers.'

'Are we . . . I mean . . . I don't . . .'

Poppy turned to John for help and realised that he seemed to be enjoying the confrontation. He had the look of a child who has done something unspeakable, deliberately, in order to become the centre of attention, and isn't remotely embarrassed or ashamed but interested, pleased, stimulated. Derek was like that sometimes.

'This isn't a game!' Poppy snapped.

His eyebrows rose an Olympian, unforgivable fraction. Poppy controlled her fury and returned to Mrs Capstone.

'Your husband and I have made love, once,' she enunciated. 'I don't think it's going to happen again. It wasn't very important to either of us, and it isn't important at all now, in fact it's meaningless compared to what else has been happening.'

'It is not meaningless to me.'

'I'm sorry. I can't help that. But there've been two murders . . .'

'John. Is she quite mad?'

'Far from it. There may well have been two murders. There are indications to make Mrs Tasker believe that I, or Constantin, or both of us in collaboration, may have been involved. Mrs Tasker has told everything she knows to the police. They have already asked to see me.'

He was still enjoying himself, for God's sake! Or was he winding Mrs Capstone up, for his own reasons? If so, she didn't respond in the usual way.

'I see,' she said slowly. 'This is that friend of Peony's, in Barnsley Square? And the man in the play centre, I suppose. What are we going to do? Presumably this will be in the media almost at once. I must know where I stand.'

Her egocentricity was almost heroic. Anger, outrage, betrayal could all be laid aside, at least for the moment, to counter the threat to her career. First things first. What should she say to the journalists?

'Almost inevitably,' said John. 'The police will probably tell them, and to judge by your anonymous calls there are others who seem to know more than we'd like. What did she say to you?'

'I thought she was mad. She said all sorts of things. That you were a murderer, that you and my brother had been importing drugs . . .'

'Jeremy?'

'She said your brother-in-law, but as far as I know Jeremy's the only one you've got. She said you were using Deborah as cover for an affair for someone with grandchildren of her own, someone connected with the play centre, and who was really secretly working for the prospective Labour candidate. The calls were ridiculous rigmaroles, and naturally I paid little attention, though I already had a feeling that you'd started another affair. Then you called this evening to say you'd be late, and I was sure. I'd been paying your Access bill, and I'd noticed the cost of your concert tickets had doubled. I remembered that Mrs Tasker had expressed an interest in music. I thought I would come and see.'

He actually laughed, that peasant laugh of his, seeing the whole thing as comic opera, the philanderer caught in the wardrobe. Mrs Capstone too seemed to be deriving real satisfaction from her position, not of course the weakness of the wronged wife, but the dominance of the unmasker of deceit. How could they, Poppy wondered, increasingly angry, as though Poppy herself, and dead Laura, and all that had happened was no more than a fresh load of corn into the mysterious mill of their relationship?

'Apart from Jeremy she seems to have been remarkably well informed,' said John.

'Nonsense,' said Mrs Capstone. 'She was . . . You are working for the Labour candidate, Mrs Tasker?'

'No. Yes. No. I mean, she's my daughter-in-law and I look after her son. She does pay me, but . . .'

Mrs Capstone stared and drew breath for an outburst, but Poppy got in first.

'Listen,' she said. 'You've got to tell the police about your calls, if you haven't already. Especially that bit about the drugs.'

'What on earth are you talking about?'

'I'm sure it was Laura. She was the one who knew about me and Janet. I don't know what she meant about the drugs, but she meant something. Inspector Firth specifically asked me if I'd come across anything . . .'

'My brother is a Major-General.'

'I shall have to tell the police if you won't. I've already told them about my calls.'

'You'll admit to having an affair with my husband?'

'I told him that too.'

'Either you are behaving totally irresponsibly or this is all part of a deliberate campaign. I am beginning to think that you did indeed make these telephone calls, just as you are making these ridiculous accusations about murder and drugs. You insinuated yourself into my household . . .'

'I didn't. You told Peony . . .'

'Mrs Tasker and I met by chance at a concert,' said John.

'How do you know it was by chance?' said Mrs Capstone.

'We were further drawn together by a shared dislike of pig farming.'

Poppy rounded on him. She had been able to control her anger with Mrs Capstone by a partial understanding, almost a sympathy with her behaviour. Confronted with a failure in her private affairs she resorted to the weapons of the area in which she was confident of success. Her accusations against Poppy were like the point-scoring of the hustings, slung out to wound, without any expectation of belief by anyone who bothered to think about them. John was different. Facing the not quite smiling mask Poppy found her anger bursting out in a shriek.

'For God's sake! Can't you be serious!'

He shrugged, invulnerable even to that. No, not quite invulnerable, because the sheer volume of the shriek had produced a momentary flicker of calculation before the look of calm detachment settled back into place. He was winding her up, she suddenly realised, as well as Mrs Capstone, but not just for his own amusement. The confrontation suited him. He wanted her angry, too angry to think, too angry to remember . . . She remembered.

'Where was Constantin the night before last?' she said.

'What's that got to do with it?' said Mrs Capstone. 'I will not be distracted . . .'

'Where was Constantin the night before last?' shouted Poppy.

'Please,' said John, holding up his large hands, palms half-turned in, in a calming gesture. 'Mrs Tasker is right, my dear. We are not being serious. I will try to explain my behaviour. Give me a few minutes, please.'

'I don't see . . .' said Mrs Capstone.

'Please,' he said again, looking at her from under his heavy brows. She stared back, nodded and settled on to the arm of the sofa, falling as if by instinct into a pose which you could imagine seeing in the back pages of a Sunday supplement, this week's article in the series about how stylish people deal with the straying spouse. Poppy, by contrast, felt all tatters and confusion. They watched in silence while John moved round the room, picking up and inspecting the bases of ornaments, removing several books at a time from shelves and feeling into the cavity behind, glancing behind picture frames. He paid special attention to the music centre, the TV and the light-fittings and finished by unplugging the telephone jack. In the end he faced them with a sigh. His whole demeanour had changed.

'That's the best I can do,' he said. 'We'll have to assume that your caller was this Laura, and her choosing to ring when she did was a coincidence. Well, I'm going to have to tell you some of what I've been doing, though I'd very much rather not, for your sakes as well as mine. Neither of you will tell anyone else. I mean that. I know I can trust you not to, for a very simple reason. You've both, I believe, guessed that Constantin is a member of the Romanian secret police, the Securitate. He's not simply there to keep an eye on me. He is a trained assassin, and he's under orders that on receipt of a particular message he is to kill me and my family—you, Clara, Deborah and myself. I have been told this in so many words by my employers, but I've not been told the circumstances in which the message might be sent. You understand?'

Poppy felt blank, useless. In a way it would have been easier to accept if the threat had included her, and even Toby. She was a passenger in a car on a motorway where there's been a pile-up in the opposite direction, free only to stare or look away, and to shudder.

'Why didn't you tell me before?' said Mrs Capstone briskly. 'We must have him deported.'

She was still in the same pose, interested, aware, concentrating, but apparently not really troubled. It was as though she believed what John had told her but somehow still didn't imagine it. It didn't belong as a possible event in her world.

'No,' said John. 'For several reasons. Doing that might cause the message I told you to be sent. There will in any case be a back-up. Then my business activities, and that means our income, depend on Constantin being available. This is even truer, though Constantin doesn't know it, of what I hope is going to happen in a few weeks' time. My employers, who are effectively the family and associates of President Ceaușescu, whom Mrs Tasker and I have just been watching, have been systematically defrauding the Romanian economy for the past decade and more, and transferring the money to Swiss bank accounts. I am their main agent for this activity. For most of the period, until Natalie died, they had a satisfactory hold over me. Since then they have used Constantin. He is not only there to keep an eye on me and be a threat to me, but also because they have so organised their affairs that no serious transaction can take place without his presence. It's done by means of a voice-lock, which responds to him, and no one else, speaking the passwords. They have me, they think, in an inescapable bind. But they are mistaken.

'The situation is about to change. Very soon. By Christmas, I believe. The commentator in the news programme was saying that of all the countries in Eastern Europe only Albania and Romania will retain their authoritarian regime. I am convinced that in the case of Romania he is wrong. I have very good contacts, much better than those of the professional news analysts, better than those of the diplomats. There will be a revolution in Romania, different from the revolutions elsewhere, more sudden, more violent. Soon.

'Wait. There's something else, of equal importance to you, and me, Clara. Constantin is not a loyal servant of the regime. He would get out if he dared, but the regime has his sisters for hostages. His dream is to run a small hotel in Crete. But he has seen and believes he knows the apparent strength of the apparatus of control in Romania. He cannot believe in the possibility of revolution. I could try to persuade him. I could say "It's going to happen, and we must be ready for it." He would be tempted, but he wouldn't believe he could risk it. He would choose the apparently safer course of denouncing me to his employers. So I'm forced to wait until the moment when there comes what the astronauts call a window of opportunity—I shall have three days at the most—when Romania is in turmoil and Constantin can be persuaded that the revolution has indeed come, but before my employers are able to make good their escape and take possession of the enormous sums of money they've been salting away.'

'No,' said Mrs Capstone. 'Not if it's illegal. Not in any country. I've always said that. I can't afford it.'

'It won't be illegal. It won't even be dishonest. I'm a businessman, not a thief. I told you, the sums involved are enormous. A reasonable commission on removing them from the control of their employers and holding them safe until they can be returned to their rightful owners, the people of Romania, will be more than satisfactory. But even that is not my main motive. I have waited sixteen years for this chance, though for a long while I didn't clearly see the shape it was going to take. Only I was sure the time would come. I was born stateless, parentless, homeless, but I can't live without allegiances, so I've had to construct my own—to my family, and to this country of which I am now a citizen, but also to an almost imaginary country which I barely recognised was there when I lived in it, but which I know to exist by having met certain of its citizens—Natalie first and foremost, but also some monks who used to run an orphanage, a husband and wife who kept an illegal lodging-house in Bucharest, a priest or two, a captain of police in a small town, and others like them. Now, at last, I have my chance to help make this imaginary country real. Do you see how much it matters?'

He had spoken slowly in his low, grating voice, talking, Poppy realised, as much to her as to his wife. Was what he'd said true? Probably, she thought, though it couldn't be as simple as that. Did it make any difference, apart from making everything more difficult . . . ?

'You really think it will work?' said Mrs Capstone.

'Until this other business came up I would have said the chances were very good. Even the bankers, I believe, would have considered it a satisfactory result. Now, of course, the outcome is less certain. It depends, I suppose, on where Constantin was the night before last.'

'You don't know?' said Poppy.

'He was supposed to be with you,' said Mrs Capstone at the same moment.

'I believed he was in Portsmouth,' said John, 'staying with a woman called Bronwen. I had arranged for them to meet, a few weeks ago. Bronwen has worked in a hotel, and expresses a longing to live in Crete. I pay her a small retainer. I told you he wasn't at heart a loyal servant of the regime. On occasions when I don't need him to operate the voice-lock he has been dropping me at the airport and then driving on to Portsmouth. If he was with Bronwen then he couldn't have been in London, murdering this woman . . .'

'Nobody has told me why he, or you, or anyone should want to kill somebody else's nanny,' said Mrs Capstone.

'In a minute,' said John. 'It's very important to me that my employers shouldn't learn that on some occasions I've been leaving Constantin behind. On this last trip, for instance, I was meeting the people who I hope are going to see that his sisters are safe, when the time comes. That could put our lives at serious risk, as well as ruining my plans. As for our supposed motive, I too would be glad to have that explained.'

'Oh,' said Poppy. 'Well, you see, the man in the park, I'm almost sure it was him who followed you that evening, after we'd come back here for supper. You were very excited at first, then you pretended not to be interested. You thought you'd shaken him off, but he recognised you. He lived in a squat at Sabina Road. There was a photograph of you both on the notice-board. He was a rather hopeless, stupid young man. He wanted to impress the people at Sabina Road by finding out something important about Mrs Capstone. He'd have done just what he did here, gone and hung around your house and watched. Then perhaps he saw Constantin washing the car or something, and tried to get into conversation with him, pretending to know more than he did—the people at Sabina Road held briefing sessions on their political opponents, so he'd have some idea. And then Constantin might have decided he was dangerous, and simply got rid of him. Pretended to be friends, followed him back to Sabina Road, found out about the set-up there, and so on. But you see Laura knew the man—I think he'd been one of the babies she'd looked after. She was telling him things she'd picked up at the play centre—I mean the girls do talk, and she'd suddenly become much more friendly—and he must have told her about you visiting me. She was terribly upset when he died, and she started making all these accusations, and she asked Peony and Deborah to tea and I expect she said things then, and Peony would have told . . . oh! That's important. Is Peony all right?'

'As far as I know she's in Runcorn,' said Mrs Capstone. 'She was extremely upset by this woman's death—as you say she'd been to tea with her only a few days earlier. Then she came to me and told me her mother was ill. I didn't believe her, but she was upsetting Deborah, so I packed her off home. She was in any case having the weekend off. I expect her back on Monday. I hope you are not planning to involve her in this tiresome business.'

Oh, God, thought Poppy. She glanced at John, and had the impression that he'd looked away as she did so. She felt at the end of her strength. She couldn't face the prospect of outraging Mrs Capstone still further with the possibility that her nanny was having an affair with her chauffeur, who'd then used her to get Laura to let him in at Barnsley Square.

Mrs Capstone rose.

'John, do you believe any of this?' she said.

'I suppose it's a possibility. There are certainly members of the Securitate who would kill under such circumstances. In fact I don't believe it of Constantin. I've been watching him for over a year now, remember, and though I don't know what his exact orders are I don't think he would kill anyone in this elaborate fashion. He isn't stupid, but he's vain and lazy. He must be equipped with several simpler methods of assassination. Or he might simply strangle the woman and fake a break-in. So I don't believe it. On the other hand . . .'

'Well, I don't believe a word of it,' said Mrs Capstone. 'It's all supposition. I would like to go home. Are you coming? I have the car.'

'I'll make my own way,' said John, as easily as if discussing arrangements after a lunch-party.

'You can go now if you want,' said Poppy.

He shrugged and followed his wife into the hallway. There was a murmur of voices as the door opened and closed, and she thought he'd taken her at her word and left without even a goodbye, but he came back.

'I'm sorry,' he said.

'It's too late for that. I don't think there's anything to say.'

'About you and me? No. Not now. One day perhaps. But listen. I want to ring Bronwen. Now, on your telephone. You can listen on the extension. She may not be in, of course, but if she is I shall try to find out from her as unobtrusively as I can whether Constantin was with her on Wednesday night. If he wasn't, that's that. I shall have to tell the police what I know. It will be a risk to me and my family, but I'll do my best to counter it. It will prevent my carrying out my plans in Geneva, but I may at least be able to tie the funds up in such a way that the Ceausescus are unable to make use of them until a legitimate Romanian government is in place. If, on the other hand, Constantin was with Bronwen . . .'

'Then everything's all right and he can tell the police.'

'That's exactly what I don't want. The danger is that it will get back to his employers and they will realise that he's no more to be trusted than I am. So I'll have arrangements to make. They won't be exactly straightforward . . .'

'I don't want to know.'

'I don't propose to tell you. But I will ask you, if you are convinced by what she says, and that therefore Constantin couldn't have done what you suspect him of, that you should keep to yourself everything I've told you this evening.'

Wearily Poppy tried to think it through. If Constantin . . . all that . . . yes, but there was something else . . .

'I still think your wife should tell them what Laura said about the drugs.'

'She was half mad, rambling.'

'Everything else meant something.'

'All right. I'll talk to Clara. Otherwise . . . ?'

'She's in your pay?'

'Bronwen? And I could have known about all this, and arranged in advance for Bronwen to provide an alibi? Yes, I could. You'll just have to make up your own mind.'

'All right.'

The ringing tone went on and on. The woman wasn't in. Nothing would be resolved. Or he'd dialled a different number, where he'd known there'd be no one there . . .

A voice snapped, 'Better be good. I was in the bath.'

'I'm sorry,' said John.

The voice changed tone. No Welsh lilt. Sharp, but lively.

'Oh, it's you. Had a good trip? Get what you want?'

'I think so. I tried to ring Constantin on Wednesday night, latish . . .'

'Wednesday? Day before . . . Oh, we were in. We were in all right. I'd of taken the phone out.'

She chuckled at the memory.

'Fancies his food, doesn't he?' she said. 'Good thing I like garlic too. When's next time?'

'I'm not sure yet. I'll let you know. How's the cash holding out?'

'Not a lot left.'

'I'll send you some more.'

'Ta. That all?'

'I think so.'

'OK. See you soon.'

Poppy put the telephone down. Constantin had been in Portsmouth on Wednesday night, then . . . and, yes, before he'd left he must have said something to Peony, told her (brutally, perhaps—he was the type) where he was going, and why . . . Not just brutally? Deliberately? Was he organising an alibi, while some colleague of his disposed of Laura? Did John know that too? Was that why he'd gone abroad so suddenly? But in that case why muck around pretending to be in Geneva . . . ?

No. The missile had come to earth, detonated, caused the predictable ruin all around. Only the target had been elsewhere.

8

There was a mystery about Saturdays which Poppy had never resolved. Some streets nearly emptied themselves of parked cars, every household having migrated to some country retreat, causing whole urban vistas to change as the original proportions between road, pavement and buildings came back into uncluttered view. That was explicable. But why should other streets, not much different in apparent wealth and social level, actually fill up, with inconsiderate double parking, leaving the owners of imprisoned vehicles to start the neighbourhood's day with flurries of honking as they tried to draw the attention of whoever had jammed them in? Poppy's street was one of those. She woke to the infuriated sound and lay looking up at the ceiling. The fury had existed in her sleep, an apoplectic staff officer with a panto-size syringe, farcically phallic now but full of menace in the memory, injecting drugs into a window-dresser's naked dummy, which then began to twitch with life.

No one will ever love me again, she thought. I shall never get a job. Janet will get into Parliament and I shall go on looking after Toby till he's too old, and then I'll become like one of his cuddly toys, once loved and depended on, now, though still in a vague way thought of as loved, irrelevant.

She got up and went into the kitchen. Twenty to eight, a soft, calm morning by the look of it. A good day for a country walk. Elias was attentive, but only in the hope of food. You couldn't call that love. She drank pineapple juice, ate muesli, made strong tea. Poppy Tasker, she thought. Idiotic name. Lot of idiotic names about. Why do women marry people and give themselves idiotic names? Clara Capstone for God's sake! Mrs Gally! The Hon. Mrs . . . of course the Hon. made a difference to some people—maybe you'd be able to stomach a bit of stupidity for an Hon. Now if Hugo had had an Hon. would Janet . . . ?

In the middle of these ramblings the name slipped into Poppy's mind. Mrs Ogham-Ferrars. Just like that, without the style or husband's name. Somebody had said it. She was having a party. They didn't want a lot of kids rioting through. Sue. Little Sue. 'I've got Mrs Ogham-Ferrars staying—Pete's gran . . .'

The scene swam back into memory, the clamour inside the play-centre hut, Toby experimenting with ribbon and the plastic engine, Deborah glorying in her scream, Nelson coming for the ravished tortoise, the clatter from the Lego table, even the odour of that longed-for rain on the parched turf outside. Sue coming up and giving her message to Nell. And earlier to Big Sue, with Laura listening. And Laura's face.

They'd called him Jonathan at the Sabina Road squat. It sounded right. Jonathan Ogham-Ferrars. And Mrs Simpson was his sister. Quite a bit older. Jonathan had been an afterthought, like Pete (how such patterns run in families). Laura had been hired to look after him. Her first baby.

And the scene in the playroom at Linen Walk, when Laura had looked as if she was about to burst out to Mrs Simpson with some dotty grievance of her own . . . Not dotty. Not at all.

Idiotic names have their uses. There weren't even any Oghams in the London telephone directory, let alone Ogham-Ferrarses. But she was staying, Sue had said—up from the country for a few days, presumably, and seeing some London friends. Quarter past eight. The library wouldn't be open for an hour. She washed up, dressed and did some perfunctory housework. I won't tell anyone till I'm sure, she thought. I'm not going to be a missile this time, ruining lives and hopes and loves, because of a few wild guesses. But it was strange how much better she felt.

Climbing the library stairs to the reference section she remembered the Hon. That meant they'd be in *Debrett*. No need to work through the complete set of telephone directories . . . .

Yes . . .

'Surnames of Peers and Peeresses, where different from title, in order of final names.' . . . '*Ogham-Ferrars: Blissege, B.*' (B for baron.)

BLISSEGE, BARON (Ogham-Ferrars)
Bevis Wibbley Fallowen Ogham-Ferrars, 7th Baron: b. 18 Sept. 1949.

(Much too young. And he lived in Montreal.)

SONS LIVING . . . DAUGHTER LIVING . . . SISTERS LIVING.

UNCLE LIVING (Son of 5th Baron)

(Ah.)

Hon. David Fallowen *b.* 1918; *ed.* Cheltenham Coll., formerly Capt. Rifle Brig. (Prince Consort's Own); *m.* 1950 Brenda Elizabeth da. of Hon. Gerald Penton (*see* Cussington, V.) of Threep Park, Wagley, Salop and has issue Jonathan Fallowen *b.* 1967; Rosemary Ida (14a Mells Parade, Bath) *b.* 1952; Marigold Elizabeth (27 Addison Crescent London W11) *b.* 1954, *m.* 1976 Giles Robert Simpson and has issue Robert Fallowen *b.* 1976, Hugh Michael *b.* 1978, Christopher James *b.* 1981; Susan May *b.* 1956 . . .

1956! What . . . ? Oh, it was all right. A whole generation in a semicolon. Susan was Marigold's *sister.* What had happened to little Pete? Poppy looked at the spine of the volume. 1988, but it would have gone to press the year before, so Pete wouldn't have been born yet. And the Simpsons had been living in Holland Park. Addison Crescent—beautiful houses, selling for a million and a quarter at the height of the boom. They could have cleared more than a million moving to Linen Walk, and they still hadn't had the roofs there fixed. Private education for three boys ate your money up, and so did running a yacht in Turkey and not having a proper job, but not that fast, surely.

Poppy ran her eye down the rest of the paragraph. Susan had married Captain John Tollery and had produced two daughters and a son, and Diana, born in 1958, had married Count Alessandro Fernandez-Boiardelli and was living in New York, apparently childless. The entry ended by returning to the living uncle, the Hon. David Fallowen:

Residence—9 Winchester Road, Abbots Charity, Hants.

Dutifully, then, a succession of daughters, at neat two-year intervals. (What had been Mrs Ogham-Ferrars's recompense in the off years? Skiing, probably. Or sailing, or both.) And then a nine-year gap, and the girls off to school, nannies dispensed with, nursery become a bedroom and then—what a trick of fate it must have seemed—she was almost forty for heaven's sake—this late, unwanted pregnancy. But behold, a boy! Fourth in line for the title! He must bear the full family name, he must have a new, young nanny . . . And Mrs Simpson was Marigold. Rosemary hadn't married, apparently.

Poppy photocopied the page on the library machine and then found a road atlas. Abbots Charity was about five miles from Winchester. She looked out of the window. Still a pleasant, soft-seeming day. It was not yet half-past ten. She put the atlas back and found the railway timetable

Confidence had evaporated well before the train reached Winchester, and been replaced by the sour awareness that all she was doing was trying to run away from what had happened yesterday. What could she possibly do? Knock on the door? 'Excuse me, but have you got a son you've lost touch with? Disowned, maybe? You have! I just thought you'd like to know he's dead.' Ridiculous. Much better simply wander round Winchester, look at the cathedral, or perhaps take a bus a few miles out and walk along lanes for a bit, since she'd brought the shoes and clothes for that.

There were taxis waiting, empty. Other passengers took the first three. While Poppy stood hesitating the driver of the last one sized her up.

'Lost then, love? Winchester not what you expected?'

'I just wanted to go for a walk somewhere.'

'Run you to the edge of the town. Three quid.'

'Oh, all right. Can we go towards Abbots Charity?'

'Any way you want, love. Drop you where you can walk along the river a bit, shall I? It's going to rain, mind you.'

'Thanks. I'll be all right.'

He was fatherly, despite being half a generation younger than her. He took her well beyond the last houses and dropped her off in a lane where a footpath led down to the river. It was early afternoon now. She sat on the trunk of a fallen willow and ate the salad roll she'd bought at Waterloo. The river was about fifteen yards across, shallow all the way, with tresses of dark green weed streaming in the clear, quick water. Trout, or grayling perhaps—she didn't know the difference—moved in the open patches, shadowy, unhurried, as though the current had no effect on them. They didn't have to thresh against it or scurry with it— they just willed their place above the gravel and stayed there. It was like time, Poppy thought. You don't usually feel time streaming past you. You seem to be staying where you want, the same person in the same place for as long as you want, only you aren't, you aren't.

When she moved on she found that the path didn't follow the river all along the bank but twisted away between fields. Where the tractors had used it there were wallows of deep mud she had to pick her way round. The valley air was close and heavy. There was no one about. Too soon after Saturday lunch, probably. About a mile more and it started to rain, lightly at first, but soon a fine but dense, almost stifling, downpour. Not good. Her anorak, though bought as rain-proof, was proof against only the right sort of rain—light, and lasting not more than ten minutes. This rain was clearly going to last all afternoon. She wondered whether to turn back. It shouldn't be more than a mile on into Abbots Charity. There must be a call-box. She could ring for a taxi from there.

The path returned to the river, whose surface was now opaque with rainfall. Poppy squelched on, encouraged by the memory that the village lay on the river so she wasn't going to miss it. There ought to be signs of it now, surely. A figure appeared, moving towards her through the rain, a man, an old man, doddering along under the willows, with no hat, and no coat, and, now that he was almost on her and she could see, a bedroom slipper on one foot, and just a muddy sock on the other. The question about the distance to the village died on her lips.

'Are you all right?' she said.

'Yes, yes,' he muttered gruffly.

'You shouldn't be out in this,' she said.

'Oh, all right, all right, I'll come back. I know when I'm beaten.'

He took her by the shoulder and leaned heavily on her as he limped along. She spotted his other slipper lying in the path and persuaded him to put it on.

'Bloody British weather,' he said. 'Never catch anything except a cold in this, I tell you. What's the point?'

His voice was humorous, military. His limp had become a shuffle. The path joined a road which ran on beside the river. A woman with an umbrella was hurrying away from them in the distance. Something about her gait, the panic and desperation of her movements, made Poppy call out.

'I've got him! He's here!'

The woman turned, peered, and came back towards them.

'Oh, thank God, where was he?' she said.

'Ah, Brenny,' said the man. 'Where've you been all this time? Just popped out to look for you.'

'I found him on the footpath by the river,' said Poppy.

'Oh, darling!' sighed the woman, without reproach but in tones of pure despair. 'He usually goes the other way. Come under my brolly, darling, and we'll take you in and get you dry.'

There was a row of newish brick bungalows by the road, facing the river, only vaguely noticed till now. The woman held the umbrella over the man as they went through the gate of the tidy little garden. There was a 9 on the gatepost. This would be the road to Winchester. The man continued to grip Poppy's shoulder and lean on her. She could feel how exhausted he was, how soon he would fall. The door of the house was open and somehow the three of them, moving together as if in a complex version of a three-legged obstacle race, manoeuvred themselves into the tiny hallway and on into the living-room, where Poppy and the woman, each holding the man by an elbow, lowered him into a chair.

'That's better,' he mumbled. 'Let's have a cup of tea.' 'I'll get some dry clothes,' said the woman. 'Keep an eye on him, will you?'

She left. Poppy removed her anorak. Her clothes were wet through but not actually dripping. The room was very warm—they'd keep it like that for the man.

'Just time for one more dance before the ferry goes,' he said, and fell asleep.

Poppy looked round the room. The green carpet was stained in places, but the furniture was good, walnut and mahogany, with brass fittings. Everything was polished and carefully kept, but the pieces were rather too large, or otherwise inappropriate for the living-room of a new brick bungalow in a row of others at the edge of a village. This was not the social context they had been made for.

The woman came back with pyjamas and dressing-gown and—Poppy already realised that this was typical of her—dry jersey and slacks for Poppy.

'I think we're about the same size,' she said. 'We'll put yours on the boiler.'

'Oh, thank you. But I mustn't stay. If you're all right . . .'

'Nonsense. I think you may have saved my husband's life. He could easily have fallen in the river. Usually he goes the other way, into the village, and someone sees him and brings him back, but you couldn't expect anyone to be out in this. The least we can do is dry you off and then get Tony Waters to drive you home.'

She was kneeling by the man while she spoke, removing his slippers and socks. Then she stood and began to ease his arms out of the sleeves of his jacket. He mumbled occasionally but did nothing to help, so Poppy went to the other side of the chair and together they stripped him of his clothes.

'You're so kind,' said the woman. 'I can do it alone—and when he's awake, of course. But when he's like this it's a bit of a struggle. He used to stand six foot four, you know, and weighed sixteen stone. Not an ounce of fat, either.'

He was soaked right through to his underclothes, thermal vest and long johns.

'I'll do this bit,' said the woman. 'If you wouldn't mind looking the other way for a couple of minutes . . .'

Poppy turned. She could have used the opportunity to put on the dry clothes the woman had brought for her, but she was determined not to stay, to be out of the house as soon as she'd helped get the man dressed again. There was a half-oval table against the wall, with photographs on it in silver frames, the head and shoulders of a handsome young woman, three wedding scenes, grandchildren. Behind her she heard the guggle of an incontinence bag being changed. The bridal couple on the left were the Simpsons, he already balding and bearded, she with her coarse mane, tough little chin and royal-visit smile.

'Those are my daughters,' said the woman by way of a signal that she'd finished with her privacies. 'The eldest never . . .'

'Don't tell me! Don't tell me anything! Please.'

Poppy realised that she'd shouted. She turned and saw that the woman—Mrs Ogham-Ferrars—was staring at her.

'It's all right,' she said. 'I'm not mad. I'll just help you get his clothes on, then I'll go.'

They dressed the man in silence, working easily, like a team who were used to each other. When they'd finished Mrs Ogham-Ferrars took his hand and his fingers closed round hers in his sleep.

'I ought to send for the doctor,' she said, 'but it doesn't seem fair on a Saturday. I don't think he got cold inside. He can't have been out that long. I don't think he's ready to go yet. He's still surprisingly strong, in spite of the operations. Will you tell me what's been going on?'

Poppy stared at her. Mrs Ogham-Ferrars met her gaze with the unrufflable calm of true despair.

'You were coming to see us, weren't you?' she said. 'I think I'd guessed already, but when you shouted just now . . . The police telephoned yesterday, you see, about Laura. They wouldn't tell me anything, but I know it's got something to do with Jonathan. It's always him. I told them he was in Canada. That's what I usually say. What's he done now? Please. I do think I've got a right to know.'

'I'm afraid he's dead.'

Mrs Ogham-Ferrars looked down at her husband.

'I'll tell him,' she said. 'When he's in one of his clear patches. It'll be such a weight off his mind, just for a bit. He won't remember, but perhaps if I keep telling him . . . What happened? Please? I'd much rather find out from you than anyone else.'

Poppy told her everything, except the possibility of the two deaths being murders. Her clothes steamed. The man twitched and muttered in his sleep like a dreaming dog. Mrs Ogham-Ferrars sat on the arm of his chair, one hand still in his and the other round his shoulder. When Poppy had finished she shook her head.

'I sometimes think we loved each other too much,' she said. 'We met at a dance, and by the end of the evening we both knew that neither of us would ever look at anyone else, and we didn't. Even now, when everything seems so dreadful and we're just waiting for the end, I know it's all been worth it. Only really we shouldn't have had any children. We didn't have anything to spare for them. All we wanted was each other, to be together and do and see things together. The girls were fun, of course, when they were small, but Jonathan . . . I should never have gone through with it . . . they had just changed the law, of course, but David . . . there's no point in making things up about what might have happened, is there? And anyway, it's over now. You haven't told me your name.'

'Poppy Tasker.'

'Were you coming to see me?'

'No. I mean, that's what I meant to do when I left London, and then I realised I hadn't got any right, and then . . .'

'I'm glad you did. I'm glad it was you. You'll at least let me give you a cup of tea, won't you, and I'll see if Tony's free to drive you to the station. He's not really a taxi, but he does it for me once a month when my eldest daughter, Rosemary, takes a couple of days off— she's a management consultant and can work as it suits her—and looks after David while I go up and stay at my next daughter's—that's Marigold—I don't know if you know her. She lives quite near you, I suppose, but she isn't often in England.'

'I've met her, and her husband, and I know your grandson quite well because he's in the play-group. He's a very nice little boy.'

'Isn't he? I hardly know the others. I never imagined I'd mind . . . Now I'll put the kettle on if you'll keep an eye on

David. He'll wake up for the tea, and then, for about ten minutes . . . you'll see.'

It worked as she said. At the chink of the tea-tray Mr Ogham-
Ferrars opened his eyes, sat up and looked around.

'Fallen asleep again?' he said. 'Bad sign. Bad sign. Hello, I don't
know you, do I? Been out in the rain? Hey! What the hell am I doing
in my jim-jams? It can't be bedtime yet.'

'You went out for a walk without your mac, darling, and Mrs
Tasker found you and brought you back. You might have fallen in
the river and drowned.'

'Good riddance. Oh, Lord, the things I get up to. Bloody nuisance all round, aren't I? Come to think of it, there was a fellow called
Tasker, ah yes, Djibouti. You remember, Brenny, he'd been in the
Fore-and-Aft alongside me at Salerno, and we worked out we'd actually been taken into the same field hospital on the same bloody day,
only we hadn't met then, and then we go and bump into each other
at Djibouti, of all places. Lord, we had hangovers next day. If ever you
find yourself in Djibouti, Mrs Tasker, don't have a night out on the
local plonk. Brenny swore she was only having a migraine, of course.
Any connection?'

'I don't think so. It would be someone in my husband's family,
but I don't remember any of them being soldiers.'

'Long shot, anyway. Ah, tea. Maketh glad the heart of man, as
that American preacher-fellow used to say. Belonged to a sect who
swore that every word of the Bible was dead true, every darned word
of it, except when it had anything good to say about alcohol. Know
what the good Lord did by way of a miracle at Cana, Mrs Tasker? He
turned bread into raisin cake. Fact.'

He lifted his cup with quivering hands and sucked enthusiastically
at it. Life energy shone from him, not just in the rattling anecdotes

but in the feeling he gave of enjoyment of everything that happened, the hot liquid, the company, his memories, even the fact of his having gone rambling and helpless off in the rain. You could see what fun he must have been as a companion, easy and sweet-natured, and how Mrs Ogham-Ferrars could complete a wholly self-sufficient pairing with him; and now how the memory of such a life could give her the courage to see it through with dignity.

'And what are you doing in these promiscuous parts, Mrs Tasker? Not that our charming little river has much in common with the great grey greasy Limpopo, eh?'

'I was just out for a walk and got caught in the rain,' said Poppy. 'And then I bumped into you and your wife was kind enough to ask me in.'

'Of course, of course. Ah, well.'

And the flame had died, without even a last flicker. Mrs Ogham-Ferrars took his cup from him and put it on the tray, then gave him a digestive biscuit which he broke in two and ate slowly. They drank their tea in silence. A car hooted in the road.

'That'll be Tony,' said Mrs Ogham-Ferrars. 'Are you sure I can't lend you some clothes? You could always take them down to Marigold's and I could collect them on my next jaunt.'

'No, it's all right. I'm almost dry. Goodbye, Mr Ogham-Ferrars.'

He mumbled what might have been a farewell. Mrs Ogham-Ferrars went with her to the door.

'I suppose I ought to tell someone about Jonathan,' she murmured. 'Marigold's still in England. She could go and identify the body. She wouldn't mind.'

'Do you know who to ring?'

'The policeman left me a number. He had an odd name.'

'Caesar?'

'That's it.'

'Ask to talk to Detective Inspector Firth, if you can. He's very sympathetic, I think. And if you can get away without saying anything about me being here . . .'

'I'll see. And thank you for coming, Mrs Tasker. Goodbye. And . . . oh, I don't know if I ought to say this, but I'm going to. Don't waste a second. Not one second. It's all so precious, and there's never as much of it as you think.'

'Yes, I know.'

The train was fairly empty and Poppy had a four-seat section to herself all the way to London. Passengers got on, but none of them seemed to fancy sitting with a bedraggled, wet-wool–smelling middle-aged woman. Poppy thought about time, and there never being as much of it as you think, and the trout, or perhaps grayling, in the river. David Ogham-Ferrars would have been a child like Toby, she fancied. Very like Toby, handsome, strong, eager, intelligent, thoughtful, experimental. With Janet's genes in him Toby could grow to six foot four, sixteen stone, and not an ounce of fat. You could put the two images into either end of a family album and almost without further help reconstruct the arching life between. Not really, of course, any more than you could put, say, little Pete Simpson and dead Jonathan at the opposite ends of some short and ill-built span and know that that was what must happen. Being an afterthought, an accident, with a doting nanny and uninvolved parents didn't necessarily make you an inadequate, or a paedophile. It might drive you instead to self-sufficiency, ambition, achievement. Marigold Simpson, for instance—of course she'd had siblings nearer her own age, and had had to compete with them for affection and attention, the scraps and leavings of their parents' passion for each other. Hence the chin, and the will, and the chilliness.

Was it doomed to happen in certain families, generation after generation, passed on, almost as if in the genes, this stunting? Even Toby? Could you see it already latent in him, and trace it back through Hugo's coldness and Janet's outward-turning energies, and then through Poppy and Derek (they'd chosen each other, after all, and not just for a shared interest in music, surely) right back to Poppy herself being an afterthought, late-born, fatherless, and with a mother obsessed at first with her ailments and then with her Old Spots? Was this what the mutterer beneath the stairs foresaw?

Poppy shook herself inwardly, though the train was for once well heated and she was steaming peacefully. She wasn't going to start brooding yet again on her own emotional inadequacies, without even a gin bottle to hand. She'd walked that path too often. Yes, she'd been too timid to give her emotions much chance, but one day . . . One day soon it would have to be . . . stop it!

The Simpsons. Had they literally not been aware that Jonathan was living, and had died, so close? Well, they hadn't been in England that much, and the family seemed to have written him out of their lives (his mother usually told people he was in Canada—no photograph on the half-oval table) and you couldn't imagine Mr Simpson wanting to have much to do with such a brother-in-law .

'Brother-in-law.'

The still-damp hair on Poppy's nape prickled erect. She was aware of having spoken the words aloud—the man across the aisle had glanced up from his crossword. She dropped her eyes and gazed at her folded hands. Not John Capstone's brother-in-law—Jonathan's. Laura had just said 'his'. The him in her life was Jonathan, but Mrs Capstone had understood it as the him in her own life. John and Mr Simpson were bringing heroin into the country together.

No. Not John. She made the effort of trust and reconstructed in her mind what had happened the evening before. His excitement had been real. Something was about to happen, soon, involving a lot of money; he could even have prepared his speech about his Romania of the mind; much of what he'd said could have been true, merely omitting the fact that one of the sources of his employers' treasure hoard was using diplomatic bags and such to smuggle drugs—they certainly weren't above that, by the sound of it. But no. It still didn't fit. It was like a piece of a jigsaw which you try and try to lock into the obvious-seeming place, but one small projection refuses to locate—not anything John had said, but Mrs Capstone. 'Not if it's illegal. Not in any country. I've always said that. I can't afford it.' Of course John could have been cheating on her still, but he wasn't. That was an absolute. Laura had just been lashing out, accusing everyone of whatever Jonathan might have told her.

Still, he must have told her something, about someone. The Simpsons, for instance. What did they do for a living? They lived in a little house close to the railway, its roof leaking in several places, but at the same time they kept a yacht in Turkey and sent three children to boarding-schools—and where was all the money they must have made from the house in Addison Crescent?

Mr Simpson, standing by the rain-smeared window:

'What did he look like, then? White? Yellow? Green?' A weird question, unless he already knew, knew how Jonathan had died, wanted to check that the signs of apparent suicide were still visible. And Marigold Simpson too, how quickly she'd snatched at the notion of accident or suicide, and the body being moved. How unextraordinary it had seemed to her. She'd known, too. She'd known . . . actually eased the needle into the vein with her own steady hands while he held her brother still? . . . Shadows, imaginings, but they'd known all the same, both of them, how Jonathan had died.

Doomed, hopeless, inadequate Jonathan. Ah, let him at least have been happy, once, for a while, happy in his bond with solemn young Laura, complete to each other for those first few years. He'd have been too young to remember, but still . . . let it have been the case. (Can you pray for something to have happened, in the past? She still hadn't sent a Christmas card to her brother Philip in his seminary—it would be something to ask him, for once. He'd know.) No photographs anywhere, no images, no imprint. They'd taken the ones Laura had hoarded, all her past too, the pictures of other families who had been her life. There'd been no time to pick and choose. All gone.

Poppy found a damp handkerchief and pretended to mop her face with it, removing the gathered tears in passing. It was dark now outside, the train swaying through suburbs, past lit back windows, every bright rectangle signalling a set of lives, unknowable. A figure against the light, young, but boy or girl? The gesture expostulation or boasting or laughter? You could picture a parent sitting at a table, a checked oilcloth on it . . . but already you were into the realm of fiction, the odds against your imagination mapping any actuality too high to be worth thinking about. How different were her guesses about the Simpsons? How much more damage might she do, even if she happened to have guessed right?

She thought of Mrs Ogham-Ferrars, with whom she'd felt such instant and admiring affinity, a really lovely woman fighting to cherish her husband's last few scraps of worthwhile life. No hope, not much money (never had that much, probably, and spent it all living the life they'd wanted, plus the wedding expenses of three daughters). How much more could she bear? Learning that her son-in-law had killed two people, one of them her son, and that her daughter had helped him? Having to give evidence? The thought was appalling.

I shan't do anything about it, Poppy thought as the train eased at last into Waterloo. Mrs Ogham-Ferrars will tell the police that Marigold can identify the body and they'll learn about the connection that way. Then they'll start to ask questions. They'll work it out themselves. It's all in the past. It's nothing to do with me any more. I shall go home and have a deep, hot bath and decide what to do with the rest of my life. There's never as much of it left as you think.

JANUARY 1990

Crowds on streets again, but not peaceful. The camera jerked and wavered, snatching at images. Gunfire rattled off-shot. Groups huddled into doorways. A body lay face up, arms spread, crucified to the earth. Three exhausted men were dragged from some hole and hauled away. Securitate the voice-over said, being taken to military courts, but it looked as if the noose would get them first. This was Romania, and it was different. John had been right. He couldn't have known, not this. There must have been something else, something planned.

The bell rang. Poppy turned the sound down and went to the door. She felt excited, confident, amused at herself in her new role, She-who-knows-what-she-wants-and-is-going-to-get-it. Mr Firth was waiting on the doorstep. She took his drizzle-dampened coat and hat, led him into the living room and gave him the magnet. He flipped it up and down in his palm.

'Thank you very much,' he said. 'I'd forgotten I'd only lent it to him. I've survived without it, somehow.'

'It was just an excuse to get you here,' said Poppy. 'I hope you'll stay and have a drink. It's all right—I shan't ask you to talk work.'

He showed no reluctance or surprise. She had phrased her telephone call carefully, so that he could understand, if he chose, that this was what she had in mind.

'There's not much choice, I'm afraid,' she said. 'Gin or red wine.'

'I'd like wine, please.'

That was a good omen. She'd guessed his tastes and bought a bottle of Rioja. He settled into the armchair and tried to persuade Elias to come and be petted. Elias cut him dead. He didn't seem to mind.

'Did you manage to see your daughters over Christmas?' she said.

'They came down for a couple of days in the New Year. It went as well as you'd expect. I don't know how to talk to them. I wish I could understand their tastes in music. It would probably have been the same if the family had stayed together, I suppose, if not worse. They're not bad kids, and as it is they feel they've got to make some sort of an effort for me, whereas if we'd been living in each other's pockets, not hitting it off . . . How's young Toby?'

'Boisterous. Talking away.'

'Driving everyone mad with questions, I expect.'

'Oh no, not Toby. Toby *tells* you. I think he was trying to explain to me in the park today that the trees were there because a helicopter had come and put them there. Helicopters can do no wrong at the moment.'

'It's a marvellous age.'

'For the lucky ones.'

'Yes, we've got a vile little case come up in Widmore Street—you don't want to know about that.'

'Not really. But I do worry about Nick. Mary Pitalski's son, I mean—I must have read the father's name somewhere, but I've forgotten.'

'Lewis.'

'Oh, of course. I rang a couple of times last month but only got an answerphone. They haven't been to the play centre. Do you know?'

'I'm off the case now. Internal police politics. But I sat in for a bit, handing over. Last I heard the kids had gone down to Lewis's mother, somewhere near Chichester. He keeps a boat there.'

'They usen't to take Laura?'

'She didn't get on with Mrs Lewis. Granny had views, know what I mean?'

'Do I not! My mother-in-law . . . No, I'll let you off her . . . So Laura could stay in London and meet Jonathan?'

'In the Shepherds Bush MacDonald's. The staff remember them well. They'd stay for hours and she'd keep buying things and trying to persuade him to eat something . . . Was it you told Mrs Ogham-Ferrars to get in touch with me?'

'I asked her not to say.'

'She didn't. But she wouldn't talk to Bob Caesar. It had to be me. And she hasn't time to read the papers.'

'Did you actually see her?'

'I went down. Last thing I did before the hand-over, as a matter of fact.'

'I'm glad you met her. I thought she was marvellous. I can't bear to think what she must be going through now, on top of everything else, knowing about her daughter. It's like Faust, or something, having to pay at the end for all the good things you've had before. And knowing it was partly things she'd told you herself.'

'I'm afraid so, but I don't agree about Faust. All that's just random, as far as I can see. I know one old boy whose life had been mostly hell—orphanage, married just in time for the war, Jap POW camp, came back to find his wife had bolted, leaving him with a daughter—probably not his, but he took her on. Never any money. Daughter turned out schizophrenic, and hanged herself, and so on and so on. He was living next door to a Pakistani couple. He'd had a leg off and was starting to go blind. The Khans gave him a hand, and gradually took him over. Not entirely altruistic—they've spread into his spare rooms, but they treat him right. He goes along to the mosque, and so on. So his last five years haven't been too bad, but if he'd never met the Khans he'd still be in hell, or dead. You can't point to him as an argument for wisdom and serenity being the reward for a life of suffering, any more than you can with Mrs Ogham-Ferrars the other way round. Do you want to know about the rest of it?'

'I'm sure you're not supposed to tell me.'

He shrugged.

'You won't pass it on.'

'Won't they want me for a witness?'

'Only if they want to bring up about the man who followed you being the same chap. I doubt it. They've got a lot of stuff. The drugs people were on to Simpson, you see, coming from the other end, so to speak. They'd had an eye on him since a few years back, when they got wind he'd been doing some small-scale drug-running out of Turkey. That seems to have been a sort of trial run, to make the right contacts and so on. Then he lay low for a bit, and then, last year, somebody seems to have staked him with real money . . .'

'They sold a house in Addison Crescent and moved to Linen Walk—at least that was their address in last year's *Debrett*, but it didn't have little Pete in it, so it must have gone to press before he was born. They could have cleared a lot of money—it depends on mortgages and things—but getting on for a million, I'd think.'

'That would be about right. Anyway he bought a bigger boat and set up a serious operation. He didn't know our people were watching him. He was all ready to go when *that* blew up.'

He nodded towards the TV. The documentary Poppy had been watching had flashed back to the Berlin Wall coming down.

'What's that got to do with it?' she said.

'You'd be surprised. You don't read about it, but one result of the frontiers opening up is that new routes became available for getting drugs through to the West. Heroin's the main one.'

Oh God, thought Poppy. John Capstone. Had Laura been right about *everything*? Her shock must have shown, to judge by his look of query.

'Did Mrs Capstone tell you about her telephone calls?' she said.

'Did she not! Ah, yes, I see what you mean. No, it looks as if your friend's in the clear. I'm afraid that's all I'd better tell you about that side of things.'

'Oh . . . Look, this really isn't why I asked you round—I'm not seeing him any more, as it happens—but well, the evening after I'd come and told you what I knew, he was here—Mrs Capstone turned up as well—and between us we made him tell us what he was really up to—you know, why he wanted me to lie about him being followed, and so on. If he was telling us the truth, and I really do think he was, then it was worth it. I'm not being inquisitive, it's just so frustrating not knowing what happened in the end. Whether he brought it off, I mean. Do you know? Do you even know what I'm talking about?'

'I'm glad that in your opinion it was worth it,' he said, very drily indeed. 'I won't ask you to tell me any more. This was one of the reasons I was taken off the case. No policeman likes to be told what questions he can and can't ask.'

'I'm sorry.'

Once, years ago, Poppy had seen a whale. A client of Derek's had offered them an almost-free Caribbean cruise in a merchant ship fitted with a few passenger cabins. Derek's response to the material realities that underlay his business had been to retreat into the sphere of total abstraction and attempt to write a thesis on the philosophy of music, though both he, in his heart, and Poppy too, knew that he wasn't intellectually up to it. His failure to achieve what he wanted came out as irritation with her, so she spent much of her time alone, and coming to terms for the first time with the knowledge that she didn't, after all, love him, nor he her. Waking early one morning she had gone on deck to watch the sun rise. Down there in the tropics it seemed to take only a few minutes for night to become day. The stars went, the sea silvered, in the distance like stretched silk, taut to the horizon, but close to the hull moving in immense slow undulations, still with that same glossy, tense surface that looked as if it could carry weight. Then, twenty yards from the ship, without a ripple of forewarning, the surface had blistered, risen to a mottled, sliding hump, which narrowed, rose clear, and only as the huge flukes had plunged out of sight had Poppy understood what she'd seen.

In a way the encounter with John Capstone had been like that. He wasn't the whale. The whale was the incomprehensible forces of control which have their lives below the visible surface of events. Such momentary revelations are all most of us will ever know of them. She had been very close indeed, very lucky. Perhaps her life had been changed, as she felt it had been by the whale.

'You were explaining about drugs,' she said.

'Oh, yes, I was talking in general terms,' said Mr Firth. 'Drug dealing's a business as well as a criminal activity. There are cartels, multinationals, spot markets and so on. You won't find many pro-Gorbachevs among the big dealers. All he's done for them is unsettle the trade, and when that happens it isn't the lawyers they send for. There's been some rough stuff, and the syndicate Simpson had been in touch with to handle his goods was one of the ones that lost out. He'd come home, urgently, to see what else he could set up. He must have been extremely jumpy. He can't have relished hearing from Jonathan at that point—Laura must have kept up with their movements and told Jonathan.'

'No,' said Poppy. 'She heard Little Sue at the play centre talking about Mrs Ogham-Ferrars. I saw her face. She hadn't realised till then who the Simpsons were. There's lots of Simpsons around, and she wouldn't have expected them to have a baby as young as Pete.'

'You know, the drugs people say it was a difficulty pregnancy. They did a lot of flying to and fro, for check-ups. She's a real tough.'

'You're saying she started another baby as sort of cover! If that's true, it's, I don't know . . . What a reason for being born!'

'You want us all to be children of love? I know I wasn't, for a start.'

'I think I was conceived because my father knew he was going to be killed in the war. But do you know what's happened to Pete? Big Sue at the play centre says Little Sue took him down to his aunt— that would be Susan, I think Tollery, wasn't it?—but she wants to adopt him herself.'

'Not my pigeon. I could find out.'

'It's all right. I'll ask Big Sue again. I've just thought of something. Little Sue would have told Laura when the Simpsons were back—just play-centre gossip—and she'd have passed it on to Jonathan. But where had he been? Why didn't he know about the Simpsons before?'

'He was in Canada, then the States. Mrs Ogham-Ferrars was extremely open about him. She says he was a sweet, quiet, timid child but then he became a difficult adolescent. He was thrown out of several schools. He had a minor drugs problem but managed to stay out of trouble. A few summers back he went out for a holiday with the Simpsons in the Aegean, there was some sort of row and he split up with them and disappeared. This turns out to have been just about the time when Simpson was doing his earlier drug runs. The next thing Mrs Ogham-Ferrars knew was when Laura got in touch saying Jonathan was now an addict and she was looking after him but she'd had to give up her job to do it and she needed some money. They hadn't any money to spare, so in the end they sold their home and moved to Abbots Charity. They sent Jonathan to a private rehabilitation centre, and otherwise allowed Laura to take charge.'

'I expect she was the only person who could deal with him.'

'It wasn't just that. Mr Ogham-Ferrars had been getting a bit absent-minded, she says, not enough to worry about, you'd expect it at his age, and so on. The move seems to have tipped him over the edge.'

'It's like a family curse, isn't it?'

'Again, I can't think like that. I just know it's a pattern with old people near the edge, when they move out of some familiar set-up. Anyway, Mrs Ogham-Ferrars had her hands full, and she left things to Laura. Jonathan was cured of his addiction, but after that things didn't work out. The Ogham-Ferrarses couldn't afford to go on supporting him and Laura indefinitely, but that's what he expected and Laura backed him up. Nothing was ever his fault, in her eyes. He'd turn up at Abbots Charity and simply yell at them. Mrs Ogham-Ferrars says she thinks Laura was egging him on, because she wanted him for herself. And it had such a distressing effect on her husband that in the end she had to hide away anything that might remind him of Jonathan.'

'It makes one's own problems seem nothing at all.'

'A lot of my work's like that. It's one of the things my wife found difficult. In the end Mrs Ogham-Ferrars saw nothing for it but to stop the arrangement. There's a nephew in Canada who found Jonathan a job, and they shipped him out, but of course it didn't stick and he bummed around for a while. That's when he seems to have started taking an interest in children. There was a so-called orphanage in Philadelphia where he worked, illegally of course—he hadn't got any papers—Laura used to get postcards from Philadelphia according to Mary Pitalski—but last spring it blew up into a public scandal with local politicians involved. He was lucky just to get slung out as an illegal immigrant.'

'I keep seeing him in my mind's eye as a child Toby's age, or Nick's, or Pete's. It seems so unfair.'

'The hardest thing for us to accept about the universe is its sheer bloody randomness. Our minds are programmed to look for reasons, for patterns, for purposes, for justice. They're simply not there. If we want them we have to create them. Justice is a man-made thing, like a toothbrush. If I do my job right Toby, and my own grandchildren if I've the luck to have them, will grow up in a marginally juster universe. But it will still be local, trivial, weightless compared to the massive randomness of the rest of things.'

'You don't believe there's a God?'

'I wouldn't know. But if there is, he's looking the other way.'

'How can you live with such a depressing outlook? I know I couldn't.'

'I don't find it depressing. Quite the opposite. The fact that I can make minuscule differences, that I can create my scrap of justice—you've got a lot of tapes, haven't you? You listen quite a bit?'

'Yes. All the time. What they call standard classics, though I'm prepared to be a bit more adventurous when I feel up to it.'

'Jupiter Symphony?'

'Yes, of course.'

'Why does that matter to us? I'm not saying what is it, but why do we care? We care because it's an assertion that it is possible to create patterned, elaborate, multi-dimensional forms of order by extracting particular sounds from the random noise of the universe. It's not immortal. If it had only been played once and then forgotten it would still have mattered. There must have been a Mozart-equivalent in Nineveh. Despite the randomness of things, despite lives like the Ogham-Ferrarses', we aren't wholly the slaves of chance. We have some control.'

'Oh, I hope that's true!'

'You know it is. After all, you've done a number of things in the past few weeks, some of them pretty painful to you, because at bottom you felt there must be a difference between right and wrong. If we have no control, right and wrong are meaningless concepts. Do you want me to finish?'

'I think I know quite a bit of it. I keep realising things. For instance Laura didn't just want to look after Toby on Saturdays so that she'd have extra money for Jonathan. She was hoping to find out things about Janet for him to impress the people at Sabina Road with. And he told her things too, I suppose, about the Simpsons smuggling drugs, for instance. Did he find out about that when he had that holiday with them before, and ran off?'

'That's the sort of thing we'll never know, unless Simpson tells us.'

'It seems a bit crazy of Mr Simpson to involve someone like Jonathan at all.'

'He had his kids out there. He wanted it to look like a family holiday. My own hunch is that Jonathan realised what was up, nicked a parcel of heroin and left, and that's when he became an addict. As I say, Simpson can't have been at all pleased when he turned up in London, with the whole of his operation on a knife edge. I should think Jonathan made out he knew a bit more than he did, too. I don't think it's surprising he decided to get rid of him.'

'Do you think it was just him? I had a mental image of him holding Jonathan down while Marigold put the heroin into his arm.'

'Don't know. She was at Barnsley Square—we've got fingerprints. That's the part of the case we're concentrating on because we've got it pretty well sewn up. You were right about the oven, by the way; there were the kid's prints inside.'

'Why did Laura let them in in the first place? There's a security chain. She'd already decided they were enemy. She'd have recognised her—I don't know about him.'

'Parcel to deliver? Needed a signature? Something like that. But with Jonathan I should think Simpson acted friendly, said he needed his help, asked questions, found out about the Sabina Road van, said it would be useful, persuaded Jonathan to take a shot of heroin to nerve him up, and then simply gave him a massively stronger shot than he said it was. The next we actually know was a chap at Sabina Road hearing the engine running in the small hours—they kept the van in a shed at the end of the garden—and going out to see what was up. The last thing they wanted was police at the squat, so they took the body along to the play centre, shaved the beard and dressed him up fancy to distract attention. By the time we'd sorted that out, Laura had been ringing round all the people Jonathan had been interested in, accusing them of murder. You, the Capstones, the Simpsons. I don't know how the Simpsons realised it was Laura—maybe something Jonathan had said . . .'

'I suppose Marigold might have recognised her after all, or realised later who it was. I mean, if Sue had just mentioned the name Laura . . . We were all round at Linen Walk the day after Jonathan's body was found . . .'

'Yes, that nurse, Little Sue you call her, says Mrs Simpson started asking a lot of questions about the people in the play-group. She actually remembers telling her about Mary Pitalski spending a lot of time in Cardiff on this opera production . . .'

'I'd love to see that when it comes to London.'

'Oh?'

Poppy felt she had heard enough. She was tired of it now. It was all past, over. At odd moments, no doubt, further connections would strike her, but not now. Now she was more interested in him, in the two of them, his nature, their possibilities. She took the chance her unplanned interjection had given.

'Do you know about opera?' she said.

'Not much.'

'Oh, well, it's something called *Euryanthe*, by Weber. I've got a tape. The plot seems to be almost total nonsense, but . . .'

'Aren't they all?'

'Well, some of them, rather. You've got to get used to the conventions.'

'My wife was into ballet. I used to think it was the worst way of telling a story human ingenuity could conceivably devise.'

Poppy laughed, rose and filled his glass, then hers, going easy on the gin without any effort of will.

'Opera's not that bad, mostly,' she said. 'Of course there are some . . . but really the logic's in the music. You're not tone-deaf, are you?'

'You are speaking to an ex-chorister of Ely Cathedral.'

'Heavens! It didn't put you off music for life?'

'Not music, only religion.'

'That's rather a big only. What do you like listening to?'

'Classics a bit. I used to like jazz. I don't really have time these days.'

'I'm sure you don't. It's very good of you to spare me the time now.'

'I wanted to see you.'

She waited but he sat in silence, watching the credits reel up over a long wide shot of Wenceslaus Square, packed with its enormous crowd, Dubcek (was it?) tiny on a balcony, Havel (perhaps) beside him.

'Where are you?' he said.

She knew at once what he meant.

'Down there, of course,' she said. 'Tears streaming down my face. Aren't you?'

'I'm behind one of those windows,' he said. 'That's my office. I'm looking down. Policemen are different, you know. Even my daughters know I'm different. We stand between the rulers and the ruled. In an ideal democracy, where the rulers are the ruled, we'd still be there, at the window, looking down.'

'What are you thinking about?'

'Why did it take so long? Why didn't they do it before? They must have known, oh, for years now, they could if they wanted.'

'Last time, Russia sent tanks in.'

'That was twenty years ago. Half my life, almost.'

So he was in his forties, several years younger than she was, though they looked, she thought, roughly of an age. She felt easy with him, anyway, as he seemed to with her.

'What were you doing then?' she said. 'Can you remember?'

He told her, and then other things. He wanted to talk, clearly. Gradually, from fragments, the shape of a life emerged: parents divorced and remarried, a horde of step-siblings, himself not belonging in either brood, so a childhood unmagical and unregretted; nothing yet about adolescence, courtship, marriage; but then two adored small daughters; otherwise workaday years, subfusc, dutiful. But he wasn't a boring man. Some combination of genes, some fluke of nurture, had made him humorous, aware, flexible, decent. He stayed almost an hour and drank two-thirds of his bottle. She could have offered him food but decided not to. She was convinced, by tone and gesture, that he knew as well as she did what was going on between them and was prepared to enjoy these formal preliminaries. She had thought, before he came, that probably she was going to have to make all the running at first, but now was confident that this was not so.

When he'd left she put on the Mahler Fifth and, by way of giving Elias an equivalent treat, opened a can of mackerel fillets and gave him half. His purring joined the wash of sound. She carried her own meal—self-indulgently instant, curried lamb in a bag—back into the living-room and drank the rest of the wine with it. By the time she'd finished she was distinctly woozy, but for once unashamed. She-who-know-what-she-wants was in charge, and had chosen to get a bit high, and that was all right. She wasn't really listening to the music, just letting it happen. The television was still on, soundless, a cackling comedy series at odds with her mood. She flicked across the channels and found a news programme, the sobrieties of debate in a chamber of deputies or something. Russia it must be as they'd shoved a hammer and sickle in the corner—yes, there was Gorbachev . . .

She dozed, and for a moment—it couldn't have been more—she was part of what she'd been watching and talking about, moving in an immense crowd, joyful, through unfamiliar wide avenues, bullet-marks pocking the stucco of the buildings, towards some vaguely felt promise. To her left, with shouts of self-encouragement, citizens were ripping down a towering hoarding which showed the sinister-benevolent features of the toppled tyrant. The face was so well known that she didn't take it in. Only after she'd turned away did the realisation strike her and by the time she looked back to check the hoarding was down, and the people who'd demolished it had become a horde of small children who were scampering to and fro trailing long strips of the poster behind them, gaudy streamers of celebration.

Her head was already shaking in denial as she woke. No. In spite of what John had once said, Derek had not been her Stalin. The choices had all been hers. It was she who had put the posters up, she who had helped organise and then accepted the repression. Why hadn't she acted before? Why had it taken so long? She had known, oh, for years now.

Well, those years were over. What next? Not John Capstone, supposing that had become possible again. It was not in her personal culture to live for long at his level of self-impelled, self-justifying individual freedom, independent of any norm outside his own single will. But I *will* will some things, she thought. Tomorrow I'll tell Janet to start looking for a new minder. Then the hell with the visit to New Zealand. Anna doesn't want me. We'd both be play-acting. As soon as Toby's fixed I'll spend that money on a trip to Poland, by coach, and short-let the flat so that I can live dirt cheap and talk nothing but Polish and come back not just fluent but understanding something outside my own little cosy bubble. I'll go in the spring, and by then . . .

I think he'll suit me very well indeed. Not just that I need him and he needs me, that's not enough. I like the way he thinks. I like his sense of order, structure, the feel for the network of other lives you've got to respect and cherish if you're going to live well among them . . . Classics a bit, used to like jazz . . . Not Gilbert and Sullivan, anyway, though even that wouldn't have mattered. It's only one way of relating. He . . .

Good heavens! I don't know his first name. I bet it's Gerald. Well, if he can love a Poppy (which he's going to, or else . . .), I can love a Gerald. This is going to be an interesting year.

About the Author

Peter Dickinson was born in Africa but raised and educated in England. From 1952 to 1969 he was on the editorial staff of *Punch*, and since then has earned his living writing fiction of various kinds for children and adults. His books have been published in several languages throughout the world.

The recipient of many awards, Dickinson has been shortlisted nine times for the prestigious Carnegie Medal for children's literature and was the first author to win it twice. The author of twenty-one crime and mystery novels for adults, Dickinson was also the first to win the Gold Dagger Award of the Crime Writers' Association for two books running: *Skin Deep* (1968) and *A Pride of Heroes* (1969).

A collection of Dickinson's poetry, *The Weir*, was published in 2007. His latest book, *In the Palace of the Khans*, was published in 2012 and was nominated for the Carnegie Medal.

Dickinson has served as chairman of the Society of Authors and is a fellow of the Royal Society of Literature. He was made an Officer of the Order of the British Empire in 2009 for services to literature.

EBOOKS BY PETER DICKINSON

FROM OPEN ROAD MEDIA

These and more available wherever ebooks are sold

OPEN ROAD

INTEGRATED MEDIA

Open Road Integrated Media is a digital publisher and multimedia content company. Open Road creates connections between authors and their audiences by marketing its ebooks through a new proprietary online platform, which uses premium video content and social media.

Made in the USA
Middletown, DE
31 October 2015